"Comic and terrifying and profound."
> —Rachel Kushner
> author of *The Hard Crowd: Essays 2000-2020*

"Wolfgang Hilbig is an artist of immense stature."
> —László Krasznahorkai
> author of *Baron Wenckheim's Homecoming*

"In a flurry of travel and binges, [Hilbig's C.] is both seduced and repelled by the West's novelties and permissiveness—a funny yet anguished mind caught between competing visions of the world."
> —*The New York Times*

"Out of the ugliness of history and the wasted landscape of his home, [Hilbig] has created stories of disconsolate beauty."
> —*The Wall Street Journal*

"[Hilbig writes as] Edgar Allan Poe could have written if he had been born in Communist East Germany."
> —*Los Angeles Review of Books*

"The most important work of German fiction of the past 20 years."
> —Ingo Schulze, author of *Adam and Evelyn*

"Bilious and bleakly funny...Hilbig is one of the essential voices of the Cold War and deserves to be as well known in the Anglophone world as Thomas Bernhard or Günter Grass."
> —Hari Kunzru, author of *Red Pill*

"Hilbig's was among the most significant prose and poetry written not just in the GDR but in all of postwar Germany—East or West."
> —Joshua Cohen, author of *The Netanyahus*

"Hilbig's antihero is all of us, a stranger adrift in the modern world. Wolfgang Hilbig was a visionary, each of his novels awash in prophecy."
—Mark Haber, author of *Saint Sebastian's Abyss*

"Unexpectedly gripping—an unconventional inquiry into one man's morals and sense of home.... A searing trip into the recent past and into one man's inner landscape."
—*Kirkus Reviews* (starred review)

"This engrossing work from the late Hilbig continues the author's dedication to narratives of life in a divided Germany...a wily tale, smartly told."
—*Publishers Weekly*

"The late author's 2000 novel may well be his best... *The Interim*, for all its bleakness and melancholia, gleams brilliantly with the incandescence of an all-consuming inferno."
—Jeremy Garber, Powell's Books

" *The Interim* is the revered German writer's most complete and erudite of his works translated into English. Isabel Fargo Cole doesn't miss a beat of Hilbig's humor and disorientation. *The Interim* reads like literature crawling out of the drain."
—Spencer Ruchti, Third Place Books

"An absurd, poignant exploration of being 'stuck,' and one man's struggle to understand his life and his art."
—Lori Feathers, Interabang Books

"A transcendent reading experience... A masterpiece of one of European literature's finest authors."
—Matt Keliher, SubText Books

THE INTERIM

THE INTERIM

WOLFGANG HILBIG

TRANSLATED FROM GERMAN BY
ISABEL FARGO COLE

TWO LINES
PRESS

Originally published in German as *Das Provisorium*
from: Wolfgang Hilbig, Werke. Band 6
Copyright © 2000, S. Fischer Verlag
GmbH, Frankfurt am Main
Translation © 2021 by Isabel Fargo Cole
Design by Sloane | Samuel

Two Lines Press
582 Market Street, Suite 700, San Francisco, CA 94104
www.twolinespress.com

ISBN: 978-1-949641-42-4
Ebook ISBN: 978-1-949641-24-0

Library of Congress Cataloging-in-Publication Data

Names: Hilbig, Wolfgang, 1941-2007, author.
Cole, Isabel Fargo, 1973-, translator.
Title: The Interim / Wolfgang Hilbig ; translated by Isabel Fargo Cole.
Other titles: Provisorium. English
Description: San Francisco, CA : Two Lines Press, [2021] | "Originally
published in German as Das Provisorium"
Identifiers: LCCN 2021015368 (print) | LCCN 2021015369 (ebook)
ISBN 9781949641233 (hardcover) | ISBN 9781949641240 (ebook)
Classification: LCC PT2668.I323 P7613 2021 (print)
LCC PT2668.I323 (ebook) | DDC 833/.914--dc23
LC record available at https://lccn.loc.gov/2021015368
LC ebook record available at https://lccn.loc.gov/2021015369

1 3 5 7 9 10 8 6 4 2

The translation of this work was supported by a grant from the
Goethe-Institut, and this project is supported in part by an award
from the National Endowment for the Arts.

"To write my collected works I have offered up my biography, my person. You see, I felt from an early age that my life was staged for me so that I could look at it from all sides. This reconciled me to misfortune and taught me to see myself objectively."

> August Strindberg
> *Black Banners*
> translated by Donald K. Weaver

"I walk in the dark.
But I am guided by the smell of broom."

> Nicolás Gómez Dávila

In Nuremberg, in the ambivalent light of a so-called *boutique*, something had suddenly happened to him: he'd been going down the broad, shallow steps to the lower level, rounding a narrowing turn in what was a sort of spiral staircase, his tread inaudible on the carpet, its rhythm irregular because the steps with their differing widths threw him off, when abruptly he felt an attack from behind. An opaque shadow overtook him, he sensed a hand raised against him, armed or unarmed, and quick as a thought he spun on his heels. In the next moment he saw to his amazement how splendidly his instincts still functioned. Automatically his left hand shot up from his hip, crossed the menacingly raised arm, and landed with a crack on a chin he hadn't even quite glimpsed. It seemed that should have done the trick, but with knees flexed for power he followed up with his right hand, hitting the guy in the midsection; he grazed the horn button of a casually fastened jacket, the exact spot he'd aimed for, and with the rest of his momentum he jerked his right fist up the fellow's body; the button flew off, the jacket burst open, the uppercut lifted the guy off his feet. And with a short step back, bobbing from foot to foot again, C. landed another direct hit, a left cross to the unprotected head. That finished him off; he broke apart.

With a groan the guy fell against the railing, jackknifing over it, then seesawed back and clattered down onto the steps, coming to a rest on his belly after an inelegant backward somersault that overturned and extinguished a floor lamp. Even in the semidarkness, C. could see fragments of shattered limbs slipping from the figure's coat sleeves, and the face, twisted around on the neck, displayed a reproachful grin. Through the cloud of dust, shrill cries resounded from the sales floor of the boutique downstairs; C., brushing off the plaster dust, stepped over the wrecked mannequin he'd felt attacked by, and took off, ignoring the chaos behind him; with a quick but casual stride he stepped back out into the bright afternoon sunlight on Breite Gasse. He shook his head and looked around nervously, swallowing something that resembled a strange sense of guilt: no doubt about it, his counterattack had been much too fierce, just the first right and left would probably have done the job.

Nothing had happened, it was a normal afternoon, everyone acting as normal as could be, Breite Gasse filled with the everyday crush of consumers that allowed him to slip away unnoticed. Now, just a few hours before closing time, the rush was especially heavy; no one strolled along the gleaming row of stores, they all hurried and hustled, their faces radiating the certainty of serving the world's most righteous cause: shopping. Down on the corner the taxis never stood for long; the moment one stopped, bulging plastic bags were tossed into the back seat or the trunk; car after car filled with customers, and car after car slipped away, smooth and playful, making way for the next; the taxis purred off toward outlying neighbor-hoods or the suburbs, where they loaded up with new, as yet unappeased consumers and drove them back to the pedestrian mall. So it went, to and fro, a constant flux of doings and dealings—as some president, a bank president or the West German president, once said in some speech, suavely conservative as he did deals of his own—and the trams that pulled up at the train station opened their doors and disgorged floods of consumers who dispersed at once into the pedestrian mall. And underneath the pavement the subway trains raced up and released more droves of consumers, conducting them, marshalled by the voices from the PA systems, to the densely thronged escalators, which catapulted the masses of humanity right into the bright glare of the shopping district. And there the contented mingled with the discontented, and the other way around; the deceived joined together with the undeceived, embracing their deceivers in delight when they entered the Boutiques, the Emporiums and Markets and Gallerias, and they bought and paid and paid again, signing their checks with a flourish. And back outside on Breite Gasse they beamed in the radiance of their liquid-ity, and all were distinguished and important enough to bear God's favor in their hearts. So they strolled, over-shadowed by the nearby cathedral spires...

Meanwhile he sat sweating under one of the umbrel-las that shaded the tables outside a pastry shop, nursing a lukewarm coffee; the glass of water he'd ordered along with it had gone down in one gulp.

There are certainly plenty of people here! he thought aggrievedly, watching the bustle of humanity. Plenty of characters, there were more than enough characters for even a hefty novel. Enough to satisfy even the critics, the literary critics who've been obsessively counting the dramatis personae of narratives ever since the good old days of the stagecoach. Personae, personae, and more personae, always the same old line... But why should I play that game anymore... What I really need to do is make myself back into a personage. And I gave up my battle with the critics before it even started. – This sort of grandiloquence was a habit of his when he was alone with himself, exchanging views, usually on literature, with a shadowy interlocutor, often while recovering from some excitement that had passed.

Where he happened to be looking, a direction he couldn't quite determine, somewhere above the tall buildings to the left of the station, the sun had dropped into the haze that hung over the city, and in this haze, as though with the last of its strength, it rekindled its effulgence, and heated colors seemed to spill down slantwise into the street. Evening was falling, and the bustle all around showed the first signs of fatigue. In what just now had been a solid wall of cars along the curb, parking spaces opened up without being filled, the human tide into the pedestrian mall ebbed, and more and more people started leaving. Suddenly, seats freed up outside the pastry shop, and now that the rush was over the staff became lax about bussing the tables. A young couple sitting at his table suddenly up and left as if an alarm had gone off in their heads. Just a moment before the two had been stuffing their doggedly determined faces with hunks of strawberry tart and whipped cream. They left more than a third of it behind on their plates—first tearing it up and smashing it with their cake forks to render it unfit for further use. Had they taken C.'s gaze for that of a starving man, watching mesmerized as they stuffed themselves? They'd thought wrong; what gleamed in his eyes was thirst. But their headlong departure had a different reason—disappointment that it was 6:30 and time to leave the shopping district. The men with the keys stood outside the big department stores, opening the glass doors one last time for the stragglers from the merchandise labyrinths, releasing them, crimson-faced, onto the street: it was all over! The evening was empty, the night to follow would be without end. The darkness to come, bordering on the void, was tenacious and oppressive, and the question of tomorrow being just as fine a shopping day was unanswerable. Skeins of clouds might be gathering in the dark above the city—oh, this capricious September! Exuding a toxic red-gold tincture, the sun had crawled into the haze, its vestigial heat now powerless to burn off the smells in the city's crannies. And these smells now ventured forth: the inexplicable stench of old cooking fats rose from the gutters and settled like soapy sweat on the woven plastic patterns of the café's tablecloths. The warmth had melted the raspberry-red glaze on the leftover strawberry tart, making puddles on the plate in which yellowjackets twitched, caught in the trap of colors and aromas. The café wouldn't close until eight, but that man left sitting by himself, who had spent the past hour with a half-full cup of coffee on whose pale brown surface swam a drop of yellow fat that had failed to dissolve when he stirred in the cream—that man who refused to order anything more had long been drawing dirty looks from the staff, one blonde and one brunette, both of indeterminate age. What was the man thinking, loitering at the edge of the shopping district, evidently without a car? To be sure, he had nothing to transport; his sole loot consisted of a plastic bag, about 12 by 12 inches, holding something square-shaped and flimsy. In all probability he'd bought just one single record, and here at the café table he'd ordered just one single cup of coffee and a mineral water, and had paid as soon as he was served. Without any tip at all. It was hard to place the type of guy he was—judging from his dialect he wasn't from Nuremberg. From the East, that might be more like it, but how did he get here, to Nuremberg, from the East? Something was wrong with this picture.

In manner, too, he didn't compare with the three beer drinkers who'd taken seats at a table over by the curb, tossing their car keys down on the tablecloth. Three younger men, but not too young, and three different car keys, embellished with the corporate emblems of the automobile brands and decorative key rings that glittered gold or silver. Blasé, they toyed with the jingling metal—nothing cheap—now and then twirling it jauntily around their fingers. All three wore brightly patterned shirts, unbuttoned nearly to the belt, showing salon-tanned skin and curly blond or dark chest hair: you could tell they took care of their bodies. The short sleeves were closely fitted, stretching over the muscles of their shoulders and upper arms; two of them sported colorful tattoos, all three were decked out with golden watches and fine-linked bracelets, also gold, and more gold chains glimmered amid their chest hair. When they topped off their glasses, they held their beer bottles with three fingers, wrist jewelry glittering in the evening sun, focused on keeping the foam from spilling over the rims of the stemmed glasses... Watching them drink, C. sensed his own thirst; the way they drank was so calculated and well-measured—well-heeled was the word for that type of drinker, a type C. had never been. They paid him no attention, conscious of the two waitresses giving them the serious scrutiny that was their due, while they conversed, intent, yet rather offhand. Only one ever spoke at a time, with the others listening and now and then, as though in unspoken accord, taking a drink from their glasses. The one without tattoos, whom C. could look at head-on, followed each swig by fastidiously wiping the foam from his moustache, then twirling its pointed tips, meticulously and absentmindedly, and the long upward-curving tips of the moustache on his over-short upper lip bobbed when his turn came to speak, and C., spellbound, followed that bobbing motion like a vulture flying away. Smoothly swaying, the waitresses slid their hips around the uncleared tables. They stacked dishes on a tray and brushed crumbs from the weave of the tablecloths, now and then vanishing into the café. The remnants of the tart were left sitting next to C.; feeling he had slipped from everyone's awareness, he thought: It's all over...

Over! he repeated, and already it was like an echo from his slumbers. Over, and too late for me to pick up the thread again. In a few moments I'll disappear into this city in some direction or other. Something has broken off, something has shifted. Maybe I'll suddenly open my eyes and see what that thing was...

He was in Nuremberg, which he still couldn't quite comprehend. He had come from somewhere else, but now he was in Nuremberg, the city boasting a special breed of youngish male monsters with knock-off Kaiser Wilhelm moustaches. Nuremberg was a city of mementos, a city of reconstructions; his sense was that every grain of human nature had been mass-produced here for sale in the boutiques.

So he'd arrived in a city where, with absolute certainty, you could vanish without a trace. If he vanished to the right, toward the Old Town, he'd retrace his steps through the pedestrian mall, nearly deserted now, and soon reach the foot of the so-called Castle Rock, where all paths led steeply uphill. Here every stroll turned into an arduous climb, ill-suited to the capacity of his lungs, which had once been the lungs of an athlete. That belonged to a different life. Before the late-summer twilight descended, in the open areas at the foot of the castle fortifications, the people referred to as backpackers congregated, along with large groups from that sector of Nuremberg's youth that regarded itself as unconventional. It appeared, was supposed to appear, as though a whole army camp of deserters and stragglers had spread out on the rough cobblestones, basking in the last rays of the already setting sun. The attitude of rebellion convinced itself that up here, while the light briefly lingered, a stand was being made against the frenzy of consumption that had just subsided one level down, on a stratum of the city less difficult to scale. Amid the throng of wine and beer drinkers someone was having a crack at his guitar and seemed to be attracting attention. He even managed to make C. slow his step… What was the point of that musical statement? At the moment all it did was remind C. of his record, which he intended to put on as soon as he got home.

Between the people squatting or lying on the cobblestones wandered others who were merely taking in the scene, and C. wasn't one of them either. These were people who were better or more expensively dressed, or who at least no longer felt obliged to signal a certain social identity by donning denim or scuffed leather, squeezing into those ideological straitjackets; people, that is, who had satisfactorily completed their shopping and dropped off their loot at home. Now they strode tall across the Castle Rock, exuding tolerance from every pore and unmistakably demanding it back in the form of indifference, which was generously granted them. And so, heads held high, they strolled through the grilled sausage fumes that floated at nose level atop the beer vapors, circling the Castle Rock. All the nearby kiosks were open, and on this late-summer evening they had no dearth of customers. C. wanted to go home and listen to his record, he kept repeating to himself. He did *not* want to stop at one of the beer kiosks. He belonged neither to one group nor the other, neither to the people lying around nor to the people strolling between them and taking it all in. The freedom here was not for him, because he was much freer. He was unfree by virtue of a far greater freedom, because he belonged neither to this side of the world, where people lay and strolled around, nor to the other side, where people yearned to be lying here…

Now he moved quickly, seeking the shortest path between the seated groups, stopping only once, when right in front of his feet an empty wine bottle rolled down the sloping cobblestones, clattering along until someone stopped it. The record swung against his left thigh; he'd slipped the handles of the plastic bag over his wrist and put his hand in his pocket, and with his free hand he was smoking, which complemented his purposeful face. By the time he'd left the Castle Rock behind him, he could no longer deny that what he mainly felt was intense thirst. Two or three times he stopped outside one of the pubs, whose doors stood wide open, evidently to let in the fresh evening air. Forcing himself to walk on, at last he found a taxi and got in.

The driver had just a short way to chauffeur him, and there he was, back at his place. He recalled—it was a while ago already—that for a time, completely disoriented, he'd taken taxis back nearly every night. And so often the grinning driver had merely turned two corners, driven down a tiny side street, and stopped a minute later at his front door. He might have been disoriented even without the vast amounts of alcohol he drank; he couldn't get the hang of West German cities. For ages, for months, he hadn't had the slightest grasp of Nuremberg, any more than he'd had of Hanau, near Frankfurt, in the months before that, though Hanau was a small and seemingly straightforward town. West German streets were never dark, and they were flooded with an inflationary quantity of lettering, emblems, pictograms, and other symbols; it was impossible to extract and retain any reference points from that superabundance of signifiers. There was an inflation of reference points, and accordingly every reference was simultaneously correct and incorrect; the writing system had regressed to a medium of illiteracy.

He still had no real grasp of Nuremberg...now that it was high time for him to get a grasp of things, because it looked like he'd have to get by here on his own now. But it had looked like that several times before, and hadn't ended up that way. Nor did he have a grasp of time, he was disoriented about the space of time he'd already spent here. But that was less crucial; he was here, that much was certain, and he was here in the present time, in a time that was newly present every day and that he had to cope with. When asked, he'd often responded that he'd been here for a year or so…only to realize a moment later that it had been two years already. Or even more…it was as though he were refusing to wake up and find out for certain just how many years of his existence he'd already spent in Nuremberg. How much of his life had already passed here. In his mind it was still just that one year… and it seemed possible that even after the third year had passed, in his mind it would still be no more than that, maybe not even after five years.

He'd started off this way, he'd arrived here in a blackout of awareness, for months keeping his move to Nuremberg a secret from everyone. And, as though to keep up a front, he'd held onto his tiny apartment in Hanau; months later most of his mail was still being sent to his Hanau address and forwarded by the post office. He'd arrived here as though under hypnosis. What had hypnotized him were his own thoughts, and they revolved around the figure of a woman. They revolved around her figure and her image, and he'd been utterly unable to allow her to become a real woman for him. He'd never been able to do that with any woman.

When the fact of his move had become impossible to hide, he'd mumbled something about a cheap apartment into the phone and it wasn't even a lie. – But your apartment in Hanau was cheap, too, said the woman's voice at the other end of the line. A lot cheaper, actually. – C. was quite aware of the muffled undertone in that voice; a tension was building and could turn shrill at any moment. He'd been fixed up with the apartment in Nuremberg, he explained, it was an offer he couldn't refuse. Besides, Hanau was too much like Leipzig for comfort. – So you never did like it in Leipzig, said the disappointed voice—and maybe you never liked it with me. – Nonsense, he said. You aren't Leipzig, you just live there. – And because you don't like it in Leipzig, you'll never come back. – That was always what you were afraid of. – Anyway, you were fixed up with that apartment in Hanau too, how is this possible? You won't ever want to come back when people keep fixing you up with apartments. – To his horror C. heard the voice in Leipzig fill with sobs. Hoping to head it off with a stupid joke, he said: So I have a few benefactors somewhere. It's easy for them to find me something for a year. But when the year's up, things will start getting serious, and you know where I stand on that… – You have a benefactress, that's what you meant to say! You're trying to tell me that when the year is up, when things could get serious, you'll just walk back out on her…

What a load of bullshit he'd talked! Of course no one had fixed him up with the flat in Nuremberg; the search for it had been hellish. The only reason he'd said that stupid thing was to distract from the real reason for his move to Nuremberg. He'd failed, and the voice in Leipzig had broken down in tears.

After one of those conversations, unable to stand it in the apartment another minute longer, he'd go straight to a bar. There, as though soothing a sick man, he'd tell himself it really hadn't been a lie to say he'd moved into the flat just as an interim solution. Bit by bit the alcohol would make him block out the thought of the woman in Leipzig, and the woman in Nuremberg would regain the upper hand. But she couldn't stand it when he showed up smelling of alcohol.

At the same time, though, the alcohol increased his love for her, past the bounds of what even he considered plausible, to the point of an eloquence alien to him. When the alcohol's effect wore off, his feelings sobered too, and he was alarmed by all the things he'd told her in the past few hours. He worried whether it would be possible, after the limited time of his stay here, to set those feelings aside, the way he'd file away some workable story material in his mind. He asked himself if he could manage to leave his feelings behind when he moved away from here.

As far as the apartment was concerned, that probably wouldn't be hard. He'd never even lifted a finger to make it habitable. For the first several months the rooms were completely empty except for a mattress on the floor. He'd taken forever to buy tables, chairs, and bookcases; by that point his time in Nuremberg was nearly half over. The bookcases had been set up, but the books hadn't been shelved; the shelves held pots and pans, and one was for the pile of his shirts and underwear. The plastic cutlery tray was left out on the kitchen table, though there was an empty drawer to put it in, and the knives and forks were grouped around the tray rather than in its compartments, rendering the table top unusable. It was as though he constantly had to signal the interim nature of his existence. As though he had to work to persuade someone of it. Persuade whom? Himself?

But in fact it was just a case of depressive inertia, exacerbated by the alcohol and still more by the sobering-up phases, which he couldn't cope with at all anymore. In those phases several moving boxes kept catching his eye, ones he shunted from corner to corner without unpacking. Filled with books, they robbed him of his peace of mind, or rather they wouldn't let peace come anywhere near him. He bristled whenever someone commented on the symbolic value of those still unpacked boxes. Or when he recalled them himself, unable to overlook the symbolism of the situation. It was two boxes in particular…they were *the things that hadn't been dealt with.* They were present, standing in front of him, standing in his way, but they were the presence of a loss…

The point had long been reached where most of his deliberations could end only with a question, extremely simple and applicable to all sorts of things: Where should I go? – Actually he felt he'd always been driven by this question, but now it drove him to the exclusion of all else. It posed itself every few steps he took or tried to take. The less he wished to answer it, the more it beset him. He suppressed it, but it followed him even when he went out to run a few innocent errands; worse still, it assaulted him right in the middle of his apartment. Now that he occupied an apartment with three rooms plus a kitchen and a shower—commanding a space of hitherto unknown, overwhelming dimensions—it would suddenly happen that, amid his wanderings across the parquet, he'd freeze into a pillar of salt as though he'd involuntarily glanced back at Gomorrah, and he'd ask himself in confusion: Which room should I go to? – You should go to your desk! he'd reply. And he would, but after writing just a few sentences, he'd feel that thirst rise inside him, yanking him up from his chair. Extreme discomfort regularly overcame him when, down on the street, he'd find himself heading—as automatically as though there were no choice—toward a small square called Schillerplatz. He went there five times a day to circle around the square; like someone hypnotized, like a wind-up automaton, he kept heading back to Schillerplatz. But no one was waiting for him there today! That summer something had broken off, a gulf had opened up between himself and the woman who lived there. Their conversations had turned monosyllabic, dealing only with practical things; when he asked her something, more and more often she'd reply: You needn't bother with that, I'll manage. Or she'd say: You don't have to worry, I'm doing better than you think. – She'd often asked him to leave her alone for a while, but this time there was a different quality to her resistance. And then all of a sudden he'd learned she wasn't there. She'd gone on a trip… That must have been true, since her car was no longer parked in front of her building. After incessantly questioning all her acquaintances he was finally told that she was staying in Munich, partly to put more distance between herself and him. And that if he could make up his mind to leave her alone a while, she was sure to come back one of these days…

So he turned around. And because he'd pass nothing but bars if he kept on going that way, he retreated to the apartment to pace up and down the rooms. – In the next yard, under the window of the room he'd chosen as his study, the butcher's hound dogs barked until late that night.

He had an idea where she was staying in Munich, but he didn't dare call. She was friends with a married couple there who lived in separate apartments, and since the husband took long business trips, his apartment was often free for several days, sometimes weeks.

C. had stayed there too once, for two or three weeks that past winter; later he'd put it in poetic terms: he'd been brought to Munich by fate. Munich had always enticed him, albeit not exactly in wintertime, but in the spring and the summer the trajectories he was on had always bent around the city. What he'd read about it nourished the remnants of romantic feeling inside him: for him it sounded almost like *Italy* (*Vienna*, incidentally, had a similar effect), and he'd arrived at its main station with that overblown optimism in his heart.

The first thing that caught his eye was the gigantic sign under the station roof extolling Munich as *the city of world-famous beers*…it was a time when he was already starting to see his unbridled alcohol consumption as a problem. Never mind the art museum—the breweries were the apex of that city's world, that was made amply clear before you'd even left the station. And for him the time that followed became a battle with the city's claim to fame, which was not without irony, considering that he hardly ever penetrated Munich's world anyway: for all intents and purposes his journey had ended at the station.

He no longer felt he belonged to any world at all. He'd realized that during those winter days in Munich; or maybe he hadn't even quite realized it, but he'd started acting like someone from the Siberian backwoods whom fate had dumped down in a modern western metropolis. Two years of experience with the West suddenly availed him nothing; he'd been sucked into a strange maelstrom that irresistibly dragged him back and down. All at once it struck him that he actually came from another country… over the past year he'd nearly forgotten, and now that forgetfulness seemed like a malady. Though he couldn't quite substantiate it, he suspected that for the entire past year he'd simply been no one at all. Two years ago, the year before last, things had been different; he'd had a visa then and had spent all his time staring ahead to the end of the period the document granted him. In the end he'd ignored the lapsing of the visa and stayed in West Germany: in that moment his amnesia had set in.

Some days he forgot why he'd been given the visa. He'd applied for it and received it in his function as a writer; it had been a complicated procedure, but that was what it ultimately came down to. But in the past year his function as a writer—in his unnecessarily unwieldy phrasing—had receded so far into the background that you almost had to say it was lost. In the country he was living in he wasn't functional as a writer, he thought.

Suddenly he'd begun wondering where that function had originated, but he couldn't get to the bottom of it. He saw a kind of shadowy forest when he thought about those origins, a forest where darkness was gathering... that region, that mental region lay apart, beyond a boundary he couldn't cross. How could he, here, where he was living now, find his way back to his writing function when the origin that seemed like a proof of his existence—however vague and diffuse that proof might be—was cut off from him forever?

He'd really come to Munich to collect his thoughts, and if possible to write them down, yet every possibility of doing so seemed to have been shut off...in this city he'd drifted still farther from his beginnings.

So every night he ended up at Munich's main station; when the crowds of travelers ebbed from the vast cold hall around midnight, a certain kiosk would still be mobbed by kindred souls who found no peace within their own four walls...if they even had four walls of their own. From that kiosk he could read the departure boards at the ends of the platforms, and while he drank he stared at the names of the destinations that were so familiar to him: *Leipzig Main Station* or *Berlin Main Station*. Or perhaps they only showed the trains' arrival times... One night he'd witnessed an episode that gave him pause. He'd made a note of the incident, the only piece of writing he produced during his time in Munich. – From one of the last trains to arrive, around midnight, a young man had clambered down onto the platform and, feeling solid ground under his feet, instantly threw his arms into the air and burst out in frightful howls that attracted everyone's attention. He marched toward the exit, windmilling his arms with his meager pieces of baggage, while to the rhythm of his steps—he was imitating a military march, slamming one foot down on the concrete floor while hoisting the bent knee of his other leg up to his chest—he bawled over and over: *Down with the GDR!... Down with the GDR!*—C. immediately realized what special type he was looking at here: the guy making all that racket was an émigré; that is, someone who had managed to cross the border and make it to Munich, whether by applying for permission to emigrate or by some other arduous method. And now, giving in to his feeling of freedom, he voiced it resoundingly under the placid roof of the Munich train station. As he came abreast of the beverage kiosk, caterwauling, the first policemen came rushing up; they quickly surrounded and subdued him. Even as he was frog-marched away, he kept braying: *Down with the GDR... Down with the GDR!*

Watching that scene, the station started to give C.

the creeps. He bought a bottle of vodka from the kiosk, hopped into a cab, and went back to his place.

The fracas had haunted him for some time—and ever since then similar scenes were probably coming thick and fast at stations throughout West Germany. For some time the press had been filled with reports that younger citizens of that "single-party state" over there were applying to leave the country in droves; that refugees were fleeing to the West German embassies in Budapest and Prague; that more and more of them had to be allowed to emigrate. The term "mass exodus" had cropped up before, but never yet buttressed with so many facts. And the GDR was dealt with so gingerly that everyone could draw their own conclusion: things over there were unmistakably disintegrating. Earlier, when people had talked about signs of disintegration, C. had always regarded the conjecture as wishful thinking. But now the Soviet Union had a new General Secretary, speaking words that could no longer be ignored: Life punishes those who come too late… Though surely meant in a spirit of self-criticism, the statement inevitably hit home in the GDR. For some it must have sounded like a death sentence.

C. was reminded of another little significant-seeming episode: Once he'd had to spend a night in jail in A.— the main town of the district he came from—and realized right away that he'd never get a single minute's sleep in the hole they'd locked him up in. His cell was probably used as a drunk tank; traces of the catastrophes attendant to the drying-out process were visible all around… In the GDR, thought C., succumbing to alcohol still made for indelible images, so it was not entirely unreasonable for writers and artists to spend their time drinking. The cell whose door slammed behind him consisted of several cubic yards of bad smells, and contained a cot, a broken-down chair, and a cracked toilet that wouldn't stop running and stood in a puddle of sludge. On the wall behind the cot, a broad swath of vomit trailed down, already dried; the dim light of a 25-watt bulb showed the walls covered from top to bottom with unidentifiable filth—possibly human excrement—spatters of blood, and countless inscriptions: scratched messages and addresses. It was enough reading material to last him all night. One of the first slogans he read stated straight out: *Long live capitalism.*

Today at the station he'd heard the second part of that statement—and now he knew the sum total of what young East Germans cared about these days. – It seemed to him that he'd read that slogan on the jail wall back then with an upsurge of malicious glee. But now a few oddly theatrical tears welled in his eyes; the poignant drama at the Munich station had kindled something like homesickness. And homesickness was what you needed to grasp, at long last, your arrival in the West. In this moment, C. was just another West German writer weeping into his beer...

That was a quote from the culture pages of one of the major newspapers; now and then it would subject West German writers to a scolding of which fortunately no one believed a word. Likewise, C. would merely shake his head, dump the teary beer down the drain, and pour himself a new one.

For several evenings after that, he showed up at the station with his bag packed, believing his last chance at salvation was to flee back to Nuremberg. But he never got any further than the kiosk at the head of the platforms.

When he'd missed all the trains, it was time to head back to the place where he slept, carrying a new bottle of vodka; the bag served only to smuggle the *stash* into his Munich apartment unseen…suddenly he knew what it meant for an alcoholic to describe liquor as his "stash." Each time he hoped he wouldn't find the key he'd hidden under the doormat. Then the friend whose apartment it was would have returned; then C. would have to move out, he really would have to go to Nuremberg. Each time the key was still there, lying under the straw mat by the threshold; by the time he fumbled it out, he'd be so far gone that he'd have to lean his forehead against the doorframe to keep from falling over.

The empty bottles standing by the trash can in the kitchen were still readily countable: if it was true that he needed two days for a bottle of vodka—or rather, that he needed a new bottle every other day—then he'd been here for twelve days. He might have missed several bottles that he'd already tossed in the trash bin outside; aside from that there'd been lots of beer, and sometimes he'd resorted to wine. If his calculations were correct, it was now several hours into December 22…though possibly it was already December 23. He'd resolved to give up booze for good on Christmas Eve, and he couldn't let himself get the date wrong…though maybe the kiosk at the station would be closed on Christmas Eve anyway. It had to mean a caesura; suddenly he began believing in Christmas Eve like believing in Santa Claus…

In the year of his visa, that is, almost two years ago (Was it really two whole years already? he asked himself), he'd gotten a stipend, quite a generous monthly stipend from a literary foundation, and then he'd requested an extension of the stipend and gotten that too. Money he couldn't use up had accrued in his bank account. Then he'd won a large cash prize in a competition; the other entrants had resented him for it…and rightly so, he told himself; he'd come to feel that most of the finalists in the competition had presented better work than his. And so he could have spent those years practically without cares, writing a new book… It hadn't worked out that way, something uncanny had happened to him, something with a thousand explanations but no real reason. Meanwhile, money was virtually slipping between his fingers…

He had to keep from thinking about the money, at the word *money* he had instant surges of panic that only alcohol could fight down. The cause of that panic was a nearly indescribable shame… What had he done? – He'd done nothing, and being a do-nothing was what aroused the sense of shame. He'd taken the money, stipends and literary prizes, and then he'd frozen up and stopped writing. Sometimes, when he was drunk enough, he hoped he was already dead…only as a dead man could you opt out of society's financial doings and dealings. But you couldn't know that that hideous sense of shame wouldn't persist even after you were dead, you couldn't know for certain…

There's still the late train from Munich to Leipzig, he told himself. The one that doesn't get there till morning… or am I mixed up, and that train starts in Nuremberg? He mustn't go anywhere near Nuremberg when and if he suddenly vanished from West Germany in the middle of the night. When and if he vanished as though he'd suddenly died. Why was he incapable of moving away from this kiosk even once to check the departure times? Maybe they'd let him cross the border without any problems;

after all, he still had a GDR passport, and maybe they wouldn't even notice how long ago the visa had expired. But probably he could even get through with his West German passport, of course he had that too…once in the GDR's cage, he'd be in for good. And dead and gone from the West…

He'd even thought up a reason for his drinking (which really did take stamina): he wanted to return to the GDR without any money. There ought to be just enough money for the ticket…one way. Maybe a few concealed hundred-mark notes for his mother, but not a pfennig more. There was no doubt about it, the authorities would be after him when he got back. He couldn't rule out the possibility that some of the bureaucrats who had it in for him—and there were plenty—felt that he'd "deserted the Republic." That was the established term for people who left the country in unauthorized fashion; if you chose to look at it that way, he'd been guilty of that offense for over two years now. Quite apart from the fact that he loathed the thought of propping up the GDR economy with an influx of hard currency—however modest the sum—the possession of western cash was the worst conceivable basis for making a fresh start over there. If he didn't wean himself off that money, sooner or later he'd start building up his Western connections again. He'd slip back into the cycle of shame…and if the devil had a hand in the game, at some point they'd give him yet another visa…

Every night the trusty key was still under the mat, the apartment was still free, and so it seemed things would go on this way forever. He sat in the light of a small lamp, arduously emptying a bottle of vodka, looking out at the reflective façade of an office tower that loomed opposite his window. He drank on undeterred, though his stomach rebelled, until dawn broke and large clumps of damp snow drifted down outside. Then he turned out the light, slunk into the next room as though coming from heavy, unending labors, and went to bed.

Before the alcohol stalls the thinking machine in my skull, he thought, I want to imagine the morning of my arrival in Leipzig. Maybe I really will never wake up again—then at least I want an image of Leipzig to take with me when I die. A sun-filled morning, for only the thought of light can sustain the fantasy of returning and starting all over. – What was it that person saw when he arrived at the Leipzig station early in the morning…?

A certain shine in the station hall; he saw it, half asleep. A light detectable only by one who knows the station well and has the leisure to find it beneath the vast vaulted roof. Noticed only by one immune to the universal depression prevailing at this hour of early departures. Nobody else in the sleepy multitude astir at this hour pays any attention to the light, that glitter intensifying to splendor; it's the radiant filth of this cathedral that has gone uncleaned for over a quarter of a century. Up under the roof it begins to ignite: vapor, smoke, steam, and dust, the exhalations of humans and machines. All unseen to the people waiting, breathing out and shivering after the crush in the trams and buses that brought them here. The multitude exhales; in the trams, it seems, they could only inhale, so as to take up as much space as possible against the compression of their no longer identifiable bodies. Now, with half an hour's freedom, they breathe out, expelling the used oxygen until the vapors seethe beneath the station vault; but soon the trains will leave, dispersing them to their workplaces. – That person left almost all alone on the platform has parted ways with the working masses; it happened several years ago, a step into uncertainty that left him with the lingering fear that he'd resigned from human society the way you resign from a political party.

He's been dragged over the coals for it. Friends of his kept on going to their factories and kept on working, and maybe they've turned out to be the better writers anyway, he thinks from time to time. And now he's lost them as friends. – He is standing on the broad plateau where the platforms begin, about halfway between the east and west exits, and the station is nearly deserted; most of the early trains have pulled out amid the loudspeakers' agitated verbal exertions and taken the multitude with them. He gazes down the vast stretch of empty tracks to the mouth of the station, beyond which the rails fan out in all directions. The arched portal at the end of the train shed, looking small at this distance, is now filled with bright light. And emanating from that arch—as from a rising sun only half visible—nine glowing strips extend down the vaulted roof, gradually widening, reaching past the spot where the observer stands. These are the glass panels in the roof vault, which still admit some light, and it looks as though a sun rising from the darkness were sending long rays up and out. The sun shines in the station like the light in a cathedral. And there are nine rays, a magic number. And through that sun the trains have pulled out into the open and lost themselves in blinding light.

W hat sort of a time had he actually had in Munich? – And what sort of a time in the other cities that he barely knew, beyond their names and their train stations...? He knew he'd lived in those cities, but they'd remained strangely closed to him. His powers of observation had failed; when he speculated on the causes of the phenomenon, all kinds of things came to mind: the alcohol that dulled his gaze, his inability to socialize, his lack of human contact, his self-mistrust, the resulting perplexity.

Little by little reality slipped away from him...he stood apart, reality refused to accept him, he was unable to relate reality to himself...he didn't know how to explain it. Reality lay behind a wall, he was constantly hauling a wall around in front of him. And since that wall wasn't made of concrete, but was a mere feeling, a consciousness, or a mere feeling beneath a consciousness...since that wall itself was unreal...it seemed all the less possible to dismantle it. He couldn't abolish the wall; if he wanted to change the state he was in, all he could do was abolish himself...

In this frame of mind he had begun searching for his memories, out of a strange desperation, as if some shabby memory were all he had to fall back on…and he surrounded himself with notes, little pieces of paper with the fragments of his memories; the next day, when he read the barely legible, drunkenly scribbled sentences, he usually threw them away: they were written in a vein of half-hearted cynicism he found insufferable…

But he'd lacked reality even in the cities of the East, in Leipzig, Dresden, East Berlin…that was clear from the mere fact of how poorly he remembered. And now? Probably these cities would cease existing for him. Or they'd exist only as fantastic spirit forms from a past he no longer recognized as his…as virtual forms that his alcohol-tormented brain was barely able to retrieve. He no longer saw himself in those cities—any more than he saw himself in the new, West German cities—in the East German cities he was a ghost, a coincidence, a temporary figure; perhaps no one had even noticed that he wasn't actually there. He'd have to write about that…if he were able to, if he were able to write again some day! But more and more he was coming to suspect that he could write only in those cities themselves…

For him, he sometimes thought, those cities were as they'd been at the end of World War II. They'd been obliterated, no one knew whether they'd ever exist again. They could live on, if at all, only as other cities…and it was almost as if his thoughts had frozen at the end of that war: that was when his consciousness, his sense of the world, had taken form…and for him those cities had now been obliterated yet again, more effectively, it seemed, than by carpet bombing. More effectively, because this obliteration had caught him at a moment when he lacked all solidity. It had taken a state border (an uncrossable border, now that his visa had expired), a wall, a belt of bureau-cratic regulations. That needed to be written about, no matter how…

What actually kept him from starting? – For one thing, his girlfriend Hedda was withholding herself. She'd taken flight…he had no desire to put the matter more precisely. It was not the first time it had happened; and the more urgently, the more desperately he tried to restore contact with her, the more incisively she insisted on keeping her distance. She had vanished…it seemed she was in Munich, but when he showed up in Munich, she'd already moved on. No, it wasn't the first time she'd told him (or had someone tell him) that she needed time to think, that he had to leave her alone temporarily. And she was convinced he ought to think things over too…

Temporarily, that was the word, he'd been living that way for quite some time now. Only drinking kept his chin up, but she said she couldn't stand to watch while he tried to destroy himself with alcohol…

It was the most cowardly way to kill yourself, so Hedda said. She had a grudge against alcohol. That was because of her Russian father, who had made her spend her childhood watching him drink. The result of that spectacle, besides an aversion to alcohol and men who drank, was a skepticism, never entirely suppressed, about the so-called "Russian national character"—whatever that meant—which admittedly was her character too. Hedda wasn't her real name, it was a pseudonym; she'd chosen it on her publisher's advice, her real name being too complicated for book covers that were supposed to entice German readers.

C., she'd said, definitely needed time to think as well,

he had to decide whether he really wanted to live with her. Clearly he didn't know. Which meant that she no longer knew either. And he should ask himself whether he really drank because he couldn't write these days—as he'd once claimed—or whether it was the other way around: that he couldn't write because he was too busy drinking.

There were more things to consider: maybe he couldn't write when he was living with a woman, or imagined that he couldn't. Or not just with a woman, maybe he couldn't stand any kind of human closeness when he was trying to write...

But we don't even really live together, we have separate apartments, he countered.

Thank goodness! said Hedda.

His stay in Munich would have been a chance to think those things over; possibly that was even the reason why he'd gone there. Maybe, if he'd actually done it, he would have come to similar conclusions...they would have been hard realizations for him to take. Granted, he'd thought things like that before, but why was it so? Why couldn't he stand closeness? Because with other people around you need good arguments for writing? But when a person was sitting there, writing and keeping relatively quiet, why did he need arguments, why did he have to justify his writing? He'd never had any argument in its defense, much less any that was satisfying. Arguments all but cried out for contradiction—contradiction was there in superabundance, you could help yourself. He himself was filled to the brim with contradiction.

In Munich he'd been all alone and still he hadn't written. There it might at least have struck him that with Hedda, who also wrote, he didn't need any argument.

The reason he wasn't writing was that he got in his own way; that was all. A seemingly trivial incident had caused ill-feeling that turned into a confrontation, a stress test: he'd forgotten Hedda's birthday, and the alcohol was to blame. During this confrontation Hedda had demanded that he leave her alone for a while; the awful thing was that she hadn't wanted to say when that period might end.

In those dark days in Munich he'd felt like a prisoner sent into some indefinite time of banishment: his behavior would determine when it ended…but he didn't know how to behave. The more he drank, the more he was possessed by the sense of being cast out…forever, he was condemned to languish in banishment forever. The thought fueled a crippling horror that only alcohol could keep at bay…

The end of his time in Munich was confused; he'd had no hand in it, but played a kind of main role, which made that end perfectly in character for him. Several vivid, almost lurid images lingered, but they loomed in zones of fog, disjointed and nearly impossible to bring into sequence. – Woken by the ringing of the telephone, he'd gotten groggily to his feet. If he hadn't had a flash of hope that Hedda was calling, that she'd been trying to reach him for ages, he wouldn't even have picked up the phone. It was dark again already, late afternoon, the rooms were freezing cold. I'm in Munich! he told himself; each day that was the first thing he thought. And the first thing he felt was a splitting headache, to combat which he always left an inch or two of liquor in the bottle. Desperately he searched the three rooms for the persistently ringing telephone; at last he got his hands on the receiver and answered.

A woman's voice filtered through to his ear, talking much too fast and in sentences that refused to finish. It wasn't Hedda. After a while he grasped that it was meant for him, and that the woman on the phone was the wife of the friend whose apartment this was. – She was afraid he'd have to move out...out of the apartment, that was... today, unfortunately, there was no way around it. But of course it was just temporary, she said...

What? he said.

Just temporary! For the time being, just for the holidays, maybe until the beginning of January. Her husband was back from his business trip, he'd arrived that morning. And he'd called over and over again, but no one had answered the phone. Now he was already in the car on the way to his apartment...that had been the agreement, after all, that he was coming back on Christmas Eve. She was sorry, she was afraid this might all be rather sudden... rather difficult for him.

C. had only a dim memory of these Christmas Eve arrangements. – No problem, he said, I'll just pack my things in the meantime.

There really wasn't *that* much of a hurry. Would he like to come by and have a bite to eat before they drove to the clinic? Her husband had already talked to him...or hadn't he? No? Oh dear, what a mess! Well, her husband was good friends with one of the doctors at the clinic, he remembered that, didn't he? And the doctor had agreed to take him on today at short notice, he had to remember *something* about that! Nothing? But it was all right, wasn't it? Of course he'd have to go entirely of his own free will, to the clinic, that was. She was convinced it was the right thing to do...Hedda would definitely think so too. Her husband had informed the doctor about the alcohol problem, and he'd agreed there was cause for concern.

Have you spoken to Hedda about it?

She'll think it's the right thing to do, you can take my word for it.

What kind of a clinic is it?

A special clinic, one of the best in Munich. At any rate he'd be in good hands there, and he'd be able to rest. He could stay as long as he wanted.

A clinic for addicts? asked C.

Her husband had looked into all the details, and the doctor, her husband's friend, had assured him that he'd be able to leave the ward at any time.

If you say so, I'm sure that's true, said C.; at that moment the doorbell rang and he hung up.

It was her husband, looking at C. with self-control suffusing his features.

Your wife warned me about you, said C.

Then I'm glad you're still here—the tone was slightly ironic. C.'s friend made a quick circuit of the apartment, then declared: You're already packed! We really had better hurry, after all, it's the twenty-fourth of December.

I've been packed for a month, said C.

You haven't even been here for a month, don't you realize that? Still, I'm sorry it had to be the holidays. But that'll mean you'll have some peace and quiet in there.

I don't mind about holidays, said C., I always forget them. Which sanatorium are we going to?

Sanatorium—that's a nice way to put it! It's called *Haar*, and it's pretty well known. Funny name, of course. It's in a very quiet spot outside Munich.

C. remembered having heard the name *Haar* before.

He asked: Is that the insane asylum where the writer Bernward Vesper killed himself?

Yes...the friend looked surprised. You know your stuff! He was committed to Haar, and admittedly he had nothing nice to say about it. Actually, the suicide was only after he was transferred to Hamburg. And the clinic in Haar has long since been modernized, now it's first-rate...

In his car they drove through the night; nothing stirred on the streets of Munich, and C. felt that the city was completely deserted. His friend fiddled with the radio, getting nothing but the same caterwauling Christmas carols on all the stations; meanwhile C. kept dozing off in the passenger seat and starting awake in confusion. The ache in the back of his head had faded, but it took him a long time to grasp the situation he was in. He felt sobered and defenseless, switched off like the now-silent radio. – It seemed to have gotten warmer, the wipers swept a grimy deposit of water and snow to the edge of the windshield. Now they were driving down country roads edged by thickets and bare bent trees; the water seen in the headlights, through wisps of fog, trickling from the branches, glistened like a strange organic slime. C. had the creeps here, outside the bounds of civilization; there was no oncoming traffic on this road. He felt they'd been driving like this for an incredibly long time, and he hazarded a joke: I feel as if we're about to reach the border...

What border do you mean? asked the friend.

They stopped at a closed boom gate that seemed to have appeared out of nowhere; to the right and left of it an oddly innocuous-looking fence vanished into the darkness. They were at Haar; outside, the friend was negotiating with a gatekeeper; C. thought of grabbing his bag from the back seat and fleeing sideways into the bushes. As he looked around for the bag, the boom gate rose, and his friend took the wheel again. They drove through a jumble of buildings that looked to C. like haphazardly placed cement blocks; hardly a single window was lighted. Then they stopped at an entrance with a sign that read *Admissions* beside it. In an enormous dimly lit corridor filled with whole parks worth of leafy, eternally green plants, C. was delivered like a package…or so it seemed to him. It must have been obvious why he was here; the helpless way he stood by, his lack of resistance announced it. His ID card was requested and vanished a moment later. The friend asked about the doctor he claimed to have made the arrangements with, but got only a shake of the head in reply. C. felt one last stirring of hope that they'd send him away again, but suddenly his bag was picked up from the floor and he felt a solicitous pressure on his upper arm; a nurse who must have slipped up unnoticed maneuvered him to the elevator, whose doors closed before he could say good-bye to his friend. Several floors up his bag was returned to him; it had been searched, C. noticed later.

His friend had been mistaken—in the belief, that is, that Haar would be especially quiet over the holidays. If anything, the clinic seemed overfilled. A perpetual madness was on the simmer here, an undercurrent, but ready to explode at any minute, kept down only by the nurses' constant vigilance. C. remembered how empty the city had appeared to him from the car; the reason for that seemed to lie here. That segment of Munich's humanity not currently sitting in front of lit-up Christmas trees had turned up at the asylums for addicts and withdrawal patients to subject itself to the procedure known as detox that took days, sometimes weeks. Here they were corralled, all those who weren't busy peeling the gift wrap off consumer goods, who weren't chiming in on the thousandth chorus of "Silent Night" but instead striking up quite an unconventional kind of Christmas carol. By the time C. reached his floor, most of the inmates were already in bed, and it was impossible to tell whether they were asleep or tossing in the throes of their delirium. In the two dim rooms—separated only by an open sliding grate and with two empty beds to choose from—he was met by a seething mass of noise whose human origin was not immediately apparent. It was like the suppressed howls and hisses of captive beasts that should not have been cooped up in the same room together. Here lay more than a dozen men of all ages, snoring, wheezing, yammering to themselves. Some released a continuous strained whimper, as if their chests had been equipped with a peculiar mechanism that went on whistling and squeaking without their volition. Taken all together, it was a song that seemed to rise from the nethermost unchristian hells. Others babbled unbroken inextricable sentences that were laments or curses, mad appeals to nonexistent listeners; they were "making speeches to the masses," as it was called here. And sometimes those speeches swelled, mounting to a bellow to which the neighbors, without actually waking, instantly responded with anxious whimpers. At such moments a blind would rattle up behind the glass of a semicircular booth that commanded a view of both rooms. The nurse on duty, a stout middle-aged person in a dark-green smock, could be seen looking up from her book and reaching for a bell-button. With the other hand

she'd aim the beam of her desk lamp outward; by swivel-
ing the lampshade, she'd search the row of beds for the
excited bundle from which the cries were emerging. This
in itself would be enough to reduce the yelling to the level
deemed tolerable. The beam of the makeshift searchlight
would swing back to the booth, first moving appraisingly
across the other twitching and trembling bodies that lay,
side by side but without the slightest contact, indulging
in their most intimate torments. The cries grew softer and
softer, the surges of excitement ebbed back into the men's
bodies and they writhed a while longer in terror; the blind
slid down again.

When day came, C. realized that he hadn't slept a
single minute all night. He'd lain there dried-up yet
drenched with sweat; his body seemed to void moisture
through every single pore, and he felt he was wallowing
in puddles unabsorbed by the synthetic material of the
mattress. His sweat seemed to mingle with the bitingly
acrid and sweetish secretions of all those who had occupied that cot before him. After a while he calmed himself,
reflecting that he'd slipped into a sort of cyclical process
in which all distinctions were suspended. – Happiness, he
thought, doesn't suspend the distinctions, on the contrary,
it's most solidly grounded on the misery of the subjugated.
Misfortune alone obliterates all classifications.

He felt a sudden tranquility at the thought that he
was lying in a bed whose material was saturated with the
vital fluids of whole hosts of generations that had gone
before him. Many had fought for their lives here, had
succumbed or gotten away with it one more time... And
when others came after him to live or die in this place...
he would have existed somewhere in the middle, sensing

the silken thread on which each hung. There's no need to sleep, he thought. He was here to listen to the great noise of torment.

The sleepers in both rooms had finally grown so weak that they merely hummed like heavy torpid insects. Now came the night's quiet phase... There's no saying, thought C., that by morning there'll still be life in all the figures in the beds. Feeling relatively stable, he got up quietly and began to roam around the rooms. The beds, set as close together as possible, were arranged in two rows so that they could easily be observed from the glass booth, and C. tried to move as noiselessly as possible. The men lay as if broken by torture, some covered, others nearly naked; many wandered open-eyed in sleep or half-sleep, their pupils darting restlessly. But rather than waking up when C. came to their beds, they gave him mad, defensive stares; clearly he was a monster to them, or he took the form of their death. He bent over an old man in concern, wondering what was wrong with him; from the long thin martyred figure stretched on the rumpled bedclothes came an uninterrupted tremor, by turns growing and fading in intensity. The man was scantily dressed, with ankle-length gray long-johns and a gray cardigan on his naked torso; an undershirt lay under his head. His mouth foamed as if he'd drunk acid, his eyes flickered wildly. And then it seemed to C. that the old man was desperately trying to stammer out a few words through the choking foam. Was he trying to tell him something? C. bent down closer and thought he heard: *Nazis...Nazis...Himmler...Hitler!* Thinking he'd misheard, C. held his ear still closer to the old man's mouth. Again he thought he heard: *Hitler... Himmler...SS...Reichsführer SS!*

What's wrong, whispered C., what are you afraid of?

The old man trembled all over, and, with a violent effort, stammered out the word *catastrophe*.

What catastrophe are you talking about? What do you think might happen…?

The man's limbs were racked so violently that the iron bedframe began to rattle. And at once his fear infected the sleepers next to him; a general agitation spread. Afraid that the night attendant's blind might snap up again, C. retreated to his cot.

There were hours when C. was over-alert, almost hallucinating; he found himself in other spaces that were like enormous train stations filled with people. The people lay on the stone floors of the gigantic halls, trying to sleep; even the broad stairways leading into the depths were completely filled. But none of the stations were familiar to him. – He lay on his bed in Haar and listened to the bridled raging of these men whose sleep was visited by fiends, phantasms, demonic faces. The noise came in waves; after moments of quiet it rose like a distant storm, towered over an invisible horizon, and raced forward; under its barrage the bedframes stamped and jangled, the sleepers clung tight, each on his own on a nutshell of a boat, whirled off by the waves, and they joined in with the noise, all yowling at once, but each in his own fear, each picturing his own solitary destruction. Only to slacken again, subsiding as if in a sheltered bay. No notice was taken in the night attendant's booth.

These oscillating waves electrified every floor in the gray cement block…and probably, he thought, in all the other buildings at the Haar Clinic. That was how they kept in touch, he thought, with this speechless demonic howling. And somewhere, in this wasteland far outside Munich, the vibrations focused like electric energies and communed with an equally speechless God.

You stayed at Haar until you'd spent yourself, until you were burned out, emptied of the rage within you. Then you could go, hollow and extinguished – and, dried-up as you were, one day you'd have to fill yourself back up with drink. Change back into the dog who howls to God…

It took three days for C.'s body to reach a state in which it could stomach sleep again. Before that he'd occasionally lapsed for a few hours into an oblivion that amounted to absolute apathy. He'd lain on his back with eyes half shut, observing the goings-on around him through a reddish haze, unable to make any sense of it all. For three nights and nearly three days the icy cold of Munich's central station lingered on inside him, his feet numb, still seeming frozen fast to the concrete floor of the station. When at last those feet seemed to breathe out a little warmth again, he fell asleep instantly.

On the morning of the fourth day he got out of bed; a nurse told him he'd slept for more than fifteen hours. He was told to take a shower and was handed a small razor. He barely recognized himself in the shower stall's mirror: he was a grotesque ghost with a wild, matted shock of hair and gray beard stubble a quarter inch long; his eyes were bloodshot and surrounded by quince-yellow bags. After his shower he felt the fact that he hadn't eaten for days, at least not that he could recall; hungrily he devoured the colorless, odorless gruel that was doled out each morning along with a heap of sliced bread. After breakfast the ward filled with rapt silence, an almost church-like atmosphere. He'd already asked two days before for permission to spend time in the corridor. – He couldn't cope with confinement, he'd announced melodramatically, after the life he'd left behind in the GDR. And to his surprise the doctor had assented. This promoted him to the group of people whose detox was progressing successfully and who were granted corridor rights. For nearly sixteen hours of the day they could be seen wandering through the halls, close-lipped and humble.

Initially C. had gotten hopelessly lost in those halls, but at last he identified a kind of circular route and kept to that, always taking it in the same direction. It was the outer corridor, running like a gallery along all four walls of the block. At first he'd walked fast, hurrying with his upper body bent forward, but he soon sensed that he couldn't keep up that pace. So he adjusted to the shuffling trot that was the norm in the ward. It was a kind of jog, but slower than a leisurely walk, and the soles of your feet never left the floor. It was an almost mechanical mode of locomotion with which you seemed to cross eternities. But first you had to practice; after fewer than ten rounds C. would be exhausted and sink down on a bench in one of the smoking areas. There he'd wait for his unrest—of which he harbored an inexhaustible spring—to rise once again and propel him to his feet.

Something in him kept on striving to overtake his fellow patients; a nurse admonished him to settle down. Maybe his compulsive pugnacity upset his fellow circum-navigators. But he seemed to have lost all capacity for rest; he'd hurry onward until he was wheezing and coughing. He counted the laps and managed fewer and fewer, but even at the smokers' tables he could only hold out for a few minutes. And he took to mumbling a phrase to the rhythm of his shuffling steps, a phrase that was a conclusion, the end product of forgotten thoughts: It's over, it's over, it's over…it was like an echo, like a quote.

One time, turning a corner of the bright, sparkling clean corridor and charging toward the blinding bank of windows, he'd run head on into a specter who turned out to be that gaunt, spindly patient whose sleep he'd spied on that first or second night—a shameless thing to do, it seemed to him now. – Excuse me, C. mumbled. – The other man said: Aren't you the guy who's still got cigarettes?

C. had cigarettes; he'd forgotten his shaving kit, reading glasses, and reading material, but he'd tossed a few packs of cigarettes into his bag. C. saw that the man was by no means as old as he'd thought; now he had shaved too, and the madness had receded from his face. Here in public he was still wearing just the baggy gray cotton long johns, and matching them, in the same color, an undershirt made from a sort of potholder material. A pilly cardigan swaddled the crooked and extremely fragile torso, and on his sockless feet he wore battered slippers. C. was sorely tempted to ask what he'd meant by "catastrophe," what "Nazis" he was afraid of, but he didn't want to raise the subject of his eavesdropping. He didn't know what to talk about; after they'd smoked sheepishly for a while, he asked, for lack of a better idea: What do you do otherwise, what are you going to do when you get out of here again?

The man shrugged, and C. repeated his question.

I'm an alcoholic, said the other guy.

C. grinned as if that had been a joke. – But not by profession, are you?

Once an alcoholic, always an alcoholic, came the reply. And the big shots who run the economy can be glad

we exist. That's why they keep fixing us up again here...
same thing with smoking, by the way.

C. offered him another cigarette; he took it and said:
And what about you, what do you do on the outside? I
noticed already—you're from the East too, but you haven't
been over here for long. You're one of the ones who made
it. And you've wound up in Haar already, pretty damn
quick. So when did you come over?

I've been here for two years...wait a moment, two
years, is that even right? And you sound like you came
over at some point yourself...

I came twenty years ago, more or less. It doesn't really
matter how long you've been here. Over there it mattered how much longer you'd be stuck there. The whole
time: How much longer, how much longer...and then you
were through after all. You don't seem like a professional
alcoholic, you bounced back quickly. What do you do
otherwise?

C. hesitated: I write...I wrote. I'm an author, if that's
the kind of thing that rings a bell.

An author, he repeated, an author! Are you planning
to write about the conditions in here, is that what you're
after? I don't think we're exactly a trendy topic for the
papers.

No, I write books. Only sometimes for the papers...
maybe sometime I could write about Haar.

Yeah, maybe, said the other guy. But be careful, don't
go naming any names. This is a good clinic, and we're all
glad to be here...there are worse places!

Dialogue between two East German comrades in
a West German detox center! What a highly symbolic
anecdote of destiny. – That very same day he went to the

head nurse who supervised the floor. He asked her to look and see what job description had been entered on his admission form—it seemed a mistake had been made. Astonished, she asked his name, opened a metal drawer, and leafed through a long card file. She pulled out a card: Here it is, you're an author. Committed voluntarily. You signed it yourself.

Could I ask you, said C., to cross out the word *author*? It's a fraud, it was a mistake.

She accepted his explanation as calmly as though fraud were the most ordinary thing in the world. – But I have to put down something, she said.

Cross it out and put: No profession.

As you like. But your data is in the computer, too, and I can't just go and change it there.

Please try, said C., thanked her, and left.

He recalled how embarrassed he'd always felt to call himself an *author*…and the word *poet* was even more embarrassing. People would look as if you were trying to attract uncalled-for attention by giving that response when they'd just asked a casual question. And when you'd lisped it into somebody's ear, it would visibly put them on the spot, as though the fact of being faced with an "author" compelled them to express themselves in print-worthy form, to conjure up a comment that melded essayistic expertise with admiring erudition. That wasn't so bad, you could listen in mute submission; the most hideous thing was the ever-lurking question: What do you write about? – C. himself had once witnessed a harmless traveler in a train compartment being forced to confess he was an author. – Oh, dear Lord! he'd exclaimed in sympathy.

Since it seemed impossible to discuss the subject of

authors without incurring misunderstandings and psychic contortions, even long after gaining independent footing as an author he'd kept on describing himself in a way that dated him years in the past: I'm a stoker in a factory. And for educated people there was a variant: I work in the heat supply sector of the metal industry. – At that his interlocutor would be unlikely to push the conversation any further.

The writing profession was one that was constantly called into question, and C. wasn't sure that cast a positive light on him. He'd wondered if one might call it the most German of professions. At any rate, it seemed to give people pause, just as when you revealed your German citizenship to a group of foreigners. In a group of Asians it seemed completely irrelevant who was Vietnamese, Korean, or Chinese. If you identified yourself as a German, you instantly seemed to encounter a shade of surplus respect, that little bit extra that was needed to cover up a sardonic grin. And the profession of author elicited a similar widening of the eyes; it was as if you'd said: I'm an *Obersturmbahnführer*! When you announced your profession as that of an author, you simultaneously emphasized—even these days! C. thought—a kind of official rank.

Those were thoughts he dwelled on while making his rounds of the halls. He was influenced by the light, or so it seemed to him: On the side with the windows, where the winter sky's white light fell through the glass front, and where the niches with the smokers' tables were, he'd hasten his shuffling steps; he'd hurry forward, causing his soles to squeak on the parquet and drawing disapproving glances. Here he was the "author"…maybe word of it had gotten around, but at the moment there was nothing he was less eager to be asked about. On the other side, in the electric light that was always a bit too dim, he'd recuperate; he'd walk more slowly, or stop in his tracks, waiting to see how long he could stand being stationary. He'd try to muster inner stability to pass the smokers' areas unperturbed. In one of these pauses it suddenly occurred to him that about two days prior he'd mulled over an idea in a fit of logorrhea that reminded him of the "speeches to the masses" that some patients delivered as they dozed. His speech hadn't been addressed to the masses, though, and he'd been wide awake, a break in his first fifteen-hour spell of sleep. He'd imagined writing a letter to the GDR's culture ministry, and the phrases he came up with in his mind struck him as irresistible. The idea was to solicit, at this late date, an extension of his exit visa…his bygone visa, it had to be called at this point. He meant to phrase his petition with a certain irony:

Herr Minister, it may actually have escaped your notice that I have not yet returned to the GDR. If so, that is merely proof that my stay in West Germany has borne fruit. Not just from a literary perspective, but in the sense that I have come to recognize myself as an individual whom you, Sir, would describe as a *citizen of the GDR*. This leads to the question of my repatriation, which I would like to clarify with you. You may ask: Why doesn't he just get on a train and return to the GDR? The reasons are twofold: Some time ago I entered into an interpersonal relationship which I am, as it were, dependent on maintaining. The second reason: For some time I have been occupied with the execution of a substantial literary project and must avoid long travel-related interruptions, which in all probability would have a destructive effect on the cohesion of the work. For the abovementioned reasons I propose extending/renewing my visa by mail. Accordingly, operating on the assumption of your approval, I shall send my travel documents to the Permanent Mission of the GDR in Bonn so that my new visa can be issued...

He felt that the letter was quite properly worded and informed by lucid logic; as soon as possible he'd arrange his release from the clinic so that he could get to a typewriter. The decision calmed him, and he fell asleep again. – Since then two days had passed, and he'd forgotten the waking dream of that night just as he forgot all his dreams.

At his next doctor's consultation he requested his release from Haar. After signing his name to confirm that he bore sole responsibility for his departure and assumed liability for any damages that might result, the doors opened for him and he was standing outside in the frosty pale gray midday light. He walked to the station of the Munich suburban train, past the front gardens of single-family homes, losing his way several times; in this quiet neighborhood there were no people around to ask directions from. In the forbidding calm of the time between the holidays, hoarfrost covered the cars, parked halfway up the sidewalks, and the Christmas decorations in the windows glittered almost hostilely. New Year's Eve was approaching, and everyone had to finish digesting by then. At the station, C. had a cup of coffee at a kiosk. It was too cold for a beer, and though a mini-bottle of liquor with his coffee would have hit the spot, he restrained himself.

Without wasting a thought on Munich, he got on the very next train for Nuremberg. Stepping into his apartment several hours later, he was touched to find that it wasn't completely freezing: Hedda had been there and turned the heat to a moderate temperature that would take just minutes to warm all the way up. She'd washed his dishes, too, and watered the plants on the windowsills. He called her while making himself tea and waiting for the apartment to get warm. She was surprised to hear that he was back already; she said that naturally she hadn't expected him yet. She knew about everything that had happened in the meantime. She said that, annoyingly enough, she had theater tickets for that evening, but of course she wouldn't go. – He said she should go ahead and not let the ticket go to waste. – No, she said, you know I don't really want to go to the theater, I was just talked into it. I'd be happy for you to come over.

He spent that night at Hedda's, in her little apartment over on Schillerplatz, with a sense of warmth he hadn't had in ages. The light burned in the kitchen, where he sat lost in thought while she slept and dreamed in her tiny bedroom in the back: Hedda dreamed every night, and in the morning she could remember it all with total clarity; he admired her for that. Inside him was a sense of shelter, of appeasement and contentment, that lasted as long as he was there, and he spent almost a week without going back to his apartment on Kobergerstrasse. During that time he didn't talk much; he listened and watched as she bustled around him with affectionate reproaches. He didn't feel like contradicting; he sat meekly at her table while, with much headshaking and comical handwringing, she analyzed his alcoholism and waxed indignant about the mechanisms of his self-destruction. He never tired of the sight of her, conscious that for him she was the most beautiful woman he'd ever met…he'd never doubted it, he just hadn't reminded himself of it every day. If he lost her some day, he thought, the years with her would still stand as the part of his life that made it worthwhile.

Hedda wasn't the least bit convinced of her beauty, and he kept on her case for that. But he ran up against a wall; it was as though he had to defend her against the verdict of a third, objective voice. C. simply knew better; he'd invoke his male gaze, which by its nature had the edge over her or anyone else's objectivity. Hedda would reply, laughing: You're nuts, you aren't even a real man. – And I don't want to be, either, C. would say.

Her beauty was that of a woman you'd no longer call "young"; her figure was on the full side, in a quite unobjectionable way, and that seemed to lend her a force that he found rather daunting at times. Against that life force she sometimes emanated—when she feels loved! C. thought—he, usually seen as the "strong one," suddenly seemed shaky or frail. What was more, Hedda's vitality spread heedlessly, as it were, virtually in spite of herself, which made her seem all the more inexhaustibly bountiful. When he was alone he would often see her before him as though she were inscribing herself still more deeply inside him: the way she turned her face toward him when she spoke, unguarded and filled with Russian passion, which life in Germany had never been able to take from her; but mixed with irony, too, or with a sudden doubt whether agreement would still be forthcoming. She could say whatever she liked; you agreed when she looked at you. When you saw how her gray-green eyes seemed to open a bit wider with each sentence, or how her mouth seemed to take in life as she spoke, as though to test the truth of it within her. Fine wrinkles would appear around her eyes; there was no knowing whether laughter or sorrow had put them there. And when he spent the night at his place on Kobergerstrasse, he often thought he'd heard her voice in his sleep.

Unfortunately he'd left his manuscript and his reading glasses in Munich, he told her. – She said that you could buy glasses in Nuremberg too. And if they called her friend in Munich, she'd send the manuscript right away. – When the few sheets of paper arrived in the mail, they struck C. as well-nigh pathetic. There were just a few badly written, barely legible lines, revolving around half-baked recollections of a small town in the GDR.

Sitting in Hedda's kitchen at night, waiting to grow too tired to sit, he recalled a strange incident he'd experienced on a trip, shuttling back and forth between West and East Germany. At that time he was still living mainly in Hanau, and he'd often taken the train back "over there" – already he'd adopted the Western way of putting things. He traveled from Frankfurt to Leipzig and back the same way, and on that train, which was almost always empty, he was probably becoming a familiar face. It happened at the station in *Gerstungen*, at the border crossing to the west… doubtless the world's most dismal station, C. thought every time. The East German border officials came striding through the cars to check the passengers' papers. At the head of the squad was a woman perhaps a bit younger than C., evidently the highest-ranking officer. She smiled as she took C.'s passport and said: Well, finally heading back home? – He was startled; sitting all alone in his compartment, he was unprepared for any kind of small talk. Yes, he agreed, yes…back home!

Later on he wondered if he was wrong, if he'd actually been heading to Leipzig that day, that is, eastward. No, he could have sworn to it: he was sitting in the train to Frankfurt, and the woman asked whether he was "going home." Yet plain as day, she'd been holding his dark blue GDR passport, which no one could ever mistake for the red-brown West German one. He was so certain of the direction because he'd jotted down the episode as soon as the train started moving again. Besides, his memories of the station at Gerstungen were always razor-sharp.

On its way from Leipzig, the train entered Gerstungen clattering and rocking, its speed barely throttled; then it would stop all at once as though the brakes had been jammed on by accident. Heading toward Leipzig, the line of cars would move slowly, hesitant, almost soundless, and came to a standstill between two bare, utterly abandoned platforms. The train would coast to a stop as though with a gesture of resignation: It's all over, this iron snake will never budge again. Then for a long time nothing would happen at all, an audible silence would descend; after a while you'd think you heard the distant chirping of birds filter in. Then—the same thing happened every time— after what seemed like an eternity a timid scrape would be heard somewhere in one of the cars. And at once a man's voice would ring out: The windows stay closed!— Instantly the window would slide shut again. In the train a few terrified retirees—on reaching retirement age, East Germans were allowed to travel—would be huddling behind their tons of baggage; no one else took that train, no one traveled to the East anymore. – You looked out the closed window at a smooth pale gray concrete wall with no beginning and no end, longer than the entire train and interrupted only by its supporting columns. It rose almost to the roof covering the platform, leaving a slit through which stark concrete buildings could be seen, pale gray too and with windows of opaque gray frosted glass. At the foot of the wall was the empty, pale gray concrete platform; it was the same across the way, on the other side of the train. Siberian gulag architecture, concocted by pale gray brains out of sheer contempt for mankind, a form of spite that C. did not appreciate. Somewhere there was a gap in the roof, and you could look up into the sky: pale gray-white, like lead beginning to melt in the heat. And it seemed possible that a disheveled sluggish bird might be fluttering through that seamless, hueless segment of infinity. The only visual relief was the orange-yellow metal bins labeled Newspapers set at regular intervals. And soon you actually saw a group of men in blue-gray uniforms tossing bundles of papers through the slits of those bins. These were the West German newspapers that had been cleared out of the train: tabloids and sports magazines, the newspaper of the West German Communist Party and the right-wing *Deutsche National- und Soldatenzeitung*. Two of the men disposed of the newspapers while a third stood by and made sure that every single piece of paper vanished into the bins. Now you finally heard the barking: it was the teams of dogs that sniffed the spaces under the train cars; of course, they were only used for trains coming from the East…so maybe one of those trains was expected. Indeed—over there, invisible behind the concrete wall, a row of train cars screeched to a halt. Again it was still except for the vicious yapping of the dogs, Pavlovian reflexes fully functional. After more long minutes things got moving: doors banged, voices murmured;

the passport control officers hurried through the train. At least they managed to seem in a hurry. They were conversing, jauntily, medium-loud, as though they were carrying out orders: on their way through the train they had to chat about private things, enunciating as clearly as possible. They were making a show of sovereign self-assurance; *sovereign* was a popular adjective in the country C. was heading for. Loudly slamming the door, they left the last car and soon passed by beneath the train windows, still chatting: steps crunching on the rotten concrete, heat rising, stillness. Then movement again: now it was the turn of the customs officers, and the whole procedure was repeated. Doors opening, doors closing, the Pavlovian reflexes of chitchat, and in between came the official language rituals solemnly observed at each compartment with an occupant. You could keep count: the train had about twenty passengers. When the customs officers left, time baked down to stillness again. Heat, disintegration, existential void. The engine of the demoted express train gave its first brief sputter. Then came a rattle and clatter; the East German caterer's hard-currency snack cart was being maneuvered through the cars. Whenever the vendor spotted a few passengers, her voice rang out: Beer, Coca-Cola, Fanta, cigarettes! – Of course I only take D-marks! she was once heard explaining. Reaching C., she shouted as though to alert a whole horde of customers: Beer, Coca-Cola, cigarettes! – C. didn't stir, and she repeated her shout with a touch more urgency. C. stared out the window with sadistic composure, never moving. Now she opened the door of his compartment so he could hear better and shouted one more time: Beer, Coca-Cola, Fanta…cigarettes! – He turned to face her and said: No thank you. – She wished him a pleasant journey and pushed the jangling cart onward.

From his traveling bag C. took one of the cans of beer he'd gotten back in Hanau, now lukewarm. When he opened the can, foam sprayed the entire compartment; the beer tasted metallic and bitter. He hadn't even noticed that the train had jerked forward and was trundling at a snail's pace out of the station. At the end of the platform was the big sign he read on each of these journeys: We Welcome Our Passengers to the German Democratic Republic.

He reflected that all the procedures he'd just gone through would, in all probability, take even longer when traveling back. And he asked himself whether the verb "travel" was even the word for what he was thinking of. Traveling back, the space between the axles was examined with mirrors attached to long poles, dogs were sent sniffing under the train, the paneling of the cars was unscrewed, a man in uniform climbed up a specially constructed ladder and shined a long flashlight into the openings. – What are they doing with my time! C. thought; the question was instilled in him for good. Even when he was in bed with Hedda, the question would be: What are these creatures doing with my time? With the time that belongs to me…

Naturally he missed his connecting train in Leipzig; he had to wait for the next one, an hour and a half later. He left the train station to take a stroll through Leipzig, but the weather had changed; it was rainy and cool. The city seemed lifeless, sullen, depressed… Several weeks ago he'd been in Vienna to give a poetry reading, and that city, too, had seemed strangely empty. – There were just a few small groups of people standing at the tram stop outside the station, but over at the taxi stand a long line had formed, waiting patiently though far and wide there was no taxi to be seen. A fine drizzle had formed out of the fog, billowing through the orangey light over the tram tracks. The moisture merged with the dust on the pavement to form a slimy viscous film that made you slip. And the same slimy matter seemed to drip in fat yellow drops from the narrow roof of the tram stop; a tram arrived, a cloud of rain and dust flying up before it. Steam rose from the sodden filth that smelled of burned coal, and the insoluble slime of ash, soot, and rain seemed to spread and cover the whole city.

Less than a month prior, in a place called Chernobyl, in the Ukrainian Soviet Socialist Republic, a nuclear accident had occurred. One of the reactor blocks of the nuclear power plant had exploded, catapulting radioactive steam far into the atmosphere. Now rain clouds were marching westward. In Vienna, early that May, the whole city had panicked. People in the West stopped eating fresh vegetables, even if they hadn't been rained on yet. It emerged that certain people with money had flown to the Canary Islands; the travel agencies were doing a booming business. But in the East—where there wasn't much in the way of vegetables anyway—no one gave a damn. Stolidly they let the broken gutters trickle swill down their necks.

Since moving to the West, C. had barely followed the news in the papers. That, he felt, had been an Eastern Bloc obsession; in the GDR you felt well informed if you gorged on newspaper articles and TV news, decoding cryptic communiqués and reading the speeches of every single chairman forward, backward, and between the lines. For him it was just the opposite now, he no longer knew a thing about politics, sports, or the latest technique for sexual pleasure. – If that Chernobyl thing hadn't put people in such a panic, it probably wouldn't have registered with him, any more than, say, the Seoul Olympics…and in the old days he'd never missed a chance to watch the Olympics on TV. Now he scornfully referred to the games as the "Cold World War." And when he heard about the doping scandals, he felt vindicated…illusion after illusion was going down the drain, and he found that the resulting holes were no longer so easy to fill. There was little in the way of replacement; slowly but surely he was reaching an age where he sensed that life consisted chiefly of illusions.

Because of that Chernobyl thing, he'd started buying the papers again. But these papers caused a minor meltdown in his apartment, piling up unread in every corner and restricting his freedom of movement. The air he breathed seemed polluted by the toxic effluvia of the printer's ink; he was constantly on the run from his apartment, which had morphed into an inexhaustible archive of journalistic idiocies. Whenever he sat down at his desk and wedged his notebook, tiny by comparison, between the stacks of printed paper, he'd look up and see the lodes of unmined print matter: they harbored so many ways of botching the subjunctive case that he'd instantly capitulate.

At school he'd never managed to learn the slightest bit of Russian—for six years various teachers had struggled with him in vain—and he blamed that for his occasional catastrophic mistake of mixing up the words "Chernobyl" and "Perestroika," albeit never while sober. Or perhaps the blame went to the inventor of the newfangled expressions that Western Europeans were now affecting, accent and all. Sources close to Gorbachev—i.e., the KGB itself, thought C.—at any rate, sources claimed that Chernobyl had basically seen a few cases of slight to moderately serious burns, and that the persons affected were recovering. Meanwhile the Western press was reporting huge numbers of deaths. – From his childhood onward pronouncements from every conceivable type of authority had a traumatic effect on C....due in large part to his grandfather, who laughed at threats and broke out in a cold sweat at promises of salvation. He recalled the time when a new subject had been introduced at school, socialist studies, replacing homeland studies; it must have been some time before March 1953. A teacher, eyes aglow, speaking with spittle-moist enthusiasm, declared that the fission energy from a single uranium rod would be enough to melt the entire Arctic ice cap. Then it would be feasible—Michurin and Lysenko were already running the experiments in their state-of-the-art biology labs—to cultivate two-foot-long bananas in the Siberian tundra. There was talk of rerouting the Gulf Stream and building dams across the Bering Strait. Now one rather small nuclear power plant built in the vast empire of the Soviet Union had sufficed to explode all of humanity's belief in progress.

In East Germany the so-called man on the street, pointing to the situation in the country—in all the socialist countries—would always vehemently defend the freedom of the press. C. was no exception; he regarded the freedom of opinion and information as absolutely indispensable, and even in the West he still held to that view. But in the West, he saw the results of that freedom on a daily basis. It was no use telling himself that this reality had to be put up with, just as long as the principle was right. More and more often he wondered whether the principle even had a chance against the reality that prevailed over it. The avowed freedom of the press had unmistakably degenerated to nothing except the freedom to take anything that could be thought, no matter what its nature, and process it so it was fit to be sold. All facts, and even non-facts, everything that could be shown or verbalized in any way, had to be rendered marketable, and for that purpose all symbols and images were permitted. Anything truthful or valuable that survived that processing procedure intact owed more to chance than to the tenets of democracy.

C. had to admit that this left him bitterly disappointed. But he didn't show it; that would have drawn scorn and derision from native West Germans. With disappointment in his heart he went on buying papers, and sometimes he even read them. But all at once he was reading them differently, not to inform himself, but instead for entertainment. Things that should have unsettled him profoundly—Chernobyl, the ozone hole, drug victims, the wars in Afghanistan and Angola, AIDS—filtered through in bits and pieces, basically no longer relevant to him: he now read the papers merely to distract himself. Less and less often would he feel a sense of horror when reading apocalyptic news as a distraction.

Maybe that's a step on the way to Westernizing, he thought. Books are too difficult, and they aren't distracting. So you read the papers, which offer more and more "color."

Whenever he got to that point in his thoughts, nausea would rise up inside him, transforming within seconds into total paralysis; it was a condition he couldn't describe, all he knew was: *he couldn't take it anymore!*—If I don't do everything in my power to beat this condition, something's going to happen! he thought. As it would often take him more than an hour to get up, leave the house, and go to a bar, he always kept a bottle of liquor in the fridge.

When he was sitting down at the bar, he'd lapse into silent inward laughter. On the one hand, he'd always been skeptical when other writers talked about their torments (except for Hedda; if anything, she played down the horrors she went through); he felt that many authors used torment to justify their writing—an accusation from which he did not exempt himself. On the other hand, in some convoluted way he believed in the creative power of tormenting experiences (while Hedda disputed it, claiming that pain merely silenced people), and he'd always suspected himself of lacking that experience. – In fact he'd always written offhandedly, looking away from his words, which had flowed from him effortlessly. In his life he'd never done a stroke of real work, he'd done everything in passing, for the interim, as it were. The real thing is yet to come, he'd always thought, as though he had infinite time at his disposal. Now he was pushing fifty—just three years left to go—it was high time for the "real thing"… and suddenly nothing was coming at all!

The alarm this caused him was not so easily contained. He knew that country over there, that GDR, was a marginal, backward enclave where literature didn't actually mean a thing; all the hoopla about literature in the Eastern Bloc was a hypocritical show…but at least he'd been able to write over there, and the hoopla had swept even him into the public's awareness. But over here literature was going down the drain, he felt that was obvious. Literature that refused to serve the purpose of distraction was punished by being passed over on the market…after all, on that market all stops were pulled to distract the public; the best distraction was what sold the best. On an almost weekly basis the culture pages of the newspapers he read to distract himself informed him about the *end of literature*. He'd never taken it seriously before; you didn't get much of a sense of that end when you were surrounded by the hype of the literature business. Then it occurred to him that the literature business was so hectic precisely so as to cover up its end. Corpses were being set to banquet, to slightly misquote Ezra Pound…

Evidently I'm perfectly adapted to the end of literature, because I can't get anything done at all, he thought, laughing inwardly until he convulsed. The two young things behind the bar seemed to notice, because they were trying hard not to look. – There goes that Easterner, hitting the bottle again, they were probably thinking. How can they even drink that much if they're as poor as you keep hearing? No proper cars, but they never lay off the booze. And we'll have to get on his case when it's closing time! Just like last time, he was the last one left…like he was glued to his chair. They exchanged nods and baby-faced smiles; they must have been around thirty, but still looked seventeen. And sometimes they swayed their narrow shoulders slightly, moving with the song he'd heard in the supermarket recently. When he waved his empty beer glass, they were quick to respond, you had to give them that.

Well, there it was, that goddamned literary torment he used to miss so sorely: he couldn't put down a single line that didn't completely revolt him! And the acclaim he'd garnered for his allegations against the system and conditions over there revolted him just as thoroughly. He didn't belong in this literary society that was concerned with nothing but acclaim…literature's critical phase was over, it had passed like a fleeting fashion—a fit of eloquence that shaped the very beards people sported. And maybe he was getting as old and gray as those beards. Ultimately he no longer really belonged in that scene, any more than he belonged in this bar that called itself "Casablanca." And that was consequently crammed with pictures of Humphrey Bogart: Humphrey Bogart with or without Ingrid Bergman, that was the postmodern style…

But had he ever belonged…on either side, here or over there? To tell the truth, he would have been outraged to be pigeonholed anywhere.

From "Casablanca" to his apartment it was just a short walk, but long enough for the aggravating realization that he still hadn't had enough to drink. If his alcohol level was too low, he might yet be lured back to his desk in the hopes of writing one sentence that could serve as a start for the next day. That had happened often enough; bits of paper with those first sentences were scattered all over the desk, and all of them petered out in three little dots. None of the sentences had seemed worth pursuing; they were stilted, bogus, and bloated, and some of them barely made sense to him. Nearly all of those sentences began with the little word "I"…that in itself would rile him enough that he'd flick the notes from the desk with one finger. The term "I" instantly made him impotent…

There were plenty of other bars nearby; just a few minutes later he'd be sitting on a stool at a new one. In the mirror behind the bar he could see himself sitting there: listing slightly, trying to prop himself on his right elbow, two fingers holding a cigarette from which a wisp of smoke rose straight into the air. The beer glass, already half empty, in front of his chest; over it, his pale, slightly puffy face... A battered boxer, he thought whenever he saw himself that way. He kept a photo of himself that he never showed to anyone. It had been shot at a moment when he was struggling back to his feet after a knockout blow; he was still on his knees, one hand groping frantically for the ropes. His eyes were wide open in horror; you could tell that his gaze was returning from blackness, but still beheld no clear images. The referee standing beside him—you could tell from his emphatic gesture—had already counted him out. – C. always kept this cruel photo hidden, even from himself, and when he happened across it, he'd stare as though it showed the only moment of his life in which his *I* had truly stepped forth.

About a year ago, C. had bought himself a record player, though records were barely even commercially available now that the music industry was transitioning to CD technology. He'd gotten it practically for free, at an estate sale that he'd seen advertised in the paper and drove to with Hedda in her little Ford. They had actually been looking for a dresser (his towels, pajamas, and underpants were still balled up chaotically in the bookcases), but all he'd had eyes for was the gorgeous anthracite record player. The teary-eyed mourners at the estate sale were clearly relieved to find someone who wanted the thing. He and Hedda had driven off with the clattering boxy case and two speakers amid Hedda's despairing derision; she was endlessly irritated by his dusty underthings.

The record player was a new barrier that blocked any move toward his desk; he was compelled to spend entire days chasing through town in constant search of records, which were either being sold dirt-cheap at flea markets or offered for exorbitant prices in music shops. Though he didn't really get to know Nuremberg that way, he did discover that it had an incredible number of pubs. A genuinely menacing infrastructure of alcohol filling stations spanned the city, and it proved extremely difficult to cope with deprivation in a place with such an optimal supply situation. Again and again he embarked on phases in which he resolved to grapple with his sense of deprivation and overcome it though persistence. He'd avoid the pubs as best he could, and if he did go inside, he'd drink coffee and mineral water, which felt like an extremely dreary substitute.

One time at the north end of the city center, as he skulked conflictedly around a pub entrance, he was addressed by someone who came up beside him. A woman was standing there, signaling recognition, but he had no idea who she was. Taking a shot in the dark, he said that he didn't have much time, but he really needed a cup of coffee. Would she like to join him in the pub, just for half an hour? – Oh, she said, a bit nonplussed, do we have to go in there? I'm sure we can find somewhere else. And she took him lightly by the arm and propelled him away. The barely perceptible grip of her hand brought it back: she had led him off once before, after attending his reading at a Nuremberg bookshop. She'd had him sign a book and then offered to give him a lift to Kobergerstrasse: she lived on Kobergerstrasse too, just a few doors down. And she had maneuvered him to her car with just that feather-light hand on his upper arm. – Befuddled brothers from the East, he'd thought, have to be treated with care in this country, and if the author's spirited away right after the reading, the rest of the audience just has to live with it. – In the car she'd asked him if he realized that this was the second time he'd signed a book for her. If he still remembered his reading in Regensburg. But that was probably too much to expect, considering all the people he must meet on his trips.

He felt that his memory was fundamentally intransigent, a failing that alcohol did its best to facilitate—it could hardly be blamed on the rich variety of a writer's life on the road; that was a romantic notion. But now it dawned on him: once, a year before being granted the twelve-month visa, he'd been allowed to leave the country for a short reading tour, and spent three days in Regensburg. And after that reading the pressure of the same hand had guided him to the same car; another hand had held an umbrella over his head because rain had started pelting down and he couldn't possibly go the short way to his hotel on foot. The umbrella had blocked his view; he'd groped through the deluge blind and disoriented, relying solely on those three magnetic fingers on his upper arm; all of Regensburg, all the enigmatic West, the status quo, the Cold War and the whole idiotic world, vanished for a while in a raging tempest that erupted in lightning and thunder and deafening torrents all around the car's alarmingly small metal shell. It had taken him several minutes to notice that there was another female presence in the car, huddling on the back seat not making a noise and evidently trying to render herself invisible. Much later he learned that that had been Hedda.

And then a yellow leather jacket had been sent to C. in Leipzig—by the woman who was now standing in front of him. The letter accompanying it said how lightly he'd been dressed back then in Regensburg. And since there must be storms in Leipzig too, not just in Regensburg (which had *Regen*, or rain, in its name), he should please accept the jacket. – The package, according to the return address, had been sent from Nuremberg.

Now I can finally thank you for the leather jacket, said C., I forgot to do it before, after that reading here in Nuremberg, and I'd like to apologize for that. I didn't write to you, I didn't respond at all. And the jacket fit me perfectly, too. – That time in Nuremberg you probably couldn't even remember who I was. And it was a stupid letter; of course Regensburg doesn't come from *Regen*, it has something to do with a castle belonging to the regents. – I didn't know that either, said C., but maybe we could try this pub here? – Once again they were standing at the door to a bar, but she didn't like that one either. – Or the one over there; C. pointed to the other side of the street. There are two across the way, no, actually three…

He sensed her reluctance, but she gave in, and finally followed him. C. instantly registered the cause of her hesitation: the room was murkily lit and deserted—but for two or three beer drinkers on barstools, wearing wildly colored shirts and sporting a whole collection of jewelry on their necks, ears, and wrists—and behind the bar stood a television on whose screen a tangle of naked human bodies performed acrobatic copulatory exercises, the ecstatic wails of the actors ringing out through the mucilage of the music. Alarmed, C. looked at his companion to see if she would bolt out of the pub, but she sat down valiantly at a corner table with her back to the TV screen, and he took a seat across from her. A woman came slouching up to their table from the bar…usually he tried not to think the worst, but the only way to describe that woman was as a boozy, slimy old bag. She leaned down between their heads and asked their wishes with a grin. C. ordered two cups of coffee and paid as soon as she brought them. She slipped the coins into her apron pocket uncounted and went away; C. asked: Should we go somewhere else? – When his companion gave a timid nod, he drank both coffees and stood up. – I'm sorry, he said out on the street, I didn't realize where we were. – No problem, that was an interesting moment there, she replied. But why don't you come have coffee at my place some time, I invited you once before, after all…

Back in his apartment he tried to recall that reading trip to Regensburg. It was practically impossible; there was nothing but twilight, nebulous watery images interspersed with the blurred hues of neon signs, gleaming drenched automobiles, shop windows washed with films of water, damp constantly steaming from his clothes, the lenses of his glasses still spattered as he gave a reading in a froglike croak polluted by slips of the tongue, after which applause pattered as from several scattered fountains. Even from the train on the way back the west could no longer be seen, as perpetual squalls of rain lashed the windows of the compartment.

Just be careful you don't catch pneumonia over here among the evil capitalists, people told him. – Not a bad idea, he'd replied. Then I'd have to stay until I got better— how long would that take? – We'll find a doctor who'll diagnose you with pneumonia if you want to stay a bit longer.

Later, in Leipzig, he'd reminisce about those conversations; they cast a certain light on the West that outshone the cold rain as it washed away the rest of the summer. They had an insouciance and warmth that he missed back in Leipzig.

Leipzig had succumbed to paralysis; it was the *phase of depression*, as C. referred to this period; no one had any idea how to escape it. On both sides of the so-called Iron Curtain, the nuclear missiles—just a fraction of which could have annihilated the world—stood staring each other down. Between them was the territory where they were supposed to detonate: the two German nations. The eastern side was ruled by a burly figure called Chernenko, an ice-gray corpse with a frozen face you'd catch a glimpse of now and then up on a rostrum on Red Square, wedged inert between his generals; if that macabre sculpture made the slightest move, you would have heard a crunching and cracking like pack ice. The general opinion was that he was immobilized, attached to a wooden scaffold set up behind his back. In the western hemisphere another cancer sufferer was calling the shots, someone who seemed more agile only by virtue of being a Hollywood actor. C. had once given a reading in California, at the University of California, Santa Barbara, and had the impression that the town was still under the thumb of that president who had already left office. The town stood silent and acquiescent in the white heat, with life stirring only at the harbor front and at the university. Everyone else, it seemed, was tied up in or with the army of tanks guarding the nearby ranch where Reagan had barricaded himself.

The Cold War had grown so cold, it had turned to eternal ice. The younger generation in the GDR seemed animated solely by the desire to escape to the West; their elders, who had already settled in, could think of nothing but Western money; for Western money you could get anything overnight, any kind of bath installation, any replacement part, any kind of dentures: There wasn't a plumber, a paperhanger, a roofer who'd even dream of moonlighting for Eastern money. The West had become the meaning of life in the East…and if you said so, no one even denied it anymore.

C. was not one of the people for whom the West was the redemptive goal of all their strivings; he had actually turned down the first few invitations, squirming with ludicrous excuses. Then he'd gone on three trips after all, each for just a few days; his sole desire was to bring back books he couldn't get his hands on in the East – not even for Western money, as hard currency held less sway in intellectual circles. But suddenly he got a letter from a West German academic institution offering him a fellowship…it came just a short while after Chernenko, the hulk from the Central Committee, was officially declared dead, and was buried, and the new man who took over in Moscow started playing an astonishingly different tune. C. had always connected that with the letter from West Germany; it was as if someone were testing whether that different tune was the real thing. The fellowship he'd receive was generous, and would last for a year; it was April, and he had until November to decide…to decide whether he wanted to move to the West for a year, and see to it that he could actually pull it off. After all, the hard currency could be disbursed only in the country where it was legal tender.

After brief reflection he wrote a letter accepting the fellowship and sent it off with a reply coupon; he hadn't waited even ten days before the coupon came back signed and stamped with the academic seal of the West German institution. He decided to ignore the thought that that stamp on the little red card might have come from the Stasi…his letter of acceptance had been received, and that made his heart lighter. – At first he kept Mona, his girlfriend—he lived at her place in Leipzig, in close quarters, barely four hundred square feet—in the dark about his step on that road toward a new life. And about his initial applications for a travel permit, all the incredibly irksome paperwork he needed to do now. But of course she quickly found out, and she was furious. – You're planning to leave me all alone for an entire year! This was the sole, solitary conclusion she could draw from C.'s activities; he felt that was oversimplifying things. – Look, they've already rejected my exit visa application, he said, holding the letter from the Ministry of Culture under her nose. – You've got plenty of time, you'll manage it somehow. Might I point out that your friend would never go over there without his girlfriend…

The friend Mona meant was the writer H., who lived nearby on Georg-Schwarz-Strasse; lately their relationship had been complicated, if not to say ruptured; C. suspected it was because of his earlier short trips to the West, about which they'd argued. The friend was actually married to his girlfriend, but for Mona that distinction on paper was not a valid argument. – You mean we should get married so that they'd give us both a visa? C. wanted to ask. He let it be; Mona might have accepted the proposal.

C.'s friend held that you had to opt out of the games of power politics, the calculated carrot and stick of conceding or refusing certain privileges to artists. Otherwise you'd inevitably end up at the beck and call of the party dictatorship; he knew this was so because he'd once belonged to the party himself. The most transparent form of granting privilege was the practice of assigning visas, which were treated as acts of clemency or rewards for good behavior. And if you played along, you'd lose touch with the feelings of the average people who didn't have these privileges.

C. had tried to discuss the issue with one of those average people, a former colleague he ran into while visiting his mother, and the response he got was: If they give you a trip to the West, and you turn it down, you've got to be a total idiot!

After getting the first refusal from the Ministry of Culture, he did some soul-searching to see what his feelings were. He refused to believe it, that was his first thought. Two of his previous short trips had also been denied at first, but with persistent badgering and the help of the people who'd invited him, he'd gotten the visas issued at the last moment after all. And those first denial letters had been more harshly worded than this one was. After coming back from the pub late at night, he sat in Mona's tiny kitchen holding the brief, terse letter, and tried to find some handhold he could use to his advantage in these bleak lines issued from the heart of the bureaucracy. The denial was watertight, containing no explanation, the commas were properly placed…and yet the letter seemed to convey some minimal uncertainty beyond the grasp of logic. Perhaps because he'd gotten to know the deputy minister whose office had issued the denial…that was an exaggeration, he didn't know him, but he'd spoken to him the other times he'd applied for visas, and since then that minister had been an inscrutable monster no longer.

C. decided to renew his application, starting by stating the following: He'd worked obediently in the GDR's factories until he was almost forty years old; only then had he struck out on his own as a writer, at nearly forty, which he regarded as decidedly late. That—he would go on to say—had been a turning point for him, not all of whose consequences had been positive. Though the writing profession was what he'd aspired to, his conception of himself had been shaken. He was concerned with grasping his identity, his identity as a writer, which—as stated by the minister himself in the cultural policy directives put forth by the ministry—encompasses one's identity as a citizen of the country in which one writes. Identity, however, cannot be developed purely from the inside out, from the hermetically sealed interior; it also needs an external, comparative perspective. For that, a year is less than enough…

His friend, the writer H., was absolutely right! With a letter like that he'd be doing exactly what H. had accused him of: coming to an understanding with power. He'd be negotiating, speaking the language of power. He'd be embracing the bureaucracy's charade. There he was, spouting off about his "identity" even as he handed it over—and asked the deputy minister to affirm it…

In an attaché case he usually used to lug his manuscripts from place to place, he'd hidden a bottle of liquor; Mona had probably discovered it long ago. Now he got it out… Hour after hour he sat in the kitchen drinking; he didn't even take off his jacket. Hearing a noise, he quickly stashed away the bottle. But Mona, standing on the threshold in her nightgown, naturally smelled the booze. He was wearing the yellow leather jacket, and papers were scattered on the floor and on the tiny table, next to the ashtray with its host of glowing cigarette butts. Mona stared at him, but all she seemed to see was the yellow leather jacket. After a while she said: So now you've lost your mind!

Maybe Mona was right and he had gone crazy. In the tiny cell of a kitchen the air had swollen to a substance that was barely a gas anymore; it smelled like the scene of a fire. He sat amid the smoke, and even inside him black smoldering fumes thickened; a strange paralysis had come over him, except when he lifted the bottle to his lips, moving as jerkily as an automaton. There was an indescribable fury inside him, a hatred, grisly and grinding; it was as though—following some completely theoretical, hairsplitting edict from which every loophole had been excised with academic pedantry—they had prohibited him from leading the life that had been forced upon him, that wasn't his fault. Now, facing off against that prohibition, he was reacting with his own boundless obstinacy: You *have* to let me, there's no other way...

If you give me the visa, maybe I won't even go, but you have to give it to me. You have to give me the chance to cross the border on Kohlhaase's bridge!

Can't you take that jacket off for once? asked Mona. Or do you want to go to bed with it? – Mona had recently gone into analysis, developing a keen eye for unconsciously symbolic actions. – You're already wearing your Western skin, she said. Mona had started analysis on the encouragement of his friend H., who was close acquaintances with a psychoanalyst. The upshot was that she was supposed to undergo inpatient therapy at a clinic in Halle; it was initially set to last four weeks, but might be extended. C. pictured it as a kind of intensive care. Now the only question was when a space would free up for her in Halle. Mona had spent months waiting for news, only to hear that as she didn't rank among the acute cases, it could easily take a year or more. C. told her: Maybe it's not such a bad thing if you don't go to Halle until I've gotten my visa. – Because then you'll have to show me even less consideration, she retorted.

It was plain to see: Mona couldn't stand him in that yellow jacket. He'd worn it all summer, too; only a few days got hot enough for shirtsleeves. The jacket was a garment of soft smooth leather, almost weightless, that just grazed his belt, and it seemed so perfectly tailored to his body that he felt it was made from his very own substance. Mona insisted on seeing it as a sheath protecting him from her, from her closeness; she reacted by suddenly buying him underclothes, better underclothes than he usually wore. And he wore the thin, brightly colored things, but soon found himself sweating in them, red welts appearing in his armpits; the seams of the underpants couldn't absorb the moisture the synthetic material made him produce, and quickly turned into cords as hard as cement that chafed the skin of his crotch; his genitals were constantly in the way of the cut of the underpants, which, unable to make the organ disappear, bundled it up to form a damp, amorphous lump of whose existence he was continually conscious. Clearly he no longer fit into the GDR's latest underwear creations, though his body had not changed a bit. He regularly forgot these so-called "intimate garments" at his mother's, where he paid frequent visits that year, and Mona naturally noticed when they vanished.

His fits of rage petered out as the summer progressed, despite the alcohol he consumed in undiminished quantities. Or was it that the alcohol softened his brain? Whenever he came to after one of those nights, he shuddered: he'd never guessed what latent hatred lurked inside him. Mona would be gone when he woke up around noon; she worked in the university's American Studies Department as a kind of assistant, and she could have written a book about the way the faculty members sabotaged each other or scratched each other's backs when it came to research assignments in the USA or England: screeds and political smears were routine for those seeking to oust a colleague who was "next in line" for one of those trips. – Your party comrades ought to be horrified of traveling to imperialist America, said C. – You should see the letters they write to the "class enemy" begging for an invitation.

He still recalled the strange weather Leipzig was having at the time. It was constantly raining, ten times a day, with the sun always breaking through again. The street would still be aglitter with moisture, and the sun would blaze down onto the dripping and trickling; mud washed down the street and collected in the craters of the crumbling roadway; nettles shot up from the omnipresent rubble heaps, you could watch how greedily they sprouted in the humidity of the scalding July days. Amid the burgeoning, steaming tranquility of the sloping side street, a hellish racket had broken loose, starting at seven in the morning and lasting until nightfall. Georg-Schwarz-Strasse, where the tram ran, had been closed to car traffic due to construction, and processions of vehicles, mainly buses and bellowing trucks, now dragged themselves up the slight slope of narrow Spittastrasse to reach Weissenfelser Strasse, whose intersection, in the traffic planners' infinite wisdom, was also blocked. C. used this pandemonium to justify his almost weekly escapes to his mother in the town of M. – Mona wanted to sleep with him, he could feel it. It wasn't just her longstanding frustration at his disinclination toward any attempt at intercourse—she was probably succumbing to the most simple-minded feminine notion of how to keep a man. And it was the most simple-minded feminine mistake: A man could hold onto a woman that way, but not the other way around, C. thought. At least not a man like him, whose constant retreat in the face of Mona's needs put him in a perpetual conflict with himself. Rarely did he have moments without a gnawing guilt; the very realization that it had just dissipated made it return to the pit of his stomach. – It's four in the afternoon, he thought, in about another hour her keys will clatter outside the door. The same sight nearly every day: she'll come inside, in all her summery beauty, a bit exhausted, but laughing; she'll drop her bag and hurl herself on the couch, exhaling as if she'd just done a sprint. She'll unbutton her blouse and lift its tails to air her body, and simultaneously, with deft movements of her feet, she'll slip off her sandals… Bring me something to drink, green soda, please. – C. fetches a glass of green fizzy soda from the kitchen and sits down beside her on the edge of the couch; she drinks in tiny sips—how does she manage to drink lying down without the soda running into her ears? When she gingerly sets the half-full glass on the table, he finally gives her a hello kiss, the carbonation still prickling on her upper lip. As he leans over her, she wraps her left arm, still slightly damp, around his neck; his pose feels rather maladroit and contorted. – I'm holding on to you, she says. – Go ahead, hold on if you want. – Now that's generous of you, she says, and lets go of him. Straightening up, he notices his left palm resting on her right breast; he doesn't know whether to leave it there or take it away. – Should I bring you another glass of soda? he asks. – I've still got some…on the table. – He passes her the glass and manages in the process to make his left hand disappear. – I have to go to the bathroom, says Mona, without touching the glass. When she comes back, he's sitting at his little desk again; sneaking a sidelong glance, he sees that she has tears in her eyes. She takes a nervous pull from her cigarette; he's smoking too; nothing is said, and down on the street the traffic's grueling racket rages on.

You're welcome to go to the pub if you like, Mona says after a while. I'm not going to come; I've got things to do.

It was over a year before—before the full onset of his impotence—that he tried to teach Mona how to masturbate. Evidently he did so out of a prophylactic impulse that he insisted on misinterpreting as a desire to enhance their sex life. Mona was one of those rare women to whom—she insisted with a certain barbed indignation— *it had never occurred to do such a thing*, not even as a teenager. Even back then, albeit sporadically, Mona had been visiting that Leipzig psychoanalyst, to whom she'd mentioned, blushing—so she told C.—this shortcoming of hers. The analyst had raised her brows in alarm and asked wide-eyed: My, my! What on earth have they done to you? – That clinched it, she decided to try it out with C. – And if you watch me do it, that'll really turn you on? she asked. – You can count on it, he replied. – But you'll have to join in, you'll have to jerk off too, she demanded. – I won't even be able to help myself, he said.

Quickly he'd scribble a few words on a piece of paper and hurry out of the apartment before Mona got home. It was always the same words, he could simply have gone on using the first note he'd written: Gone to my mother's, can't write, too much street noise.

It was a sure bet that he wouldn't have managed to write even if it hadn't been for the street noise. Ever since his first visa application was rejected, he'd been getting practically no writing done; each text he began went belly up after the very first line... Once I get the visa, I'll start writing again! That was the perpetual promise he used to keep himself afloat. – No, actually he wasn't keeping himself afloat any longer. His impotence held sway in every respect. He had to change countries, social systems, political camps. But those goddamned masses didn't give him the slightest support. He had to change the weather, his lovers, his whole mental economy. For forty years he'd been stagnating in his life; now it was time he snapped out of it. Naturally he'd promised his deputy culture minister he'd come back; naturally, what else could he have done? In his old apartment in Berlin he'd had a small poster, the kind they used the English word for, showing Rimbaud's juvenile mug, under it the famous words: *I is another.* Long before the phrase became a worldwide cliché, he'd sat in front of it for nights on end, letting that thought roam his head. Unfortunately the poster had been stolen by someone or other who came to visit. Probably they'd only taken it because it was "from the West," but still it did show there were other people in the country who were skeptical of the life prefabricated for them by the state, the society, and the party.

Leaving the house, he crossed Spittastrasse and took a side street to walk down Uhlandstrasse. That way he avoided meeting Mona, who would be coming home about this time. Instead he ran into his friend H. on

Georg-Schwarz-Strasse. – Ah, H. said, what a miracle to see you around still. I thought you'd gone West long ago. – You'll be seeing me around a while yet, said C., they turned down my application. And I submitted a second and a third application, but still no reply. – Then it's not looking good, is it? – The bureaucrats are playing dead, that's nothing new. – Do you think they'll come to life again? Why are you bargaining with the dead? – People are hearing that it's starting to loosen up, you can practically smell it. People are hearing about more travel permits being granted…of course, you never hear about the ones that get denied. – Come on, let's go for a drink, tell me all about it. – No, said C., I've got to get to the bus station, I'm going to visit my mother. – You never have time for anyone. No one's buying it anymore. Are you writing at least, do you have time for that? – I'm trying… – That doesn't sound very convincing. Now take me, I'm always writing, I'm writing lots, and I still have time! – I've got to get going… – I just ran into Mona, she was on her way home, you must have seen her too. She said she wasn't doing so well with you. – Oh, she said that, did she… I've got to go now. – You don't care how she's doing anymore? – You care, that's enough…see you! – You've got plenty of time for the bus, don't worry. Besides, you can afford a taxi. – Yes, I can. Say hi to Mona if you see her. – You don't want to belong with us anymore, I can tell by looking at you. – I don't belong to anyone. – You're misunderstanding me on purpose; you're learning a thing or two from those corpses of yours. – You're the one I learn the most from… C. flung one arm into the air, a car stopped, wheels screeching. – Hurry up, the taxi driver yelled, there's no stopping here! – In the car C. turned around and saw his friend standing on the curb, smiling and waving after him.

He got there in plenty of time for the bus, but he missed it anyway, hunkered down at a restaurant in the train station. He'd been looking forward to the bus. After leaving the south of Leipzig and passing through long bare expanses that stretched to the horizon—the former coal mines, stretches of which resembled a desert on the moon—it passed through an area that seemed to him like an idyll. The moldering backwaters in this southern tip of Saxony nestled between green hillocks; narrow roads with hardly any traffic wound sinuously around dense primeval stands of trees, between which little valleys lay, abundant with water and overgrown with dark-green rushes. Suddenly, these landscape remnants broke off, and the sandy chasms of the strip mines gaped; the bus driver, his view now unobstructed, stepped on the gas, and the old rattletrap barreled forward, swaying perilously along the brinks of the chasms. Then it slowed down again, lurching and screeching along the endless switchbacks where the insatiably growing greenery, already shading into dark blue, surged up on both sides. – He was coming home, he could smell the place already, he smelled the sand, sand mixed with ash, and the sulfurous water of his childhood, the smoke in the air and the hard dry poplar leaves whose bitter tang wafted across the road… Gottfried Benn was wrong to ask who saw poplar woods—you saw them here. Of course it was a stunted weedy breed of gray-yellow poplar that grew on the slag heaps; it snowed in May or in June when myriads of white blooming tufts rose from the poplars into the air, so light that the heat bore them up and carried them for miles over the countryside; in the evening, when it grew cool, they sank down and lined the roadsides like little snowdrifts.

H.'s mother was a writer, and he hated her, or at least he liked to claim he did. C. had met her a few times; she was small and very spry, incessantly radiating conviction and the unwavering will to edify. H. writhed in agony whenever he was forced to hear her adamant opinions on everything under the sun. And yet, C. thought, H. was fascinated by his mother. – She likes you, she has a thing for men who aren't intellectuals, H. told C. one day; watch out for yourself, next thing you know she'll try to get you into bed. – So, said C., what could be the danger in that? – She eats men up, you'll have to share her with half a dozen others. – Do you really think she can eat me up so easily? C. asked. – And you wouldn't have any problem getting involved with a dyed-in-the-wool Party member? – I can't possibly come to any harm, said C., with you spotting all the pitfalls ahead of time. – Another time they'd gotten to talking about his mother again, and H. asked: Do you want to know what she said about you, or would you not be able to take it? – When C. said nothing, H. went on: I was talking to her about your writing and praising your poetry to the skies. But she just shook her head and said: You can't fool me, he doesn't have the *eyes* of a poet!—C. listened impassively without replying, but he keenly felt H.'s scrutinizing gaze…presumably fixed on his eyes! At the corner of H.'s mouth he noted a slight tug of irony that he knew could quickly turn to sarcasm: maybe H. actually believed his mother's words a little. Though generally he insisted that her lips could issue nothing but lies.

C. was liable to fall into a lasting malaise over certain personal remarks, and perhaps H. was one of the few who knew about that weakness. It never occurred to C. to ask how the eyes of a poet were supposed to look. He sensed what a struggle he was going to have with the remark. First it made dismay creep over him, then raging fury that finally changed into despondency; only days later did he manage to put it out of his mind. – It was several years before he was able to say that her words exemplified the mindset of the East German ruling elite. In a social order based on scientific materialism, they claimed the ability to do without arguments, spitting out mystical pronouncements instead. Earlier on, when he was still naïve enough to send his work around to East German publishers, he'd gotten replies that were cast from the same mold and plunged him into the same depression. The diabolical thing about those unexplained rejections was that you ended up searching for the missing arguments yourself… and naturally you found them! For you never felt the rejections were groundless, not by a long shot, it was just that the grounds went unnamed…there was no point in naming them, hopeless cases aren't worth arguments. The distribution of hope was strictly regulated in this dictatorship. – And it was just the same with his applications for an exit visa: no one saw the need to reply…

When he missed the bus, he took the train to the town of A., where a suburban train took him to his destination. At the Leipzig station he'd washed the uneasy thoughts out from his skull, and during his hour's wait in A. he did a bit more drinking. Arriving at his mother's, he immediately collapsed into bed; before falling asleep he pondered what ought to happen now. It was a strange feeling, lying in this bed and thinking about the future: he'd been born in this bed…

He'd had his beginnings here in this bed, and yet he didn't know how he'd begun…he didn't know how he'd become what he was, he didn't even quite know what he'd become. Envy and resentment gnawed at his life; the writers, like a herd of swine, bit each other in the snouts fighting their way to the feed trough. Back before he'd been an author, a prominent author, they'd thought him good enough to serve as a cause for protest letters declaring to the state how art was being suppressed. Now that he'd become that prominent author, now that he was trying to go his own way, a way that often found him groping through utter darkness, he no longer suited their plans. He was no longer any good as a figure for polemics that let people pose as resistance-fighters. He had to escape from this state of affairs, he had to vanish from this country, he was repeating himself…

He felt as though the fellowship he'd been offered could bring a solution to all these problems. – He told himself he needed a break to collect his thoughts. To gain some detachment. To reflect on what he really wanted, what direction he really wanted to go in. A year was a good amount of time for those reflections. When the yellow leather jacket had arrived from Nuremberg, Mona had remarked with a certain undertone: What a nice transitional jacket!—He wasn't sure whether the undertone was just derision, or also fear. Her intuition had been correct; like her, he understood the word *transitional* to refer to more than the seasons: for a year he'd live in a transitional time. It wasn't just that he'd give the West a try, he wanted to find out where he stood in life, however empty that phrase might sound. – So you've decided to embark on a kind of interim solution? Mona asked.

– You're right, that's pretty much it, he replied. – But is it also a transitional time for you to switch from one woman to the next? Mona asked. – He recalled giving a reply that sounded like a definite promise to come back to her once that year had passed.

Just as he dozed off, he had an image of H.'s mother, a sprightly woman, barely five feet three inches tall, who seemed ten years younger than she was, and who, as a writer, had acquired a certain leadership role in her local district. H. was constantly preoccupied with her, not so much for the understandable reason that she was his mother but out of concern for his little brother; he felt their mother was exposing him to the worst conceivable influences. She lived with her underage son in a house by a big lake in Mecklenburg; the house, nestled into the woods surrounding the lake, was rather isolated; she'd often mentioned, H. said, that the place sometimes gave her the willies. Then she ought to move to an apartment in town, she's got several of those in addition to the house, said H. But she won't do it; out on the lake she feels free from being watched. And it gives her an excuse to keep hooking men to guard her and the house. – C. had once been asked to play that role; he was supposed to protect the house from burglars while repairing the drafty windows before fall came. But when he and H. arrived at the house on the lake, another man had already settled in. An instant stab of disappointment showed he'd had high hopes for the rendezvous. It was true, he hadn't been able to forget H.'s remark that his mother would drag him into bed some day. No, he had no moral compunctions whatsoever! He was interested in H.'s mother below the belt; he'd hardly have any use for her thoughts. She could proselytize to him as much as she liked—with ideological cogency, with the mindset of infallibility that her Party was so skilled at, and all in the tone of maternal femininity used in cajoling a recalcitrant child: what a charming combination! But he knew she had a capricious hole between her legs, installed by a divine adversary of her Party, which could undo all the atheism of her scientific worldview. She'd whimper with lust like a bitch when the class enemy crawled down that maw of hers.

Amid thoughts of that sort, C. drifted off to sleep. – His mother woke him up around noon. That was unusual; she would usually let him sleep as long as he wanted, often on into the afternoon, knowing that he'd stay up all night to write undisturbed in her tiny apartment. It had been like that ever since his mother had retired, nearly six years ago now, and no longer spent her days in the office from eight a.m. to four p.m. The company would only call her back in at the end of the month, when staffing shortages caused a backup in the payroll accounting. As that was the case at the moment, it surprised C. to see his mother back home by noon. – Mona was here, his mother explained, she'd come with an urgent message more than an hour ago, and when no one answered the door, she'd figured out the way to the company's payroll office. Mona seemed completely distraught, she said, something was the matter, he had to get up right away. – Mona, looking pale, stared at him with wide, disconcerted eyes when he came into the kitchen at last, still half asleep, hair standing on end. A telegram had been wired from Berlin to Leipzig, and now it was lying on the kitchen table next to his still-open notebook. – It's a good thing I didn't have to go in to the university today, said Mona. The telegram came this morning, the only option was to bring it straight over here myself, it seems urgent. – The telegram said that he should pick up his exit visa before the weekend. The bureau would close at 5:30. – It was almost noon, and it was Friday… some malicious creature in that so-called bureau, an outpost of the Culture Ministry, must have delayed sending the telegram for a day, if not two. – That would have made his friend H. grin sardonically: They do that to display their power, to humiliate you, don't you see?

There was no time for thoughts like those… H. would have said: You never take the time for those thoughts! – Standing there pulling on his pants, getting tangled in his pants legs, he drank the coffee his mother had at the ready. – At least brush your teeth, said Mona, watching him with unconcealed displeasure. – No, he said, I won't have to kiss anyone at the bureau. – You have to go to Berlin? his mother asked in alarm; clearly she felt it didn't bode well to decamp in such a rush to report to the authorities. – Mona will explain everything, he said, snatching the yellow leather jacket from the hook and running out the door. – Isn't it too cold for that jacket? his mother shouted after him…

It really was getting too cold for the jacket; it was late October, and at night the temperature sometimes dropped below freezing. He took the train to Berlin via the district capital of A.; only on board did he check to see that everything was there: ID card, passport, wallet. Just after five he arrived at the main station and raced in a taxi to the *Bureau for Publishers and the Book Trade* on Clara-Zetkin-Strasse, the ministry outpost where the Deputy Culture Minister presided. At five thirty on the dot he was standing at the reception counter, behind which sat an amiably grinning pensioner. – We've been waiting for you for two days now, the old man said, sit down and have a cigarette, it'll be a moment…

Did you really think, said the minister once C. was admitted nearly an hour later, that we ever get to knock off at a decent hour around here? No, there was no need for you to rush like that. – But today is Friday, said C. – Really? Is it Friday again already…? Well, this isn't your first time here, you know what I've got to tell you. But I've lectured you often enough already, you just sign that you've heard the lecture, then go down to the secretary in the travel office, you remember her. I'll call to see if she's still in… And pick up your travel documents. Let her know the date the visa should take effect—today, tomorrow. Well then, good luck with everything, see you around…

Suddenly everything was going so smoothly, it was practically sinister. He kept waiting for a trap to appear, but there was no trap, everything unfolded without a hitch. Downstairs the secretary had him sign off on the skipped lecture, which would have gone something like this: You are a citizen of the German Democratic Republic and are subject to the laws of your homeland even when abroad in capitalist countries. You must behave there in a manner appropriate to the laws and moral values of your homeland. This means respecting the laws of your host country as well. Should a conflict arise, immediately contact the Permanent Mission of the GDR in your host country…

Half an hour later C. was back out on the street: they'd even had him turn in his old passport, which needed renewing, and issued him a new one. So they'd had another passport photo handy…when he signed for the new passport, he saw a stamp in black ink staring out at him, a rectangle covering almost the whole of page seven in the blue booklet with the words: *SERVICE VISA valid for single exit/multiple exits until…*the date that followed limited the term of validity to fourteen months; the visa began on October 31, 1985, and ended on December 31 of the following year; the words *single exit* were crossed out, meaning that C. could enter and exit the country as often as he pleased. – It was the sort of visa issued to journalists, consulate staff, and probably spies, C. thought.

He looked down the street with its bleak, forbidding office buildings: he didn't belong here anymore! It was dark already, with damp cold fog drifting through Berlin; he walked slowly down to Friedrichstrasse. A few hundred yards in the other direction he would have run up against the Wall: now it had shrunk to an absurdity for him! The question was when he'd see the Wall again, at least from that side. Would he ever come back to East Berlin? – Possibly never, he thought to himself.

He was facing his last weekend in the GDR…he couldn't get the thought out of his mind. – Who knows, tomorrow they could overthrow that Gorbachev guy and hermetically seal off the whole Eastern Bloc, he said to Mona. She slapped her forehead, the look in her eyes reminding him of the night when she'd insisted he'd gone out of his mind.

He had to struggle to remember the weekend that followed (how many years ago was it now?): indescribable unrest had filled him, submerging every detail. Mona stood by, distraught, sometimes vanishing into the bedroom for a full hour; he used that time to soothe himself with liquor. It was as though, upon receipt of the visa, a personality he'd once been able to regard halfway reliably as his own had suddenly been obliterated within him. In its stead emerged a thing that cast doubt on his every little action, criticized it, declared it to be pointless. He packed his bag, only to dump out the contents and jumble them up on the floor: What did he need with all that crap at his feet? – Meanwhile he suddenly remembered that he'd forgotten his notebook, with the text he'd been working on for days, on his mother's kitchen table. Nor had it occurred to Mona to bring the notebook along back to Leipzig…or had she left it behind on purpose?

Wouldn't that be perfectly understandable? For months, for more than half a year he'd been deaf to even her slightest objection, he'd acted like a thoughtless automaton, and now he expected her to think of his forgotten notebook. – The text he'd begun was a haphazard string of sentences with no real rationale; it was writing for the sake of writing. The only reason he'd been writing was that he couldn't do anything else…he couldn't just sit there and watch his life slip away and not write anymore! And so he'd tried to depict that very situation: In long, increasingly theoretical sentences, he tried to home in on the question of why he could no longer write in this country, this country where he crouched as though in a cage. Those sentences hadn't come anywhere near an answer…

It seemed in keeping with the whole affair that that text could perfectly well be left behind in M. – Late that Saturday afternoon he took the tram to the main station to pick up his ticket. You went to a special counter and presented your exit visa so that the ticket could be issued, and they had to be paid for in hard currency, i.e., West German marks or the so-called Forum checks that the bank gave you in exchange for your Western money, crudely printed vouchers used to buy products at an Intershop. C. had set aside about two hundred D-marks from his last trip to Regensburg, and after buying the ticket he was left with about fifty. From those fifty marks he bought a bottle of whisky at the Intershop. That led to more bad blood with Mona; she'd been planning to buy a new coffee maker at the Intershop, since her old one was about to give up the ghost. Now there weren't enough Forum checks left. – You're crying about a silly coffee maker, he said to Mona, but soon we can get a much better one. And he held out the ticket so she could see he'd bought a round trip: I'll be back in a month at the latest! – I'm not crying about the coffee maker, I'm crying about you! The tears washed the mascara from the corners of her eyes; embarrassed, she vanished into the bedroom.

By early Sunday evening he'd finally finished his preparations; at least he declared them finished. His bag stood on the floor, packed; he could barely recall what was in it. Warily he asked Mona if she'd like to go out for one last dinner and a bottle of wine at a restaurant on the east side of town that passed for pretty good and where they'd gone several times before. She agreed, and they took the tram to East Leipzig. Unexpectedly they found a free table and were served fairly quickly; the catch was that there were just two dinners left to choose from, and they were ones that Mona normally didn't eat. She ended up sawing away at a tough piece of meat buried under a mound of red, overly spicy pepper sauce mixed with unidentifiable overcooked vegetables, some greasy fried potatoes piled at the edge of the plate. After a while she pushed her plate away in disgust, and when the waitress came to clear the table, she picked a quarrel with her: the food was a disgrace, apparently even here they were trying to debase their standards to the usual Leipzig level. – Predictably, the waitress's reply was borderline insolent; C. paid the bill and they walked out, leaving the bottle of red wine one-third full. – It's actually good that we aren't getting home late, Mona said in the tram, I have to go to therapy tomorrow morning before the university, I want to go to bed on the early side.

C. breathed a sigh of relief once Mona had gone to bed and he was finally alone in the living room. Calm descended at last, as though furies had been raging around him in circles all weekend, and their howling suddenly faded. He'd braved it out...but at what cost? There was a feeling inside him as though he'd offended, hurt, alienated everyone around him, every single person who meant something to him. He'd alienated them because he was trying to find himself, or so he believed. They felt hurt because suddenly they failed to recognize him...he'd never managed to recognize himself, and that was why he'd acted in a way that suited them, suited what they thought of him; they'd made an image of him for themselves, and little by little he'd confirmed that image. One single time he'd fallen off that pedestal, and instantly they recoiled, hyperventilating. They were weeping and moaning because they thought he was deserting them. But the only thing deserting them was the image they had...what he actually was probably didn't matter one bit to them.

He opened the bottle of whisky and took a swig...he had practically nothing left to do now. He had to be at the station at six, and there was no point in going to bed now...

No, he wasn't all done, not yet, there was one little thing left: he had a letter to write. He sat down at the typewriter to answer a letter that had come about two months ago and that he hadn't responded to yet, though he'd kept meaning to. He just hadn't come up with a viable reaction, and the letter had slipped deeper and deeper into a mountain of papers that he'd set aside and would have thrown away if he hadn't suspected there might be something useful there, or unfinished business. As he recalled, he'd even shown the letter to Mona and said he had no idea whether or how to answer it. – Mona's reply was perceptive: Letters that aren't out for a clear reply are really love letters in disguise…answer them just as cagily, or not at all…

Now he answered the letter, which had come from Nuremberg. The sender's name was Hedda Rast; C. hadn't had the slightest notion who that might be. Nor was he much the wiser now: the letter said that they'd met briefly in a car in Regensburg on the way to his hotel; "met" being an exaggeration, they'd seen each other for perhaps five minutes. She'd been sitting in the back seat. In the meantime she'd learned a bit more about him from reading his books, though of course the question was: What could reading books, poetry collections for instance, really tell you about the person who'd written them?

In his first sentence he apologized for taking so long to reply; he couldn't come up with a second sentence. He barely remembered Regensburg, he eventually wrote, there'd just been too many strange people around him. She was probably a friend of the woman who'd spoken to him and then driven him to his hotel in her car, a woman who'd also been a total stranger to him, incidentally…

After practically every single sentence he typed, he

got up and roamed the apartment…it was amazing that they'd been able to install a bath in this cramped warren just four hundred square feet in size. Mona's father had managed it; as an engineer in an installation enterprise (C. himself had spent years working in places like that), he was one of those men, Mona said, who could pull anything off. C. knew him only superficially, and had always felt her father treated him with a certain condescension, probably because he'd had his factory give him his walking papers. – Your "walking papers," that was what they called the discharge papers; if you got them that easily, clearly you weren't good for much of anything.

The bath had been installed at the expense of the bedroom, leaving space for just a cot and a closet, and the path between the two was so narrow that the doors of the closet wouldn't open all the way. Now that C. had stopped squeezing in with Mona on the cot, he made a habit of going to bed only after she had left for the university. Of course, he could have slept on the couch in the living room, but Mona would have seen that as an avoidance tactic; it was better if she got up to find him still writing… or at least in the posture, pretending to write.

Each time he passed the kitchen, he took a big swallow from the whisky bottle before sitting back down at the typewriter. – It was quite possible, in fact practically a sure thing, he wrote, that he'd soon be granted permission for a long stay in West Germany, he'd been expecting it for weeks. As soon as he knew where he'd be staying, he'd write her from there. And who knew, he might even pass through Nuremberg someday…

By the time he'd finished the letter, he'd downed half the bottle of whisky. He slipped into his shoes and pulled on his jacket to take the letter to the mailbox. He might forget to post it if he waited until he was heading to the station, on what would predictably be a hectic morning. It was at most a hundred and fifty yards to the mailbox; when he stepped out the door, a heavy autumn rain was pelting down and would have soaked him even on the short stretch he had to walk if he hadn't been wearing the leather jacket. Back upstairs he hung his pants over the back of a chair and moved the chair toward the tiled heating stove, which still gave off a little warmth. Then he dried his hair with a towel...the rain had refreshed him somehow, all at once his mind was strangely clear. He opened both living room windows to air the apartment, then lay down on the sofa in his underwear. Leipzig was quiet, the almost uncanny quiet of the last hour or two before the din of traffic erupted down below on Georg-Schwarz-Strasse. He heard the rain rushing down the street.

When he woke up, bright sunlight filled the room. He instantly realized where he was: he was still in Leipzig; he'd overslept. He bolted up from the couch, dashed into the bath, and ducked under the shower's ice-cold jet. Only then did he try to mull the situation over...none of this was a problem, he could just as well leave tomorrow morning! The whole thing was a bit idiotic, that was all...

The whisky bottle was still standing on the kitchen table, he hadn't even hidden it; disgusted, he stuck it in the fridge. Before she'd left the apartment, which must have been very early, Mona had taken the trouble to put an alarm clock on the little table by the couch: it had rung at 4:45, but C. hadn't heard it. Next to it stood a coffee cup and a little thermos of hot coffee. She'd be awfully surprised if he were still there that evening...but would she be pleased? Wouldn't it mean going through the same drama all over again? All the same, he felt a sudden longing for Mona…maybe he should stay and spend the evening talking the whole mess over with her? He didn't quite know if one evening would be enough…he might have to talk to her for another whole week to bring about more than a superficial truce. He wasn't sure he'd still have the conviction to leave after that…

There were two other options: he could go to his mother's and fetch the manuscript he'd left there…or he could take the second train that left for Frankfurt that evening. But what was he supposed to do at five or six a.m. in Frankfurt…where there probably wasn't a soul who knew he'd gotten permission to leave the country? – Yes, in all the confusion he'd forgotten the telegram, the telegram to his publisher explaining that he had the visa and was coming to Frankfurt…

Exasperated, he tossed back his coffee, took his bag— completely full and quite heavy—and left the apartment. He dropped the key into Mona's mailbox downstairs… now there was no turning back! If he did change his mind, he'd have to ring Mona's doorbell that evening. After that he went to the post office to send the telegram.

He ended up standing out on the street in the autumn sun—blindingly bright, but with no strength to give warmth—completely incapable of making any kind of decision. All he felt was the piercing pain in his head, that all too familiar legacy of a certain cheap brand of whisky from the Intershop. As though he hadn't sabotaged himself enough already, he hit on the idea of visiting his friend H., the writer, on Georg-Schwarz-Strasse. Now, early in the afternoon, he likely wasn't home yet, as he worked at the metalworking shop of a nearby hospital, but maybe his wife would be at home. – He was right about that; Martha opened the door and burst out laughing when she saw him. Martha was a genial person incapable of pretense; when she laughed, you could be sure that her delight was genuine. – Have you just come from West Germany, or are you on your way there? she asked. You look a bit pale, you probably want me to make some coffee. – I'm on my way there, he said, I ought to be there already, but I overslept this morning. – Same old story, you'll never change. But it's good for me, because it means you're suddenly hanging around town by yourself, and you have to ring my doorbell…you ring just twice a year, but you end up doing it sooner or later. – I put the key in Mona's mailbox, now I'm locked out. – You shouldn't drink so much, said Martha, setting the cups of strong, Turkish-style coffee down on the table. Of course you could wait until Mona gets home, but it looks like you don't want to? – Something like that. – Your friend H. has disappeared too, it's been nearly two weeks now. He's at his mother's… – At his mother's? – Something's happened with his little brother, a burglary, or several burglaries. At any rate the kid's in custody awaiting trial… and he's only fifteen. – What's wrong with the boy, what's wrong with all the kids? – What's wrong with the whole country, and what's wrong with us?

When Martha said that H. had disappeared two weeks ago, it sounded as if she were talking about more than just H.'s little brother. – That's the question, said C., what are we doing? Is everyone going their separate ways? – It seems like certain constraints are loosening up. Everything coming from the state seems so weirdly lacking in force. And without that pressure, what breaks up first are the artificial communities people have always used to get by here. – So you don't think it's just a negative thing? – It may turn out that we aren't capable of really sticking together. That it's something we never really learned…

Martha suggested going out for dinner that evening at one of the beer gardens; there were lots of them among west Leipzig's labyrinthine allotment gardens. – We won't have much to drink, though, at most a few glasses of wine, Martha said. If you like, you can spend the night at my place. You can count on me to wake you up early.

After nightfall the rain set in again. It was easy to lose your way in the gardens' sprawling network of lanes—in the dacha owners' shadow city, as Martha put it—but now that the trees had lost their leaves, you could see the reddish fog of light over the city and get your bearings by that. In the fall most beer gardens closed by eleven; walking home, they clung to each other. From the black sky rain ran down in endless veils, and some of the lanes were impassable, ankle-deep with water; it took them half an hour to reach Martha's apartment, completely soaked. Once again, C. hung his clothes to dry beside the tile stove.

All the same, the next morning in the crowded tram they were still damp. But everything in the tram was damp; he stood in the aisle with his bag wedged between his feet, while around him people squeezed and squirmed as though to wring each other out. The tram moved by fits and starts; outside, in the dark city, you could see the streaks of rain darting slantwise through the light of the streetlamps. By the time he was finally sitting in a compartment on the "interzonal" train to the

West, he was already half soaked again.

The train seemed to be heading for a dark sky, while behind him, over the receding city of Leipzig, the first turbid light was rising. Propping his head on his right hand, he closed his eyes. There were two young men sitting across from him; after a while he heard one of them say: That's the tram to Bad Dürrenberg down there…

He looked out the window: the train was traveling along a high embankment; then it trundled with a hollow din across a series of bridges. Sure enough, down below, in a sort of valley, the two cars of a tram were crawling along; in the distance a jumble of multihued lights blinked above sprawling industrial facilities. Those were the chemical plants of Leuna, either Leuna I or Leuna II; he'd spent years working in both sections of the gigantic complex. Leuna covered the entire horizon: cooling towers, other grotesque-looking cylindrical towers, futuristic spherical tanks; the tangled weave of the struts crisscrossing every which way, pricked the sallow dawn suffused by yellow and red gas flares. It had stopped raining. C. recalled—it was seventeen or eighteen years ago now, maybe even longer—that he'd taken that tram to Bad Dürrenberg every day; he'd lived in a worker's dormitory there, as one of the several thousand installation technicians employed throughout the Leuna plants. – Sometimes that time appeared to him as a kind of virtually inexhaustible, albeit dauntingly difficult, material; to write about that could keep him busy for quite some time. He'd written very little about that period, practically nothing, he thought, but it never occurred to him as he languished away at his desk, mentally blocked, ineffectual and devoid of ideas, as his impotence gnawed on him and he gnawed on his impotence...the flares of Leuna with their Expressionistic hues never occurred to him then. He was a sinner and a squanderer for neglecting that huge part of life that after all he knew so well! But maybe he never wrote about it because in Leuna he hadn't been living in his life, he'd been living in a dormitory life...

And who'd care about that, in the place he was going to? Would any of those literature-loving women who came to his readings care? That woman in Regensburg, for instance, who asked him to autograph a book and watched him wide-eyed, fixing her gaze on his unsteady hand as he tried to write his name on the flyleaf, botching the signature that instantly struck him as a forgery... and who had then plucked at his sleeve with the tips of her fingers, nails painted pale pink, to conduct him to the car as it started to rain, placing him in the front passenger seat as graciously as though he were a dignitary, controlling him like a feather blown in the desired direction by a breath from parted lips...

He grinned: he certainly didn't resemble a feather that could be blown around like nothing at all! But perhaps the I within him was made from so light a material...

Women had never wanted him back then, when he was still busy in this chemical wasteland whose every corner smelled like a different insidious toxin; it was simply impossible, or so it seemed to him, to make any kind of contact with the female branch of humanity. As if he'd been going around with his face covered in green or purple chemical metastases, oozy eyes that squirted out ammonia, a mouth filled with acetate or phenol, a fug of gas rising from his salt-soaked clothes...a woman of the class that went to readings in Regensburg never would have looked at him. Yet back then he'd already been writing (and maybe better than now, he sometimes thought)… and now those women had nothing but commiseration for the fact that he'd once been a worker. What a calamity not to be born straight into the literature business! And their commiseration always disguised a certain doubt in his literary abilities…and of course it was the exact same doubt he had, which he went seeking obliquely in others!

Martha was the only one who sympathized when he spilled out his rancor on the subject, when the alcohol got him riled up against his deprivation…for he often saw his working years as nothing but a deprivation, as years that had been irretrievably wrested from him, and inside him raged a constant unpacified fury that he preferred to leave undisturbed; only the alcohol made it surge up. – Why can't you use the opportunity now? she asked him. Why can't you nail those women one by one and then tell them all to go to hell?

It was a fair question; he just couldn't…he couldn't reach out and take those women, he was a kind of Tantalus as far as the opposite sex was concerned…and maybe he even prided himself on the role. – Martha said: You must have hypnotized yourself at some point, in puberty or earlier, you must have put yourself through a thorough course of autosuggestion. And now you can't make your little prick wake up, and you won't let women help you…

He'd slept poorly that night, he now recalled. It was long past midnight when, lulled by the gentle noise of the persistent rain outside the partly open window, he drifted off into some distant realm and no longer knew where he was. He hadn't really woken even when he sensed a woman's body beside him, crawling underneath the coarse, rather prickly blanket where he lay in his still-damp underwear. Probably it was Martha who'd come looking for him…or it might have been the night before, and it was Mona alongside him: the two women were about the same size. Warmth flooded him when he felt her slow gentle breath on his neck. She pressed against his side, Martha or Mona, her nightgown pulled up above her breasts and one of her thighs across his stomach. He took her in his arms, ran one of his hands down her back and hid it between her thighs, resting it against the neutral spot between her two defenseless orifices. And one of her hands appeared in the same place, seized his fingers and pulled them deeper into the clinch of supply yielding folds. His fingers were thrust inside, for a few seconds the lower body at his side was set in motion, rubbing in circles against his hip, aided by the two clasped hands inside her body, their fingers interlaced, so that briefly he couldn't tell which of the fingers in the melting moisture belonged to him and which to her. Her teeth bit down on his shoulder as though she were suppressing a cry…at that moment he recalled the questionable masturbation proposal he'd made to Mona some time ago.

Martha woke him early the next morning, but went straight back to bed because she couldn't stand watching his edginess: mentally he'd already left this place far behind. He made coffee and drank it standing up, taking deep drags on a cigarette. He was at the station way too far ahead of time.

And then he didn't wake up again until the train slowed to enter the border station of Gerstungen. Laying his passport with the visa on the narrow windowsill, he settled in to wait.

For some unknown time now he had experienced the world only in train stations. He moved from station to station with rare interruptions; all that lingered in his mind were the images of stations; they had become the sole points of reference for his consciousness. Nothing in them conveyed a sense of clear contours; a rapacity held sway in the stations, you were constantly guarding something hidden in your head or your breast: it was nothing particular to you, it was only egomania. Big-city stations were the special haunt of characters who changed their sense of self like shadowy clothing; they moved as if they had eyes in the backs of their heads, always in the process of assuming a new appearance, thinking up different destinations, taking on origins that had nothing to do with their own. – C. felt that in train stations he wasn't immediately recognizable as an arrival from the East. But that wasn't the reason for the hold that train stations had on him; even in the East they had possessed the same magical attraction.

As soon as he was reachable at a West German address—first in the town of Hanau—the circus of author appearances began. From the very start the events struck him as a highly peculiar ritual that went on existing only because, once it had begun, no one knew quite how or why to put an end to it. And so those readings went on and on like a bad habit whose cause had long since vanished. But the fact was, the vast majority of West German writers earned nearly their entire living from readings, with the exception of a few stars, and perhaps those already drawing their state pension. Wasn't it inevitable that a writer in this country would feel like a completely useless figure reduced to accepting handouts? Or was it just the opposite? Perhaps leading the lives of traveling minstrels convinced writers that they ranked among society's essential individuals?

Perhaps C. had also succumbed to that delusion at first. He was flattered to be invited to lots of readings, eagerly accepting all offers. Later he restricted himself to the view that this was how he earned the money he spent... He was reluctant to use the customary turn of phrase: That's how I earn my money.

The events were sparsely attended: he was increasingly astonished that anyone at all still took an interest in literary products...and you could count on a major part of the audience consisting of colleagues; that is, writers who happened not to be on a reading tour themselves. Indeed, most of what was read, what was recited more or less fluently over a microphone into the airspace—whose receptivity was naturally limited, depending on the size of the room—most of the texts dealt with the existential conditions of the writer. Writers reported on writers, often enough with the subtler variant of an author novelizing about an author writing about the novelizing of a third author...about his difficulties in professional life, or about the circumstances that had driven him—or both of them: the narrating author and the narrated author—into the clutches of this profession. In the best-case scenario the subject was a love affair that had come about due to the fact that at least one of the smitten characters was an author; often, both of them were writers.

More than a few works hinged on the exposition of the fates that led the characters to become authors. Fate was the fitting term, for the taking of that path was generally described as inevitable, suggesting, in fact, that as a writer you'd more or less been born as such. Translated into intelligible speech, this meant nothing other than: Provide for me and pay my way—it's not my fault I'm a writer!

That was a phenomenon, thought C., that was more the exception than the rule in other professions. But of course it had to do with the nature of writing, which forced you to appeal to the public...that set it apart from other professions. A manufacturer of cooking pots appealed to the public too, but only obliquely, he needed them only as buyers for his pots. And if those pots leaked, no matter how nicely they were decorated, no one would buy them. For the writer, the crux of the matter was that he produced vessels he had to sell, content and all. Now, what happened if he could find nothing but spoiled contents in the world? It became necessary for the writer to vouch personally for the fact that it was time to look into those spoiled contents...unquestionably this implied a certain authority. Could such authority be held by a writer who proffered himself as traveling elocutionist in a completely peripheral cultural industry?

More and more often, C. looked forward to his readings with apprehension. He practically started to fear them: the closer the date of an event approached, the more he felt drained of all power to transform himself before the audience into a person who had any self-respect left. He no longer felt he had any right to claim the attention of even the tiniest group of listeners. Less and less did the figure raising its voice on the little stage have anything to do with him.

It was a kind of erosion from within, reaching its height the evenings before he left for an event; the next morning, sitting in the train, he'd slowly begin to get over the feeling…but how much longer could he keep this up? When he arrived in a city in that condition, he'd repair to the hotel where he was to spend the night, drop off his baggage, and then—on his first and, as a rule, only walk through the new city—return to the train station. He wanted to memorize the route for the next day, for the day of departure, but that didn't explain the attraction train stations held for him. Before leaving town he might pass up one or two trains just to linger a bit longer in the station. The city, its centers and its sights, didn't interest him; he'd never really get to know a city, but he knew the stations, he recognized the stations in the most obscure places, even if he'd last roamed them a year or two before. – Once the bookstores had still enticed him, the used book dealers around the station; soon he preferred to stand at the window of a fast-food restaurant on the edge of the station building and watch the world go by, gazing out from inside this refuge that was not entirely part of that world, though it was usually located on a central square around which the city's activity gathered in an arc. That activity was closely tied to the station, but he himself had already broken away; in the station he didn't stand out with his particular form of restlessness; on the contrary, here he found composure, here all he had to signify was flight and transience.

Perhaps most of the people here, those who'd taken flight into the fortress of the station, were perpetually searching for an alibi to cling to some illusory notion of life. Someday they'd change their ways—they constantly told themselves—but it's virtually impossible to change your ways in a train station. In the arrival and departure halls change was constantly being projected, yet everything always stayed the same, the minute in which everything would suddenly be different kept receding before your eyes. The plethora of orientation devices, clocks, information from loudspeakers, electronic departure boards, the perpetual semblance of reliability only anchored in the mind the provisional and fragmentary nature of human existence.

C. tried to picture the train stations in the East, asking himself whether he'd thought similar things there. He'd dreaded them sometimes, especially at night, and not just because the train service was so unreliable. The stations were more provincial, even in the cities, and were geared toward economic requirements above smooth passenger service. At night travelers were relegated to the sidelines, while the noisy business of freight traffic dominated the train yards. In general, passenger trains ran at longer intervals, but they ran later in the night... Even past midnight the platforms were dotted with people, tight knots of haggard figures who stormed the compartments as soon as a train pulled in. In no time the grimy ice-cold cars were crammed with passengers, you could count yourself lucky to find a relatively undisturbed spot to stand in the corridor. If you tried to move through the train, you had to clamber over whole groups of young people who'd parked themselves in the corridor with their bags, passing around bottles of liquor or beer. Often, after swallowing the throngs, the trains would trundle out beyond the station and wait...for what? They waited out in desolate grounds where everyone felt lost, next to lonely dim lamps through whose reddish glow showers of sand, rain, or snow sifted; they waited, and time seemed to stand still until at last some signal gave the go-ahead.

In contrast, West German train stations increasingly seemed to resemble shopping centers, distinguishable from those in the city only by their extended business hours. C. found it hard to avoid getting lost in the train stations the way he kept doing in the cities' pedestrian malls. Without thinking about it, he'd ride down the escalator to the underground shopping arcades located beneath nearly all the large train stations. Shop followed shop, a barrage of neon drove the shoppers along, rhythmic waves of colored light washing them up and down the passages, and in front of the Shops and Markets, the Boutiques and Stores, the Cafés and Bars, they were gradually divested of their selves. C. would let himself be dragged along by the crowd, panicking at irregular intervals at the thought that he'd missed his train. After just a short while, confused and depressed, he'd let the escalator carry him back upstairs.

Then an almost empty train would carry him out into the countryside: he was an anachronism, this isolated passenger in his compartment, this reader in the train who kept nodding off over the endless pages, waking with a start, looking out the window at the autobahn, parallel to the tracks, where herds of cars raced along. It grew dark; resting his head against the pane, he watched how they'd overtake the train. How they'd bolt forward as if an evil spirit rode on their shoulders, giving them the spurs, and they'd try to break away, but it would cling to them. How they'd sweep onward, around a curve, and shoot toward the railway; how they'd charge, then strike a course parallel to the tracks, almost standing still for a moment, and then, shifting gears, inexorably pull away from the train. Disciplined and united in close-massed squadrons, united for one minute, identical lobotomized brows behind the windshields, bodies perching their death-packed asses on a power that wasn't theirs, fused to a steering wheel that mastered their fists, they'd flee onward as if set in motion by the lash of a great herd-driver's whip. And that great shepherd was Capital...he said to himself each time he looked out the window of the train at the intertwined chains of dimmed headlights, a light-suffused gas-cloud over them, a cloud of sweet Arabian perfumes as of burning pipelines, a cloud of colored miasmas that drifted along with them as they rushed down the course in formation, gigantic glittering automobile hives, and the shepherd whipped them on from one gas station to the next, where they filled themselves with their manna, tanked up on their divine gas. – Stick it to them! cried the shepherd, their God, who had long since grown weary of his flock.

You stick it! Stick it to them...truly, it was that now-sluggish spirit who hovered over them in the red haze waving them on faster and faster. You stick it to them! Too sluggish to perform the last rites, he'd placed all the power into their hands. And when he waved, it was their hand he waved with. And he raised his scepter, invisible, at the exit for a gas station: Exit! Faster faster! Stick it! Stick it to them! It was the spirit of profit, their shepherd, their God, their great Schicklgruber. And he fired the starting gun at the glass-smooth exit of each gas station. – Aaah! Filled with manna they roared off obediently in close formation, with the joyful cry of death on their lips, triumphant and with a fixed gaze they bore down on the nocturnal ribbon of the autobahn. Here on the autobahn, in the drunkenness of speed, in the masses, in the toe-ing of the line between the metal barriers, in the endless tunnel of their trajectory under artificial light, they at last perceived the blind spot that they all bore within them, and that for centuries they had vainly sought to grasp. The empty space in their bodies, the abstraction—here in the midst of the squadron they suddenly knew what it was, that I, that self; it could be translated by a simple Greco-Roman word, and its name was none other than *automobile*. And when the God, the great shepherd, the great Schicklgruber waved his scepter majestically, gesturing out into the open, to the exit, to the exitus, undaunted they followed their automobile's soul and roared off again: *Aaah!*

Will we survive this century? asked the lonely reader in his train compartment. Yes, surely we'll survive this one last century.

The reader in the train was afraid. That fear was indiscriminate, capable of assailing him over and over, at any moment, from behind, from the side, unexpectedly, in moments of peace, its blows no longer predictable. It would leap out at him from the newspaper, from a book, it twisted his most innocuous thoughts and turned them into fear. When he'd dispatched a fear-triggering thought in his mind, that didn't mean it couldn't return again, bringing a fear just as merciless; there was no certainty that any thought arriving in the mantle of benignity might not suddenly bare the naked bones of fear.

After his readings he rarely went away feeling good. In the vast majority of cases he felt that his performance had been a miserable failure; there was something unspeakably false in the role he played, he was unrecognizable in it. It was as though incomprehensible circumstances unmasked him: he didn't even remotely exist in the form in which people had expected to see him…some sort of legend seemed to exist about him, a public image for which he was no match. But he desperately sought to come close; from his void, from his East German nonexistence he fled toward this simulacrum, inevitably falling short, and the audience went home disappointed and baffled. Afterward he'd sit in his hotel, annihilated: he existed neither as the person who had just simulated a literary reading, nor in any other conceivable form!

He'd ask himself what they had expected of him, what image he'd failed to match. He'd lie down on the bed in the hotel room and wait for the pathetic tremors of his wounded soul to die down…it would take a while. When the quaking slowly moved to his limbs, he'd be able to get a grip on it…drenched with the moisture of a whole series of sweats, he tore the slippery clothes from his skin where he lay, until he was naked on the cold bedspread; little by little, thinkable thoughts returned to his mind. The light was burning, and he'd forgotten to close the curtains of the hotel window; he pulled the curtains shut and dropped back down on the bed. After a while he tried to think of some woman over in East Germany; the images, of which he had a limited selection, all refused to take shape in his head. With malicious persistence, the only figure that came to mind was the mother of his friend H., her slight, always lightning-quick form decked out in Western clothes from the Intershop, only making her all the more vividly East German. He imagined her ironic gaze directed at his genitalia, soaked with cold sweat and spilling helplessly from between his thighs, and as her little round face began to move toward that organ, that ravaged agglomeration of brownish hairy skin, he covered it with both his hands.

After a while his sex warmed beneath his hands, and he felt it again…he felt it stir between his sensitive palms, coming back to him. All the back-breaking labor he'd done over there in the GDR, for the incidental benefit of GDR literature—underwriting the second and third homes of its writers that the West lionized—that work had taken no toll on those hands' delicacy of feeling.

No, he didn't have a poet's eyes and he didn't have a poet's prick of the kind prescribed by GDR literature. Nor was he capable of putting on an act as a cultural emissary of his country, as one of those writers from the GDR who had much to criticize about it, especially its cultural poli-cies, but who called the country theirs. West German audi-ences approved of that attitude, indeed it was quite well received, and he didn't stand a chance against it. He had nothing to criticize about the GDR he knew; he regarded criticism as pointless. At West Germany's universities, whole teams of literary scholars devoted themselves to GDR literature, apparently viewing it as an alternative to a West German literature they felt had reached an impasse. And possibly they even regarded the GDR as a whole—if you were able to appraise it as critically as the GDR's literati claimed to—as a political alternative to West Germany. For him, excursions into this conceptual sphere were nothing but hollow theory; at the same time, he felt that never in a hundred years could you make any headway against the image of GDR literature that dominated the market. For its dominance was beyond doubt...

Once an East German publisher had chided C. for lacking an attitude called "critical solidarity." He'd thought about the notion and was forced to admit it was true: when it came to critical solidarity with the GDR state, he could kindle barely a spark of conviction in his breast. But that was the exact attitude with which the well-recognized GDR writers appeared in front of West German audiences. And—there was no other way to put it—with their critical solidarity they'd created something like a new establishment in the West German literary market, they'd become a practically irreversible trend. He could get down on his knees before the West German intelligentsia, C. thought, but he'd go nowhere around here without solidarity, critical or not so critical. Admittedly a rupture had taken place long ago, East German writers had been banished from the country; they'd been robbed of their livelihood through expulsion from the Writers' Association and forced to go to the West. There had been a huge outcry, demands from East and West that these measures be rescinded. That, if you liked, meant yet one more bonanza of critical solidarity. When C. arrived in West Germany, people there were still smitten with a salutation echoing the title of a well-known East German book: "Good morning, sweetheart"...by that point he'd long since started greeting people with "Good night, shithead."

He had always felt a keen resentment toward what he called the new establishment—the official GDR literature with its commercial success. Of course he hadn't admitted this pathetic feeling to himself, he was trying to ignore it… but whenever he hastily retreated to his hotel room after one of his appearances, it became impossible to ignore. He was invited to Europe's most beautiful cities, had his travel costs covered, even got a generous honorarium for a trifling appearance lasting two hours at most—really, anyone would have envied him for it. Cities that other East Germans dreamed about were transformed for him into the scene of a horror story, consisting of nothing but a tiny, dark hotel room where he'd hunker sweating and stinking, waiting in desperation for his return flight. For two days he'd had a room in the best part of Zurich and hadn't even glimpsed the city. Outside, the weather was gorgeous; he sat in the hotel with the curtains drawn, a bottle of liquor clutched in his fist, his fingers practically fused to the bottle's neck. The room was befouled with tobacco smoke and alcohol vapors—dark blue, or so it seemed in retrospect—and the bathroom smelled of vomit. The telephone kept ringing, journalists wanted to talk to him, the event organizer wanted to invite him out to eat; trembling with horror he waited for it to stop. All he knew was this: these reading tours were being orchestrated in order to destroy and unmask him…and that seemed to be the very reason he agreed to appear. He failed to find an explanation for what he was going through, what he could not escape. The only recourse was to sit tight and persevere…to wait and see what would happen to him. And that was the image he embodied: a harried figure in a hotel room without the slightest notion who he really was. Perhaps he was a being lent human form only temporarily, by chance. A guinea pig of fate, a sham through and through; there was no conception of what he was supposed to have become. And all he could do was wait, he'd vomited all his wits into the toilet bowl of the hotel room, he was a pastiche without meaning or character, he could do nothing now but sit there motionless, slowly perishing and waiting for this interim to end...

Maybe it was Hedda who'd been trying to call him! Again and again he'd promise to stay in touch when he was traveling, but he never kept his promise...he was afraid she'd find out the state he was in. As if Hedda could only turn away from him in disgust if she caught him like that. But at the same time, of course, that fear was a false-hood...she wasn't able to turn away in earnest, he knew that, she'd try to get him back on his feet. And that would encourage him to go on living amid all his falsehood...

Besides, he didn't know how to explain his state. There was no explanation, just a mass of phrases that kept mindlessly repeating. One time, in a hotel room in Rotterdam, she had caught him after all; unexpectedly, she was the person on the phone. When he started to try to explain his condition, an inextricable knot formed in his throat, a gagging, burning revolt broke loose in his gorge as though he were some sort of fire-spewing lizard; he was racked by an attack of barking coughs, and only with the utmost effort did he manage to fling the receiver back onto the hook. He'd vomited into the tub, endless quantities of whisky mixed with viscous gall-bitter stom-ach acid flowed unresisting from his gullet; he thought he was bleeding to death. Then he'd crouched down in the middle of the sulfurous smelling, nearly black puddle and turned the cold shower onto his head…

Afterward he'd wandered around Rotterdam aimlessly, still plagued by remorse because he hadn't been able to choke out a single word for Hedda. An endless, arrested dusk lay over Rotterdam; it was an oppressively hot summer evening. The vast sallow evening sky appeared to flatten and sink toward the north, like a reflection of the leaden gray, motionless North Sea, and it seemed to vibrate faintly, holding a weak rumble of thunder from nowhere. C. strayed from the center of town and came across a series of strangely barren spaces overgrown by dry grass like a steppe. It looked as though this had once been a neighborhood, but now the built-up area began a long way away, at the edge of these spaces; when he walked through the grass, he seemed to feel gravel and pulverized rubble underfoot. Off to the side of one of the open expanses stood a rough wooden platform where some rock musicians were hastily packing up their instruments and a sparse audience was trotting off in little groups toward the buildings; toxic flashes of heat lightning filled the sky, a storm brewing. Evidently, the buildings that once stood here had been casualties of the German bombing of Rotterdam on May 14, 1940, just four days after Germany began its western offensive. The Netherlands had capitulated a day later. Those bombings were hardly ever mentioned anymore, all anyone talked about was the Allied air raids on German cities. Back in May 1940, C. hadn't been alive yet…

How was he supposed to explain what was wrong with him? Whenever anyone asked, he always claimed to be doing fine…any other reply would have been absurd, implausible, and completely misconstruable. And in truth he was doing fine, he was doing very well indeed, he spent more money on drink than even the average West German could afford. But the thing inside him wasn't truth. Nor could he call it unconquerable falsehood; what stirred there lay outside language. And the only possibility left was to hide from the whole world…at least until he had fumbled himself back together, put his mask back on, temporarily realigned himself with what he took to be everyone else's state of mind. When he asked himself when all this might have started, he felt it had set in as he'd slowly become a public figure. Was that it, had he been drifting into this chaos of his ever since? Once he'd become a published author who met with a certain response…

Then those people back east had been right, with their warnings and good advice…

And so the only thing that could help was what was completely and utterly impossible for him: he had to cease to be a public writer…

He couldn't do that, if only because he begrudged those people back east their truth…

One day, this much was clear to him, he'd have to describe the monster that had entrenched itself inside him, and deliver it up to the public. That public from which he crawled off to hide even as he worshipped it, adjusting himself to it with every conceivable trick as he hoodwinked it with his shrewdest maneuvers in an effort to sell himself, like a wily old Scythian horse dealer. And the authorities representing that public were the literary critics: he'd have to fling that beast down the critics' bloody gullet to feed on…

At some point he decided it was useless to keep firing up all those terrorizing thoughts in his brain. The beast he was talking about was probably just a bugbear, a delusion. This beast of prey went by meaningless names such as *God* or *death*, abstract names that were mere figments of the mind in the world outside the hotel room...

The hotel was the prototypical abode for a life lived in transience. Usually the train station was somewhere nearby; at night, when he couldn't sleep, he'd wander over to the station and look at the timetables. There were trains that left early in the morning, crossed national borders and, at some point that evening, arrived in the East, in some random city he'd once known quite well. What kept him from getting on one of those trains, letting himself be trundled off to sleep—helped along by a bottle of whisky—to wake up over there after a long journey...over in what seemed the home of the beast, whose restlessness he could no longer control?

It was ludicrous: every time he had a conflict with Hedda, the altercation ended up as a battle between East and West, a senseless proxy war between two different histories. A conflict like that had to end in a stalemate, because the histories of both sides were over and done with, and thus left no room for persuasion. Only casualties could result; each battle ended with their backs turned to each other.

It might have been one of those disputes that actually sent him fleeing from a hotel once. It was after a reading in Vienna, his second event in that city, late in the summer of his second year in the West, a reading, incidentally, which he felt had gone well, quite in contrast to the previous one that spring, after which he'd left

Vienna feeling rather despondent.

The business with Hedda preyed on his mind; he needed to be alone, but he couldn't tell anyone why. It was as though it would have been an admission of guilt. In the middle of the obligatory get-together in a café after the reading he'd excused himself, saying he'd be back in half an hour; after walking twice around St. Stephen's Cathedral, breathing hard, he suddenly found himself in front of his hotel; the deranged alcoholic in his head induced him to fetch his bag from his room and head straight for Nuremberg. There was no one at the reception desk; he took his key from the key rack himself, then laid it in plain sight on the desk before he left. In the taxi to the Westbahnhof station he already began to regret what he'd done; he could at least have left a note with the key. Soon after that he was sitting on a train to Munich, the last one to leave Vienna at that hour.

He was in Munich a little after six a.m. He headed for the station post office, intending to send a telegram to Vienna to explain his whereabouts. That didn't work out; the post office didn't open until eight… Back in Vienna they'd probably already reported his sudden disappearance to the police. Then he tried to call Hedda, getting no answer the first two times; the third time a man's sleepy voice responded. Alarmed, he hung up. He went and sat in the station café and drank several cups of coffee. He'd recognized the voice on the telephone: it was Hedda's ex-boyfriend, the one she'd broken up with, who actually lived in Munich, or rather went back and forth between Munich and Nuremberg…ever since C. had come onto the scene, that boyfriend had a rather vagrant look, as though living in an interim state himself.

Now he recalled the reason for the fight he'd had with Hedda: it was about the trip to Greece she was pining to take. Hedda had been to Greece before, and judging from the stories she told, it must have been a seminal experience for her. – She'd been dreaming of Greece ever since, she said; her desire to share the experience with C. was so strong that sometimes he practically felt hounded by it. – However, she declared that they couldn't make the trip until spring, because in summer the place she had in mind would be besieged by an unparalleled tourist invasion. And second of all, the summer temperatures were unbearable. – But next spring my visa will have expired, C. responded.

That triggered a fight about C.'s lack of decisiveness, the unacceptable way he kept putting everything off, refusing to think of the future, sitting there idly as foreseeable problems loomed, then responding with maneuvers and evasions…acting provisionally and on standby, as Hedda put it… – You aren't in the GDR anymore, you can decide for yourself what to do, she said, why can't you bring yourself to do it?

Of course that hit a nerve with him…but that was how things stood: by next spring, the time for that trip to Greece, he would have to have left the West, according to his contract with the East German authorities. Or he would have to have made the effort to get his visa extended… – It was easy to see that these discussions weren't really about his visa, they were about a kind of contract with Hedda, a commitment to her. So far he'd made no clear statement on that subject; that was the accusation that lurked behind the Greece issue. He was using that lousy stamp the East German bureaucrats had slammed down onto his passport as a device to keep his relationship with Hedda in limbo…he couldn't even bear to picture the intensity of Hedda's indignation at this behavior. The selflessness it took for her to look past it. The provisional state that he was living in, that he'd pushed so hard for, was something he inevitably ended up imposing on her life as well.

She didn't complain about it, but every argument they had quickly centered around his whole lack of belonging. There was a danger in that, with even minor disagreements suddenly turning into existential questions that bore on the survival of their relationship. He recalled that in the first year, after each fight they had, he'd actually longed for his visa to lapse…he'd never said it out loud, but he'd thought it, and Hedda would sit staring at him anxiously as though she guessed his thoughts. His indecision—his inability to grasp that Hedda wanted no one but him, even if once he heard the voice of another man answering her telephone—his corrosive mistrust, no doubt those were the reasons for his frequent trips back East, and Hedda must have sensed that as well. His precipitous departure from Vienna was one of those impulses…how many times before had he toyed with the notion of slipping off to the East to get away from Hedda? But when he actually did, thoughts of Hedda began to haunt him as soon as he arrived, and he had no idea what he was doing there.

Could it be true that he needed a woman only as a kind of dream vision? And that when he was confronted with her actual existence, he didn't feel equal to her?

And he needed her only as a dream vision in some other atmosphere, on some other level from which insurmountable forces severed him. On a stage, where he could see and desire her without being able to reach her. Or on the TV screen of his imagination, where she was a yearned-for but untouchable phantasma. Like his mother, whom he'd slept next to all through his childhood in the double bed, his back turned toward her, separated by the ineradicable distance that time and age imposed, turned away from her in sleeplessness, in a solitude that through her tangible proximity had become a merciless judgment from God...

In her exasperation at his constant evasions Hedda had told him: If you don't want to go to Greece, then I'll just go there with Gerhard again...

Now, she might not have meant those words quite seriously. Rather they came from a sense of helplessness: C.'s apathy was capable of making the staunchest character feel helpless. Gerhard, that ex-boyfriend of Hedda's who'd answered the phone in Munich early that morning, would probably have accompanied her to Greece in a flash, he'd have grasped an offer like that like the proverbial straw. But even if the trip had actually come about, Gerhard still wouldn't have posed a serious threat to C. Gerhard was a nice guy who worshipped Hedda, and who'd already taken her in twice, without showing particular signs of rancor, when she'd been trying to get away from C. Hedda didn't let on exactly how she felt about that, but she said: It won't happen to me a third time...

Though Gerhard had constantly wanted to sleep with Hedda, it happened rarely—practically never, she claimed—because she'd refused him most of the time. The alibis she gave were chronic illnesses or at least symptoms that chronically plagued her. One day she bluntly confided to C.: I never really loved him, and the way he wanted to go to bed with me every day, it actually ended up making me sick. That's how he wound up becoming my nurse… – Then why didn't you leave him? asked C. – Where was I supposed to go? I really had no one to go to in the entire country. – You're a very beautiful woman, you could have found someone in just a few days… – Anyone else would never have become my nurse!

In their relationship, even that was turned on its head: she got sick because C. didn't go to bed with her. After half a year, at most nine months, he'd realized to his horror that his desire for Hedda was waning, that he was showing signs of surfeit. It was an almost traumatic experience; he'd been through it two times before.

When this predicament began, for quite a while he made himself keep sleeping with Hedda. The first few times Hedda had let it go in silence, but then she said to him: If you don't really feel like it, then let it be. You're straining as if your life were at stake.

My life is at stake, he thought, but he didn't say it. Of course he knew that the more often his life was at stake, the more his resistance would grow. More resistance meant more straining, and it was all heading inevitably toward a collapse.

At night he'd withdraw to his apartment on Kobergerstrasse and read the tips given by female professors with three or four academic titles on the letters pages of various porn magazines and tabloids; instantly this would compound his plight. Or he discussed things with Hedda, who felt it would help to talk about his situation. Naturally he didn't share that view, believing that in his case it was quite the opposite (though of course that was just as ridiculous a notion); it amazed him, the seriousness with which women could discuss male problems. He'd always emerge from those conversations empty-headed; everything he'd had in his head sank down to the pit of his stomach, turning into a ghastly brew of shame and anger that subjected his little worm's erectile tissue to days of paralysis. All the same, he developed something of an addiction to these sessions; for a while he stopped avoiding them, until he realized that he was going along with the conversations because they facilitated his abstinence. C. and Hedda had even asked themselves whether he might actually be gay without having noticed. C.'s response was that he didn't think so; going by his gut feeling, he'd find it easier to shoot a man than to embrace him. – Hedda didn't appreciate the black humor; she was a woman, and by nature rejected irresponsible attitudes toward human procreation.

But the fact was that in the West, sexuality's promise beamed out at you from every billboard. Apparently consumer goods or public opinions could be sold only when associated with sexual fulfillment. The fact that all this didn't end in the total castration of Western society filled him with a vast respect for the tenacity of primordial human drives; the only problem was that he was the exceptional case on whom that promise had a literally crushing effect. Sexuality went hand in hand with fulfillment, and as such was the dominant state of affairs—that was implicit in every public statement. Sexual fulfillment was such a self-evident fact, its existence seemed so far beyond question to the vast majority of the public, that every linguistic act in the entire country seemed solely concerned with its further enhancement. Practically everything was proposed as a means to that end: the purchase of cars, toothbrushes, TV sets, and toilet paper. If sexual fulfillment was already a given anyway, and was constantly supposed to be enhanced, the only possible objective was its overfulfillment. And this notion of the overfulfillment of a norm presented him with the most astonishing parallel to standard GDR-speak. That is to say, the highly respected Federal Republic blathered on just as idiotically as his socialist fatherland…so he might as well just go back where he'd come from. The idiocies differed only in their efficiency, admittedly impressive in the West, suggesting that the GDR had quite a ways to go.

Going back to that creature hidden inside him…he'd called it a monster or a beast…perhaps it came from having let his own life pass him by. He'd squandered what was his—that feeling fermented inside him like a belly full of bad food. But he didn't even know what was his, no doubt precisely because he had squandered it, nor did he know exactly what had impelled him to do so or how he'd pulled it off. And perhaps he didn't want to know, as that could only mean living with an abyss of unforgettable losses… He was in the West now, with two-thirds of his life behind him, perhaps the years generally known as the best of your life…he doubted he could say that of his years. All he knew was that he'd missed out on that time, there was no doubt about it, and he didn't know if he could go on living with a vacuum like that in his head. With that ice-cold fury constantly lurking inside him, was there any way to cope with the rest of his life and not go haywire? He knew the only thing that could give him some brief satisfaction: he'd love to take all of them—the ones who'd carved the border through the country, who had built the Wall, who had justified and glorified that Wall with their poetry, their cultural policies, and their police force, and all the ones who'd built an ideological wall blocking off his poems, who'd kept tossing him out of their pestiferous editorial offices, who'd only taken a break from copulating to sign the rejection letters he received—and herd them all into a corner and mow them down with a machine gun...then he could breathe easy again.

Over there in the GDR, running idiotically back and forth between the coal cellar and his equally grimy desk, he'd had so little time and opportunity for love that he'd pounced like a raving animal on every woman who gave him the least little chance, which had quickly burned him out, and no wonder. To avoid utter disgrace, he told the writers the tall tale that you could occasionally get laid in the boiler room; in the boiler room he told everyone he had a lover in his circle of writers. And sometimes he'd wake up nights drenched in sweat, suddenly believing his own yarns.

In the heat of the bedroom his memories would suddenly be irrefutably true. He recalled walking one night at a woman's side through a town's narrow, winding streets that were as tortuous and dark as those in the small town he'd once come from...or which he had never really left. He remembered every word they'd spoken together and thought of how his gaze kept seeking the pale glimmer of her shoulders in the darkness. It was hot and humid, a storm was brewing, thunder rolled onward toward the city, but they made no effort to walk faster. Once he ventured to touch her white arm, slightly damp in the steamy air, and just as she turned her face toward him the first blinding flash of lighting descended...

He had been interrupted in the middle of writing

down this episode; his girlfriend, Mona, had noticed that while writing with his right hand, he'd shield the lines in the curve of his left hand, as though ready to cover them up at any moment. Mona had looked at him askance and claimed that he was trying to hide something from her, though he himself was utterly unaware how he held his hands when he was concentrating. – That trivial thing had started a fight; Mona felt wounded, while he was filled with guilt…instead of revealing that the episode was just invented, he acquiesced to Mona's reproach and withdrew into the sweat-stench of his guilty conscience.

Outside his bedroom window the storm was raging; he got out of bed and went into the kitchen. A whole series of lightning flashes made him turn around, and suddenly, somewhere in the bedroom's dark disarray, he saw the woman's face reappear. It was a faceless face, without mouth or eyes, like an oval draped in a white cloth… it was true, he had just thought her up! She didn't come from reality, she'd arisen from his brain, maybe not even his brain, maybe just his helplessly scribbling pen. The whole episode was invented, all his episodes were just invented, maybe all the women he'd loved were nothing but inventions.

In time all his thoughts had come to seem preposterous to him, and he clung to that perspective as though it could help him escape from his trap. But no, after all these were his feelings he was dealing with—miserable creatures, criticized to death, which he'd tried to transform into thoughts. And all these thoughts kept ending in disaster. For far too long he'd laughed off his feelings as though they weren't his—for decades he'd ridiculed them, and not just to himself, but in public, evidently with the aim of getting by in society halfway unscathed. Now all these precautions were melting away, and he was as soft as an undercooked egg. Everything suddenly seemed to be slipping through his fingers, it seemed too late for most things. He rebelled, but he should have rebelled much sooner. Now maybe his rebellion was just a song and dance.

On nights like these he'd inevitably reach a point where he'd feel he no longer had a brain in his head, just a maelstrom, a gushing, gaping hole which no answer was enough to fill anymore. That was how it was: what throbbed in that spot behind his brow was the maw of an insatiable vulva before which he, with his aborted masculinity, was doomed to failure…

Once he had a dream, a terrifying one, in a hotel room in Antwerp. As usual, he'd barely seen the city, only the station, over and over, frequenting it every few hours over the several days of his stay. It was just a few hundred yards from his hotel, and struck him as one of the biggest and most beautiful stations he'd ever seen, a veritable palace, with an enormous entry hall buttressed by gigantic columns, gleaming with marble and gold. In his dream the station suddenly vanished; instead, his path led farther and farther into a dark and clearly impoverished quarter where old, crooked lamps scattered a light that barely shone, that somehow seemed to smoke. He was starting to wonder if he'd taken a wrong turn when a figure detached itself from the shadow of low-slung houses and signaled that he could keep on going straight. The person joined him, drawing him into conversation in laborious broken German; he felt that the man beside him was mad, and looked around for an escape, but there seemed to be no way out of the narrow lane. Suddenly the man stepped in his way and asked quite clearly, now in fluent German, if perhaps he wanted to go to confession. – A Germanophobe! thought C., and looked him in the face: an older man with a white beard, quite sturdy. – Now he seized C. by the jacket and asked again if perhaps he should take him to confession. He was smiling with his flawless set of teeth, his hands were clutching the collar of C.'s jacket, his grip growing tighter and tighter. C. pushed him hard in the chest; the old man fell against the wall, but didn't stop smiling. In that instant C. knew he was facing God…no question about it, it was God, this was how he'd pictured him. In an outburst of rage mixed with fear he went for the old man's throat and squeezed. – You've got everything and I've got nothing! C. cried, but his voice sounded thin and shrill. The old man was still smiling; C. choked him with both fists, pressing his thumbs against his larynx: You've got everything, I've got nothing! he yelled again. – At that moment he saw that the neck supported a woman's head, a woman's face, laughing at him. The face was almost beautiful, elaborately and luridly made up, mouth open; under the pressure of his hands her tongue lolled between blood-red lips. And that tongue was long and pointed and moved, twitching and flicking like the tongue of a snake; there was no denying it, the woman was smiling mockingly. C. loosened his grip in alarm, and the woman asked: Want to see my asshole? Half price for looking… These words were followed by a laugh, soft and quiet, that gurgled up from the gorge behind the tongue. – At that the dream ended; he woke up in a strange, unfamiliar city…

And he recalled his first trip to Paris, which he'd anticipated so eagerly. Paris, for him, was the city of Apollinaire,
André Breton, Max Jacob, Pierre Reverdy…and so it
remained: when he finally departed, Paris was more unreal
than ever. For him it was a faded city immersed in gray
cold vapors, with the streets—or really just one street—
perceivable only in snippets, in alternating fragments,
interpenetrating or mirroring each other. It was one of
those transitional months (he didn't even remember quite
which), no longer fall, or not yet spring, with extreme and
startling shifts in temperature; you lost all sense of time
on the Boulevard du Montparnasse with its bare trees,
washed and washed out by a damp that barely let up, by
rain, by wet snow or wet fog. In the morning ice would
still shatter in the gutters along the broad sidewalks; a
little later it had melted and merged with the universal
dissolution of all solid things, their contours and colors.
The rain had begun with his arrival, the drizzle, which had
come without warning, sank and rose ceaselessly through
the mix of air and gas, and the people of this continent
of intricately nested buildings were transformed within
the space of an hour into millions of bizarre crustaceans,
swelling under dripping black umbrellas and moving by
jerks and bobs, wafting through the water like sinister
dark manta rays or wriggling onward like oddly upright
snails. The corpse-colored Seine seemed to have risen
from its bed, surging down the channels of the streets
with all its sodden, dissolving refuse, and sometimes, from
the gray-green-white veils of water suspended between
the roofs, surreal mutant cadavers seemed to grin, seeking
to engage in dialogue with him. For four days—rainy days
and rainy nights—he walked up and down the Boulevard

du Montparnasse; in cafés and bistros he drank without a pause, bitter Danish beer tasting of sulfur and urine; he would order it in a pathetic mishmash of English and French and the waiter would set it down with a look of disgust. That was all he could afford on the fee for his reading, long since past; the connection to Nuremberg was poor, with only two flights a week, and he had to wait. He waited, his clothes never having a chance to dry, smelling of mildew and moldy tobacco; he himself had long since started smelling like his decaying denim things that no one wore in France; the fabric, cold as wood soaked in water, seemed to have melded with his wrinkled skin, an epidermis roughened to permanent goose bumps, steaming and smelling of swamp; and even the bed in the little Montparnasse hotel smelled of moor and coal by now, as though he'd been stewed during the brief hours he slept, lying askew and derailed on the oddly made French bed, dreaming wild dreams of his Saxon woods, convinced he was being boiled by the electric light that set the streaks of rain aflame outside the window. And as he sweated— coal-colored tears trickling from all his pores—he felt all his inner substance leave him and ooze away into the mattress below.

On arriving he'd claimed to want to see as much of Paris as possible, to be eagerly looking forward to Paris (that at least was no lie), so the event organizers had left him to his own devices, and now he lacked the courage to call them and admit that he couldn't cope with the city at all. He lived entirely on café au lait and croissants as light as air; he couldn't fall asleep until five in the morning, long after the traffic noise had started outside, so he over-slept the hotel breakfast by hours. But the concierge at the reception, a friendly old man with a perpetual ironic grin, always conjured up a few croissants for him. With the breakfast room already being cleaned, he'd drink his coffee out in the lobby, huddling tremulously in a capacious fauteuil, sunk like a drowned man weighed down by a millstone; the concierge would watch him with ironic concern. Several times the old man, who spoke a bit of German, made a joke when C. came down to the lobby. – Ah, you have trouble waking up, Monsieur! he'd say. You've been listening to the king of the elves all night...

The bookstore that had hosted his reading was called "Le Roi des Aulnes"—the King of the Elves—and was not far from his hotel.

The longest of his forays had taken him up to the gigantic *Arc de Triomphe*; in the fine persistent drizzle he stood on the sidewalk and spent five minutes contemplating the mighty, senseless edifice. The German troops had marched through its arch when they occupied Paris; his father hadn't been among them, he'd gotten only as far as Calais before being sent to Stalingrad. When he recalled the famous photo of those parading German troops, it seemed to him that the trees lining the street to the left and right of the triumphal arch hadn't grown at all since innocently ending up in that photo...

He turned around, and was soon collapsing back into the armchair in the lobby of his hotel. He struggled to breathe; he sensed the smell of his aging graying hair; he smelled the pallid moisture of his beard stubble, the soap that clogged it, whole eons of greasy ghastly soap bogged down in his beard; and he breathed in the smell of his brain, which gave off vapors like old masonry full of molding mortar and colonized by dark dripping nests of unknown vermin.

Soon after arriving in Montparnasse he'd undergone a strange regression. On the boulevard, which he'd imagined being much larger, where the lights began turning on even in the afternoon gloom, the shop windows were already lit up, and the lamps burned in the empty cafés— in the middle of this Babylon overwhelmed by mournful wetness, he'd suddenly reverted to being an individual of his particular origins. A GDR citizen, unreservedly; once again he was what he had been, and he was lost...he had never felt his GDR identity so clearly and inescapably, not even in the country itself, which perhaps had already ceased to exist. And he couldn't help viewing this identity as *inferior*. Against all empirical reason he carried that sense around with him in his aging body, and there was nothing he could do about it...

Over and over on his reading trips he was haunted by the sense that he was getting old. It had escaped his attention, or he'd pushed the thought aside, but now a mighty indignation began raising a ruckus inside him. It yanked him up from his seat in the train compartment and he walked down the corridor looking for the bar, quick, lithe, elastic, the way he used to walk, as a different person in a long-gone time, rolling his shoulders, sticking up his chin; now and then he ran his hand through his hair as though his head were crowned with flames, and with the other hand he smoked with sweeping gestures, languid and glam like David Bowie at the mike. A moment later he saw his reflection in the glass pane of a door in the corridor: his face was falling apart, exhausted, furrowed by vexations, dark sweat-damp creases stretched down toward the depths; a short aging anxious man with his belly bulging from his jacket, that was all he was. Instantly his flatulate distention deflated, and he fled back to his seat. Horror had seized him; he was defenseless against it, only gradually did it melt into a cruel gall-bitter grief. His rage was aimed at an inevitability, and so could not be turned around. There was no way to aim it against himself and his body, against his fear, against his grief, against his *nature*…there seemed to be a multitude of wells within him from which hatred suddenly gushed forth, as from myriad opened veins whose pulsing flow could not be staunched. He held tight to the bottle that stood in front of him on the little table by the window; he froze, listening to the silent whimper that came from somewhere within his body. It took him quite a while to strangle those feelings; only then could he think again.

That country over there had swallowed up his time! That vestibule of reality. That country dripping with cretinism, crippled with age, ground down and burned out by wear and tear and stinking like a cesspit, that country had fed him with mortality and deadened his reflexes, it had sucked the desire from his veins; his brain had calcified like the workings of a sclerotic old washing machine. He'd escaped that country too late…

Actually, he didn't want to talk about these things unfolding inside him. They embarrassed him; ultimately he didn't even feel like thinking about them. They mortified him, they didn't fit him at all. It was amazing that he was immune to these attacks in the company of other people…they actually only hit him when he was alone…

Only when he'd shut himself off from everyone, when he was sure he couldn't be disturbed—and when it was easy for him to think that he wasn't even alive anymore—only then did that flood of black gall rise within him, emerging perhaps from the very dregs of his being. And that gall in turn loosed a wave of shame…if he'd had to name the reason for that shame, he would have been stricken dumb. The shame was insoluble, it could neither be penetrated nor illuminated; he was always busy covering it up or dispelling it…

And it never occurred to him to ask whether there was any reason for his shame. He harbored mental states against which he had no defenses, they'd slumbered inside him unnoticed for ages…they'd suddenly risen up to claim their territory, and he'd ceded them the field. It was a defeat, and that defeat operated as though it were part of his nature—that was how it felt, at least. It was as though creation had unexpectedly decided on some other path for him. He'd been taken unawares by it, some god had duped him…and at the same time it delivered him the shame of failing to live up to his previous role. It was a shame as though he'd been deceiving the whole world about who he was, but now his intentions had come to light…

The whole world had thought he was strong, and he'd been all too happy to play that role. And he'd probably played for too long; for far too long he'd made a secret of his weakness. Now he was afraid that *the whole world* (what a devil of an expression!) would turn its back on him. People are glad to turn their backs on the weak…he was speaking from experience: hadn't turning his back on the weak been a strength of his as well?

When he thought about it, however, he did find reasons for his shame, and they were ones he could hardly ignore. He had two boxes full of books in his so-called office in Nuremberg, packing cases around which he constantly prowled, unable to bring himself to unpack them. These boxes, as he saw it, contained the cumulative horror of the twentieth century. Soon after arriving in West Germany he'd begun amassing all the available books that described, documented, and pondered that horror. These books, he told himself, were that century's indispensable knowledge, they held the only *truly necessary knowledge of the twentieth century*. He collected these books maniacally, with almost irrepressible greed: he surrounded himself with them, he buried himself under them, he walled himself in with their rows. And then he found himself unable to breathe amid the stacks and piles, so in a panicked fit of nocturnal activity he stowed the books away in the two boxes. He closed the boxes up and labeled them. After that he felt as though he were guarding a concentration camp. And sometimes he dreamed about the boxes: they loomed in the night like darkly glowing furnaces, emitting a faint incandescence that spread sulfurous vapors. He sweated in his sleep, felt his breath failing; he jumped up, turned on the light, and went over to the boxes. There they stood, motionless. In black marker he'd written on their lids: *Holocaust & Gulag*.

There they stood, those smoking boxes, absorbing every possible reproach against the world. Faced with these boxes, filled to bursting with the unthinkable horror of the *modern* era, reduced to stammering, slapdash block letters, every grievance was rendered cowardly, childish, irrelevant. With those boxes in your home, your complaints sounded as ludicrous as the squeaking of a rat. You had to be ashamed of any discontent, you had to hate yourself if you were still able to feel unhappy, you had to keep it secret in the face of this madness that had made language lose all dignity.

And for that the powers that be could ultimately be grateful, they had to feel a vast gratitude for the *phenomenon of Auschwitz*...and so they guarded it like the apple of their eye. And he thought this not just with an eye to the East. If that phenomenon hadn't happened, they would have had to rectify the omission...but that was a thing you couldn't let yourself think if you didn't want to fall through the cracks of this society.

That's a thing I'll be left to cope with alone, he thought after a while, as the train sped him on through the countryside. He'd gotten ahold of himself and was able to think with some lucidity. Lately he'd found himself wondering more and more often how he'd become what he'd become...with the increasingly frequent misgiving that it was actually too late for these reflections. Inside him was a kind of bottomless terror that he'd missed every opportunity to realize his true calling...it was a vacuum around which he circled in panic, and that fear was inextricably entangled with another one, a childhood fear, no longer fathomable, that had survived in some hidden place within. – I'll be left alone with my past, he thought, and with my incommunicable fear. And whenever I try to speak of that fear—to any old person, a listener, a reader— all that will result will be something resembling literature. I'll make my fear into a kind of *show*; I will have had a past just to be amusing...

Really, with thoughts like those in your head you couldn't keep going on reading tours...how could he stand before an audience when he was nothing but this hollow charlatan with nothing to hold onto inside him?

He wondered how he could possibly manage to be in

any shape to appear in front of an audience by the time he arrived at the event venue. He had actually gone through trips on which, up to the very moment he took a seat on the chair in front of those two or three rows of credulous people and started reading, he was trying to figure out how to escape, how to vanish at the last moment…until he grasped that the best way to make himself vanish was to recite what he called his *text*. But his voice wouldn't play along; as soon as he started reading, something in his gullet would begin to protest, a strange refusal arising in his throat—likely in the vicinity of his vocal cords—seemingly inexplicable by simple physiological causes, a complication that could neither be localized nor remedied. It was as though his words, emerging from his chest along with his breath, had to work their way through some resistance—not a constriction, not some lump in his throat, but rather as though his words had to travel an incredibly long way, and once he'd finally forced them out into the open, they were disheveled, half squashed, and garbled by hoarseness. On their long wanderings his words had aged, grown frail. They'd had to trek through hostile atmospheres, ancient deserts, epochs of decay, emerging covered with dust and caked in salt, dried out from endlessly sifting fine sand, and when at last he deposited them in the artificial light in front of his podium, it took just ten minutes before he felt his entire body fill with exhaustion he struggled to ignore.

While he'd been running around on his reading tours, time had slipped past him well-nigh imperceptibly: two, three, nearly four years had passed and he hadn't even really looked up. In light of the words that passed through him and that he discharged at these events—those decrepit, hoarse, often barely intelligible words—and given the long-past time and the remote deserts or steppes from which they seemed to originate, there was no significance to those few years that had floated away in passing. And in that time his love for a woman had faded and he had paid it just as little mind. Hedda was gone, she'd vanished somewhere, and he didn't know her whereabouts. – No, he had genuinely failed to catch on to the fact that he loved her, he hadn't understood it, he'd given no credence to his feelings—and still less to hers, apparently—he'd squandered and botched that love, unconsciously he'd constantly been fleeing from it, he hadn't even been able to pronounce the word *love*. And if he ever did dare to do it, he suspected himself of lying… Now the whole affair was over, or at least so it seemed, and somewhere inside him he felt a dull indefinable pain in whose existence he couldn't believe either. – He tried to think what date it was today: he didn't know exactly, he didn't even know that…fall was about to begin, it was probably September 14 or 15, 1989, and it was still as hot as if it were the height of summer. Two weeks ago, at the end of August, he'd had his birthday, and on that day Hedda had left him…without a word. She'd left him; it was pathetic, he finally had to admit it. For about a week he kept boozing to switch off his brain; then, suddenly, in an attack of panic, he'd stopped drinking and began to let the whole thing sink in. It was a repulsive sense of cowardice that overwhelmed him: he crawled into hiding, but there wasn't even a chance of hiding from it. Hedda was gone, there was no way of reaching her, and he couldn't live with that, nor could he die. It had happened before that she'd vanish for a few weeks, but he'd always chased her down again by calling, by writing letters, by relentlessly interrogating her friends and acquaintances; this time his gut told him it was over.

He wavered between outrage and weepy vulnerability, hectic activity and resigned irresolution, with an immense fury at himself swelling inside him. He knew that Hedda was holed up somewhere suffering because she'd forced herself to take this step. She'd done it for the sake of self-preservation…and he felt his pity for her nearly driving him mad. But it was too late for that pity now…

He could barely bring himself to set foot in his apartment on Kobergerstrasse…he'd only ever been able to stand it there because he knew Hedda was within reach, right nearby on Schillerplatz. Now he was hunkered down in the middle of this utterly alien city and didn't know what he was doing here. When he crossed the threshold of his abode, it was like voluntarily returning to a dungeon where he suffocated in the sulfurous fumes of his anguish, able to do nothing but focus on his breath—those short, audible, arduous breaths—and where he felt that his own presence was killing him. On that late summer evening with no fixed date he walked across Nuremberg's Castle Rock, where the bustle of people, all united by joie de vivre or the craving for pleasure, put him to flight; but he took a few more detours before approaching what he shruggingly called home. There he found the shadows of aging dust dimming everything with their gray bitterness, and the dry, yellowed papers curling at the edges; the only vivid thing there was the harsh howling of the dogs in the butcher's yard. Nothing could put a stop to them, it was like a noise from the vestibule of Hell. He'd bought a record, he'd bought dozens of records, merely to drown out that whining.

During the first year, while still in possession of a valid visa, he'd regularly defected each time he had a falling out with Hedda: he had taken the train to his mother in M. That, too, was a thing of the past now: he'd kept meaning to extend his visa, making up his mind on a monthly basis for the past two years, and now he felt haunted by the unaccomplished plan… Writers he knew who had a three-year visa, or were even on their second three-year visa, had encouraging words for him: it was quite easy to pull off once you had gotten a visa in the first place, whether for one year or for three. Only he mustn't let too much time pass, or the rationale he gave would lose its plausibility. – He never did write up the application, it was one more thing he kept putting off, and for stretches he completely forgot about it—the way he forgot everything that could have brought some order to his life. And he noticed that the only time he still felt the urgent need to travel to the GDR was when alcohol made him sentimental.

Several times over the past few years his mother, who as a retiree was allowed to travel, had visited him in Nuremberg, but now he'd grown incapable of inviting her. As always, she would have been happy to come; he knew she'd taken a great, half-hidden liking to Hedda, and enjoyed being with the two of them. That was exactly what kept him from asking her to visit. He had an insurmountable dread of admitting to his mother that all was not well in their relationship, that they took turns doubting whether their liaison could last, that the ominous rifts between them hardly seemed possible to mend. Now that the relationship, in all probability, had broken off completely, he felt it utterly impossible to tell his mother the truth. It was as though he'd have to confess a misdeed, a deliberate cruelty that would disgrace him in front of his mother more than any other person. Sometimes his mother seemed to suspect his defeat, even when it was just beginning to loom; she asked about Hedda more and more often. And when his replies turned monosyllabic, she switched to tactical maneuvering, asking in a roundabout way, practically posing trick questions, and even when she spoke of other things, he sensed that she was constantly feeling him out for information about his relationship with Hedda. Suddenly she had all sorts of messages she'd instruct him to give her, and the next time they talked on the phone the first thing she'd ask was whether he'd passed everything on, and what Hedda's reply had been…he had no choice but to tangle himself in a web of lies from which he could find no escape. She'd already started pouncing on his contradictions; staying in touch with the suspicious mother who kept pressing him was becoming a horror scenario, and he started shirking the conversations. She didn't have a phone, but one of her neighbors did; she would commit C. to set times for their phone calls, and whenever that hour drew near he would sit by the phone filled with dread, afraid of its ring.

He faced the shrilling telephone without picking up the receiver...yet unable to shake the thought that it might be Hedda calling. In the pit of his stomach he felt a dull, indescribable pressure that was all too familiar to him; his heart seemed clenched in a brutal fist, his brain was drained of blood, and for no reason at all he struggled to breathe; if the pressure spread downward, it inevitably caused racking diarrhea. He sat gasping at the kitchen table and fought to get a grip on his body, to get his mind back in motion. Finally he went to a nearby café and searched his memory for things that had triggered similar panic attacks. Had it been like this long ago when he'd lost boxing matches...hadn't some of his defeats felt quite humiliating? True, he'd had a similar sense of shame, but ultimately he'd been far more preoccupied by trying to chew without too much pain despite his jaw being out of joint or cooling the big fat shiners under his eyes with slices of raw potatoes. – No, what was always much worse was when, in desperation, he hit on the self-destructive notion of typing up a few of his poems or the like on a typewriter and sending them to various GDR publishers. And when he got the rejection letters—assuming he even got the honor of a reply. It would be clear between the lines that a female editor was stifling her outrage at his molestation...almost sounding as though he'd tried to violate her. She'd spit a salvo of ideological vocabulary into his face, lecturing him about taking his happiness into his own hands by getting married, starting a family, and taking the package vacations offered by the trade union society. Right away he should take advantage of all the avenues open to him, and go look for proper, meaningful work. He recalled days when letters like that had come and he'd opened all the gas taps in the kitchen…only to realize he'd forgotten to close the windows. In the evening, arriving for the night shift at his meaningful job, that mixture of shame and panic would still be raging in his body; knowing himself, he could tell it would take a good week to die down. And he had another rejection letter or two to look forward to, since for reasons of masochism he always sent out his poems to two or three places at once; the only relief was that in most cases the replies never came at all, because his work—his be-all and end-all, his only hope of survival—had landed straight in the wastebasket. In the stifling vault of his coal cellar, once he'd loaded the first fifteen or twenty hundredweights of coal onto the wagon and paused for a moment in exhaustion, his hopelessness having sapped his endurance, he'd suddenly see—sweat flowing into his eyes, his gaze blurred in the yellow-red opacity that called itself light—the editor standing by the sooty brick wall, laughing. Of course he'd never met her, she existed only in his imagination; she was—a woman in glasses, and he loved women in glasses. She was probably laughing at him, that was the only way to picture it; with a cry of rage he rammed the shiny whetted tines of the coal fork through her neck and nailed her to the brick wall. Then he bellowed for another half a minute like a wild, maniacal animal until he felt what a fool he was; of course the fork hadn't hit anyone, it was stuck in the moldering wall, oscillating with breathtaking lightness. His bellows died away unheard; the boiler house stood far afield, on a patch of ground between fallen fences in the steppe behind the town, behind the outlying villages, out where there was nothing but dead ash beneath the stars, scrapheaps, head-high steppe grass, and filth.

Or that feeling would strike him when, yet again, the Stasi slipped a summons into his mailbox…that was later, when a few small circles of people already regarded him as a writer. The Stasi would do it a certain carefully calculated period of time before the appointment, so that you'd have a week to tremble and speculate about the reason, though the interview itself might be a banal trifle of ten minutes. But for several days before that, impotence would howl in his guts, he'd see the world as though through a fog and spill cups of coffee over his belly, and barely a line of what he tried to read would make it into his head. Then, when he arrived, he'd be led through the agency's corridors by two men who'd stay half a pace behind him. If ever he tried to turn and face them, they'd say: Look straight ahead, keep walking!—And he'd stare straight ahead and keep walking, waiting for the shot in the back of the neck.

No, his dread of his mother's calls didn't compare with that. – There was something else behind that dread, its causes lay deeper, he regarded it, perhaps wrongly, as fundamentally inexplicable. There were so many different things that could trigger that feeling, a feeling of being suddenly and inescapably defenseless, strangled by a power that pounced at random. Ultimately all that helped was alcohol; it dulled the pressure, resigned him to the thought of having to live without the slightest hope for the future. In extremely bad phases he couldn't afford to give that feeling any quarter: when the effects of the alcohol wore off, the fear would instantly close in again.

Hedda, he recalled, had often exhorted him to undergo analysis. He had resisted, telling her: As long as you stay with me, I don't need a therapist!—But Hedda had always questioned the notion that his problems could be solved so easily. – But of course, she said, when I refuse to believe in such an easy solution, right away you think I don't want to stay with you. – He smiled; he knew one of those endless arguments was looming, the ones that lasted entire nights and sent him dashing into the kitchen to the fridge early on to take the first swig from the bottle. Incidentally, she wasn't entirely wrong; the thought that she might leave him was never far from his mind. – Besides, he said, analysis would take much too long, my visa would run out first. – That took them back to the main issue: that he was unable to say where he really wanted to be, in the East or in the West. And it seemed as though he genuinely didn't know. And that actually he was the one who was constantly threatening to leave.

As a matter of fact, he felt an intense antipathy toward the psychological or pseudo-psychological banalities that you stumbled over wherever you went in the West and that the magazines made the bulk of their money on. Evidently the only thing psychoanalytical ideas were still good for was to increase the sales figures of the sort of periodical that made your hair stand on end. – Once, he recalled, he'd picked up a magazine someone had left in a train compartment, one of those lurid weekend entertainment magazines with a flawless set of teeth smiling on the front and bared breasts at the seaside on the back. As soon as he opened it, a bold title, almost a headline, leaped out at him as if it were just what he'd been looking for: *Attention Men: Oedipal Complex Causes Impotence!*— Instead of laughing, he angrily hurled the magazine into the corner. A moment later he felt a hankering to pick the rag back up and read the article. Fortunately, just then some people entered the compartment, so he didn't dare touch the magazine. Trembling, he shrank back into his corner and stared out the window... There they were again, those tremors of fear below the belt!—How could a line like that, such a primitive attention-grabber, stab him in the guts that way? How come he didn't feel that caption was completely laughable? How come he knew it was laughable, but didn't feel it?

Maybe because he himself was laughable! All the cells in his body that he'd never given any love in his life had filled little by little with viscous stupidity. The stupidity in Europe that everyone was neck-deep in found its way right into empty cells. And evidently he was filled to the brim with them. The whole thing was grotesque, he had all the trappings of a freak show.

These thoughts took his mind back to a trip, his last visit to M., his birthplace south of Leipzig, before the expiry of his visa. It was in the fall, about the time of his second reading in Vienna; it was possible that right after his defection from Vienna—as he'd taken to calling that idiotic incident—with the morning stopover in Munich, he'd traveled on to the GDR; he no longer quite knew when it had been, all he knew was that he'd been tormented by awful feelings of anxiety that whole fall; his sense of orientation had practically fallen by the wayside. His relationship with Hedda was constantly teetering on the brink; though she didn't say it very often, C. knew that she was pressing for a decision. The more time progressed, the more impossible that decision became. He drank more and more and felt like a criminal; the question of where he wanted to live, and with whom, had long since become a question of whether he wanted to live at all.

He arrived in M. late in the afternoon, taking the

train from Leipzig via the district capital of A.; en route it occurred to him that his mother couldn't possibly know he was coming, and he recalled that once when he'd come unannounced like this he hadn't even found her home, and had had to spend several hours waiting for her.

He walked the rather long way from the station through town; the yellow fall sun, already somewhat bleary, lit the street from the West. It had sunk between the buildings, but as the street ran almost straight from West to East, cutting across the entire town, he had its rays coming from behind him all the way, golden, already shading into red. There was a bustle of last-minute shopping, the town was full of people, but they all seemed so preoccupied that hardly anyone recognized him and no one spoke to him. Approaching his mother's neighborhood, he suddenly saw the old woman right in front of him. She was coming out of a grocery store, laden down with two full shopping bags. He looked her straight in the face and she looked at him too, but she didn't seem to recognize him. She looked a bit disconcerted, then turned around and headed for home. He stopped in his tracks… she turned halfway around again, squinting, blinded by the sun, while he stood there in a throng of people milling around the entrance to the supermarket; no, she hadn't seen him; slowly she went on her way, hauling her shopping bags.

He set down his traveling bag and waited. What was going on? He knew that his mother's eyesight had gotten worse in recent years; she'd complained it had given her trouble when traveling to Nuremberg.

He extricated himself from the crowd and followed about twenty yards behind her. How slowly his mother walked! All at once it alarmed him how she'd aged, in such a short time; she must have practically had an aging spurt; she walked uncertainly, overcautiously, bent under the weight of her bags, her gaze fixed on the ground, probably because of the glaucoma that afflicted her eyes… he'd learned that she'd once been knocked down by passersby while shopping, had lain there on the ground until someone brought her glasses.

Now his mother ran into an acquaintance, one of her neighbors coming in the opposite direction; the two women stopped to chat; he ducked into a side street so as not to be seen. Walking down it he came to the street that paralleled the one his mother lived on; then came another cross street that led down to his mother's, twenty or thirty yards past her house.

He saw his mother coming, slowly, step-by-step, taking an eternity to walk diagonally across the roadway and shuffle toward her front door; she seemed to have difficulty crossing the street, looking in all directions several different times. He hid behind the corner of the house to avoid being seen. She opened the front door, set one foot on the front step, leaned her shoulder against the doorframe, and lowered her shopping bags onto the step without letting go of the handles; for a moment she rested. Now she picked the bags up again and stepped inside the house; the door fell shut behind her.

He walked back up the side street, headed straight to the station, and took the train back to Leipzig. – On the train he watched the people, young people mostly— how they perched on the seats or walked around, how they talked, chattering, fast, lots and loud, blasting music from their tape players, drinking beer and telling the same jokes over and over with boundless gusto. They seemed full of joie de vivre...none of them could travel to West Germany, they were all prisoners of this *really existing socialism*, and yet they were filled with joy, filled to the brim with love and radiating pride and vigor...

He thought of Martha; whenever he came to Leipzig the first thing he thought of was Martha, the wife of his friend H.; he thought perhaps he could spend the night at her place. For Martha his problems never had any moral implications; she never tried to censor him. Martha was a delicate woman, sometimes a bit helpless-seeming due to her nearsightedness, with big soft breasts whose weight she sometimes found burdensome. C. was completely besotted by her breasts, and she'd say to him: Do you have to keep fumbling with my breasts? You're constantly reminding me of them, and they get on my nerves. – H. would turn around to look at the two of them—he usually walked a few paces ahead, he always had to take the lead—and say: Let him have his way! Otherwise he'll feel like a fifth wheel, that's what a fool he is.

In Leipzig, C. resolved to take the first train that would take him back to the West: Nuremberg, Munich, Frankfurt, it made no difference. Or Berlin, where you could reach the border most quickly...

After his visa expired, the reading tours took off in earnest. He was awarded a well-known literature prize, and invitations came even more frequently after that. He took these readings much more stoically now, submitting resignedly, sometimes even managing to give a persuasive performance of his confused non-identity (or even anti-identity) to an embarrassed-looking audience. Those were the readings he felt he could put down as successes.

He knew he'd come through the worse for wear: if all went well at those events, you were accepted, sometimes you might be admired as a writer, but you got no love there…

After those readings people would generally go to a restaurant for dinner or drinks. He'd be on tenterhooks the whole time, it cost him a frightful effort to take part in the conversation unfolding at the tables; he seemed to manage it only by disavowing his self in a way that plunged him into unfathomable confusion for hours thereafter. Unless someone drove him back to his hotel, he'd spend ages blundering around a strange, increasingly chaotic-seeming city, in panicked search of the hotel that initially had been just a street or two away.

It was around that time that various hotel chains began introducing so-called pay-per-view television. These video programs, generally a selection of four different films, could be called up on the hotel TV with the remote control; it registered when you turned it on, and a surcharge of about twenty marks would be added when you paid the hotel bill. The special offer targeted the wallets of bored male hotel guests on business trips, whose employers generally covered just the price of the room; if they wished to avail themselves of the so-called extras—phone calls, the minibar, dry-cleaning, and PPV television—that was up to them. So if a male traveler was disinclined to visit a brothel, he'd still have the choice of paying twenty marks to ejaculate in the direction of the TV screen: at least two of these video programs consisted of porn movies, one in English, one in German, not that it mattered, given that practically the whole soundtrack of the movie was a mix of pitiful wailings and even more

pitiful music. Within a short period of time, a year perhaps, all scruples about the movie selection fell by the wayside: whereas initially there'd been soft porn—harmless
little movies in which the lower edge of the frame stuck
scrupulously to the upper margin of the pubic hair—very
quickly the boundaries had fallen. Soon it was all about
putting a more or less well-lit vulva in the middle of the
frame and having it penetrated with mechanical regularity by a male organ.

The most astonishing thing about these shots was the
stamina required to demonstrate that unrelieved in-and-
out for minutes at a time, and the sustained moaning and
squealing of the female character was equally astonishing, given how you could assume that the belaboring by
the sizeable prick was having no effect whatsoever on her
erotic satisfaction. All you heard besides the background
music was a barrage of sounds to which the male actor
sometimes contributed a snort and which, as the actors'
faces played no role whatsoever, didn't even need to be
dubbed. After a while it was hard to escape the suspicion that the moaning and grunting stemmed from the
almost acrobatic efforts required of the actors on account
of the fact that their conjoined genitals always had to be
captured unimpeded by the eye of the camera. Thus, for
instance, they could not be blocked by the thighs, which
were constantly in the way and had to find a stable place,
if possible outside the picture, where they could brace
themselves, buffering the rhythmic lurches to steady the
frame of the body.

A further obstacle turned out to be the actress's hair,
in the scenes in which she used her mouth in an effort to
give her partner an erection. Again and again that blonde,

permed hair would fall like a curtain to hide the focal point of the action, seemingly at the very moment when success was in the offing and the stiffening organ began to slip more vigorously in and out of her mouth. With a testy motion of her hand she'd keep flinging her magnificent curls behind her ear, evidently on the repeated orders of the cameraman, but at her very next passionate nod the luxuriant locks would whip forward again; the actress's hair, beautiful though it was, robbed everyone—including the viewer in front of his TV screen—of the ability to focus on the essentials.

The ultimate union, the naked and indispensable sex act, formed the most tedious part of the performance, especially since, as though conforming to the dogma of an educational film, it had to be executed in all possible variants. The sequence was arbitrary or was determined by the quickest and least complicated way to effect a change of position. Each version served the same ultimate aim: to insert that roving male exteriority into the inner life of the female, an outcome hereby demonstrated in a form that rendered the notion of a higher aim obsolete.

As a rule the final variant was the one in which the woman knelt in front of the man while his penis thrust *doggy-style*—the vernacular term for this constellation— into her openly proffered body; this position seemed to enable a kind of liberating finale, evidently since it was easiest to capture on camera. But even here the actor couldn't position himself comfortably between his partner's thighs, he had to do his work in an awkward squat over the woman, almost a jockey's pose, resting all his weight on his legs, which were bent at right angles and splayed out to boot; he braced his arms on the woman's hips as though on a piece of gymnastics equipment. How hard a time he was having could be seen by the tremor that spasmed now and then through his calves, though you could tell he was in excellent shape. Now the eye of the camera would have had an unobstructed view had it not been for his dangling scrotum, which—you couldn't get rid of it, it was a fiasco that resisted clearing up—bounced around without cease and with perfidious verve in front of the woman's orifice. The camera had to film from underneath the scene, to circumvent the intrusive sack-like structure; they really should have filmed from a hole in the ground. It never occurred to anyone to take a band-aid and tape down the wrinkly bag of skin on the thigh somewhere; the makers of such movies were strangers to artistic inspiration. And after a while you asked yourself whether the awful groaning and panting that accompanied everything didn't in fact come from the person operating the camera, who might have been forced into a headstand to guide the lens into the home stretch past that obstreperous scrotum which kept crossing it.

The main question that persisted through it all was, undeniably, how to bend the human body to the will of a camera. God's creation had included no allowances for the emerging media and communication society. You'd have to develop strategies for taking the human body apart and reassembling it at your discretion; there was no other way. And if you couldn't make up your mind to do that, you'd have to accept that this highly sensitive organism wasn't good for much of anything but wreaking havoc on the best-intentioned projects.

There was no use denying it—to be truthful, he had to admit to himself that in his imagination the position demonstrated last, that pornographic final position, had always excited his senses most keenly. Now, he knew that feminists—those ideological opinion leaders in West Germany who had redefined the traffic rules for dealings between men and women—held the view that said position was degrading for the woman...as they saw it, the woman was on her knees, she lay with her face on the ground, she stretched up her defenseless rear for him, the man, to do with as he pleased...but did that view actually reflect reality? In truth the woman was bowing down to no one, she was turning her back to the man; so could it be that she was bowing to nothing but freedom?

When at last—the night already half over—he forced himself to switch off the television, the bile would rise in his throat, and he'd lapse into depression. He'd go back to raiding the minibar and castigating himself. His self-accusations were ones he normally would have regarded as unfair: for all intents and purposes, he told himself, what had lured him to the West was the porn industry. At any rate it had played a major role in what certain benevolently pontificating culture writers described as C.'s *emigration*. The artistic freedom he strove for, so he told himself, actually consisted of sitting in a West German hotel room and watching pay-per-view television...

Of course, no one ever heard a word of these self-accusations. They were left behind in the hotel room, and that was where they belonged, in that boxy little cavern, so sealed off as to be nearly soundproof. It was an interior resembling that of his skull, a place in which he lingered only temporarily, behind a painstakingly locked door and drawn curtains, in dim lighting further clouded by the smoke of many cigarettes. There he sat on a chair without making a move, even trying to muffle his coughs when the smoke stung his throat. – So that was it, that was his life in West Germany; he switched on the TV during his brief sojourn in West Germany and West Berlin, and he stared at life through the window of the screen. And he turned down the sound so that the randy women's swinish squealing could barely be heard.

Not until he was sitting in the dining room, amid the cheerful noise of the hotel guests relishing in the ritual of breakfast, did it occur to him that he'd forgotten to call Hedda. He knew that she was waiting for his call, and that she was quick to worry when she hadn't heard from him for several days. – It was even worse than that—he'd forgotten her birthday! There'd been bad blood once before when he'd arranged the date of a reading so awkwardly that he hadn't been able to get to Nuremberg until the evening of her birthday. He'd assured her that he would reschedule the date, but then forgot about it until it was too late…in the end he promised to call from the hotel at midnight, the start of her birthday (and he really had meant it!); he wasn't even back at the hotel by then, and later on he'd forgotten. He cursed what was in his mind, distracting him…and often enough Hedda sensed that that curse was part and parcel of him. She'd asked him about it, she'd practically grilled him, until they got into desperate arguments, senseless power struggles about nothing. He could have admitted anything to her, any kind of meanness or betrayal, but he couldn't confess the real reasons for his forgetting…

He hadn't been able to confess them to himself…

This time he'd meant at least to call her from the

station, after getting there in a taxi. But first he'd sup-
plied himself with drinks for the long return trip, going
to three separate kiosks on the train platforms and in the
station hall; there weren't many options in Bonn's relatively small station. He couldn't bring himself to ask for
the whole amount at any one of the kiosks: three times
he bought three cans of beer and three miniature bottles
of Underberg digestive bitters. All the while he was pon-
dering the reason he'd forgotten to call… Hedda probably
wouldn't have believed him at first, gradually she'd have
grown nonplussed, then she would have teased him a little—she had a talent for teasing him without hurting him,
it actually calmed him down—before asking with a laugh:
Why didn't you say right off that you've got this catching
up you need to do?

He never did tell her, because it wasn't just the need
to catch up; it couldn't be reduced to anything that simple.
It was some unclear thing, and he kept failing whenever
he tried to express it. He would have preferred the word
desire…he was afraid that his desire might cease. When
his desire went extinct, it would be the end of something
almost identical with his life…

He thought these thoughts standing at a snack stand,
drinking a coffee and a mini-bottle of liquor…and missing
his train to Frankfurt. There was nothing for him to do but
take another stroll through Bonn…it was a nerve center of
the Western world, but the city had a modest air. Beyond
the station square the genteel old-town atmosphere set
in; he walked down narrow streets, past perfectly restored,
bourgeois buildings; looking at them, you'd never think this
country had once lain in ruins… There's not the slightest
hint of it, thought C. – Garlands of Christmas decorations

were already strung over the streets; on the left and the right there was a multitude of restaurants, all so-called gourmet restaurants, mostly empty even though it was lunchtime; through the windows you could see unoccupied tables with their white tablecloths and bored waiters in white standing at the bar. C. turned onto a narrow side street with just as many restaurants and equally elegant buildings; as soon as no one was watching, he quickly tossed back an Underberg. At once he felt a barely controllable wave of nausea; he looked around for a secluded corner where he could regurgitate the Underberg, but a suitable corner was nowhere to be found. He swallowed and swallowed until his stomach ceased its revolt and emitted a feeling of warmth, almost heat. Then he drank the second mini-bottle he had in his jacket pocket. Realizing that he was barely able to walk on the slick cobbles of the narrow lane, he turned around, crossing a square where a table outside a bookstore offered vast numbers of remaindered paperbacks for sale. He went over and bought four volumes of the anthracite-colored complete works of Walter Benjamin, hefty paperbacks published by Suhrkamp that were on sale for a ridiculously low price. The book dealer bundled up the books, crisscrossing them with rubber bands, and handed them over to C. As he paid, the young man was already busy with the next customer, but C.'s definite impression was that the bookdealer had shrunk away from him; he'd probably smelled the revolting bittersweet cloud of herbal liqueur that C. exhaled. With a sticky mouth, weak in the knees, he headed back toward the station…increasingly he sensed that he was losing his tolerance for alcohol. And yet there was that unconquerable aridity inside him, that persistent viscosity of the bodily fluids, and at the same time an unrest that washed over him at intervals, which he could fight down only by drinking more.

In front of the station his eye was caught by the trash bins mounted on the pillars that supported the projecting roof over the entrance: they were brimming with those little dark-green Underberg bottles, carefully piled to form mounds that rose above the tops of the bins, their caps painstakingly screwed back on after they'd been drained. All the trash bins nearby looked the same: train stations were where Underberg did most of its business. And around the entrance the bums loitered, staring at him expectantly as he approached the station. Two of those bottles, empty and painstakingly resealed, were still in the pocket of his jacket (and there were more in his bag in the luggage locker); he didn't dare add the empty bottles to the mounds in the trash bins, not under the bums' voracious stares; he'd have needed the steadiness required for a game of pick-up sticks, but his hands shook so hard that he'd risk toppling the pyramid before the eyes of the bums who gazed at him, motionless, crouching on the ground like dogs with gaping mouths and vibrating tongues.

Sitting on the train, he leafed through the Walter Benjamin books, unable to concentrate, unable to engage with them at all; he bundled them back together with the rubber bands and stowed them in his bag. He was constantly forgetting about the books he bought on his trips; weeks later he'd be astonished to discover them in his traveling bag.

There they were, books he'd have given his right arm for back in the East, and he never read them. There he was, coming from that communist land of books, from that GDR that never tired of bragging about its people's hunger for reading, but all he'd known there was frustration and humiliation over the books he was constantly lacking. From the very first day he'd come to the West, he'd bought books like a madman; he never could have read them all, he didn't have enough years left in his life to properly read the books he piled up; no one understood the drive, the obsessiveness with which he bought books, wheedled books from publishers, stole and procured books by any conceivable means; no one could comprehend it, though no one even knew the true magnitude of his greed, not even Hedda; even from her he concealed most of the books he hauled back…he stowed them in a luggage locker at the station and fetched them in a taxi at night after Hedda had gone to sleep.

And then he'd realized that books had no more value here in the West. It took quite a while for that thought to gain a foothold in his mind; the shock it triggered was all the more enduring. Books were slipping away from his grasp…yet he was a writer himself, or at least he fancied he was! He'd always wanted to be a writer, his whole life long…a producer for the remainder bin! Twice a year, with a whole rigamarole of blaring advertisements, a huge quantity of new books was dumped out onto the oversaturated market; in next to no time they were turning yellow and moldy in the remainder bins outside deserted bookstores. And the so-called New Media opened their jaws for the audience; a vast flood of gaudy, twitchy images drowned people's wits, imitations of music blasted their ear canals, their brain cells, their neurons to the point of overload. People swallowed every digital daub, every tin-can installation, every rudimentary bit of background noise as the last word in culture, twitching along unresistingly. – Yes, he'd always wanted to be a writer, his whole life long, and if the profession hadn't existed, he would have had to invent it. Even as a child he'd had that fixed notion, later a crackpot notion, and it had scuttled and snuffed out his life. He'd screwed up his school years from the very start, he'd learned trades and chucked them, he'd hunkered in a noxious small-town serpents' nest until he was practically forty, in the corner of his mother's kitchen, constantly waiting for the moment when he could finally claim to be a writer; that moment had never come. He'd picked a quarrel with that cancer of a state over there, he'd risked jail and correctional labor, he'd gone around insulting people, thrown all his friends and acquaintances to the winds. No lie had been too dirty for him when it came to carving out time for his writing attempts. He'd hypnotized his prick or beaten it with kitchen spoons to make it collapse again, to keep his erections from getting in the way when he was sitting at his desk. He'd ditched all his love affairs—however paltry their number, however halfhearted they'd been—he'd left all his lovers in the lurch. So far he'd made two women desperately unhappy (at least for a while), abandoning them for fear of having to sacrifice his writing time for them; and he'd left his daughter in the lurch when she was still a small child, though he loved her dearly; now he barely knew her anymore. He'd left his whole life in the lurch and spurned his own happiness...

And now that he'd come over to the West, he listened incredulously to the claptrap about the "value" that was still placed on literature. That value was hardly worth mentioning. The word struck him as completely out of place. And yet they'd thought of everything in this country: you could buy plastic mock-ups to install decoratively in shelf systems, their visible side molded into the shape of book spines bearing the golden letters: "Goethe's Complete Works" or "Schiller's Complete Works."

He sat there on his train, racing through the dim washed-out December afternoon, filled with a mixture of dull fury and horror that threatened any moment to turn into hysterical sobs. But he hadn't cried in twenty or thirty years, there was no use in starting now. Hardly in control of his jittery movements, he emptied the bottles of Underberg down his gullet, then moved on to the cans of beer. Feeling that he was starting to smell, he hurried to the toilet and tried to vomit again, but once again he couldn't. He rammed his erect middle finger down his throat and retched until he started to black out; his stomach yielded nothing but a minimal amount of brown mucus that looked like putrid blood. He staggered back to his seat thinking that some imponderable perfidious death wish must have moved him to go West. Some beast in his soul that not even Freud could truly have explained. Some infallible killer instinct aimed against himself…

There was yet another train of thought that generally followed straight on the heels of the one he'd just had; if he was drunk enough it attacked him just as fiercely and was capable of finishing him off. Over there, in the so-called GDR, he could at least have ditched the whole writing gig, very belatedly but not definitely too late, and looked for a job again. There was no question that he would have been hired back; he hadn't been a bad stoker after all, though he'd hated the boiler houses like the plague. The West, that was a goal for his *Volk* back East, for that herd of imbeciles with their brutish appetite for

Dannon yogurt and banana-flavored condoms; it was not for him. But now he himself was here in the West, staring goggle-eyed, pupils swimming in alcohol, at the future of the proletariat. The future of the proletariat was the unemployment figures, however shamelessly they were faked. Here in the West he could gaze at the rectangle of a TV screen produced by robots and see the automobile industry's enormous, clinically clean manufacturing facilities. In the factory hall, discreetly humming and glittering with chrome, there was just one solitary guy to be seen, wearing a white smock, a tie and sunglasses, weaving his way between the switchboards and robots, pressing little buttons, checking the regularity of the energy supply, perhaps having to change a chip once a year, and that man was nervous, because his days were numbered too. Meanwhile, at the terminus of the production process the brand-new convertibles bounced off the assembly line like tennis balls. And all that was going on somewhere in the Malay Archipelago.

Workers, just like writers, were obsolete economic models; at least they had that in common. For ages he'd bemoaned the fact that he was forced to live two different modes of life—that of a worker and that of a writer—and neither of them properly...now both were shot to hell. Neither way of life had any future left, he'd been barking up the wrong tree entirely...so how many years did he have left till retirement?

He couldn't figure it out right now, he didn't even know his age anymore. But evidently he had quite some time left before he could retire; how was he supposed to get through that time? And was he even entitled to a pension here in West Germany? He really needed to get a hold of some defector from the GDR who could give him an answer to that question. And how would he ever manage to get together all the employment records he needed to apply for a pension, fragmentary and filled with gaps as they were? He could count on Hedda's help, but she wasn't exactly thrilled by that sort of thing. He probably couldn't manage it on his own, he'd need years of psychotherapy to be up to filling out a West German tax return, much less straightening out his employment records, some of which had been fraudulently obtained…

Anyway, if he went on living and acting the way he'd been doing, pretty soon Hedda wouldn't lift a finger to help him.

He'd have to try to sober up a bit so he could call her from Frankfurt, where he had to change for the train to Nuremberg. Because naturally he'd forgotten to make the call in Bonn. To get a bit of clarity in his skull, first he needed to stop complaining…or rather, stop bemoaning his fate, wallowing in his self-pity. Maybe I don't actually love Hedda, since I keep forgetting to call her, practically forgetting on principle, he thought. But I keep insisting to her that I do love her…I believe I don't even know how it's done, how to love someone. – Who does know, anyway?… The question showed clear as day that in this regard he was just a theoretician.

Every time he calmed down again, his complaints embarrassed him; he was glad that he kept them hidden, that he didn't share them with anyone, not even his girlfriend Hedda. But of course that had certain consequences: As a rule, or so it seemed to him, he was regarded as an insensitive, even unfeeling person, a hulk, a kind of victor against the odds who'd managed to dodge all sorts of problems and fight his way up from being an "ordinary worker" to become a writer—he was mistaken for a broad-shouldered tank whose steely brow concealed nothing but crudeness and self-confidence. For him, to be looked at this way was an insult beyond redress. But then he never protested, so it was his own fault...only when he was alone, all by himself (and lately he was alone with himself more and more often), would it suddenly overwhelm him, he'd sit on his chair without a sound, and there would no longer be a reality surrounding him; he'd await the inevitable onset of trembling that for a long time would be impossible to tame, a pain he couldn't articulate would ring inside him like exquisitely thin but unbreakable glass. And he'd feel the desire to break apart, but he never did break...

Lately he'd had to take care not to be caught in one of these spells. They had started to plague him even on the road, they'd ambush him on the train, in the station, in the middle of a city, or sitting before an audience trying to read from his work; he'd suddenly sense something coming at him from the text, sometimes just from a trivial phrase; a retching feeling would rise in his gullet, he'd feel incapable of saying the word *love* in public, and lightning-quick, in the middle of the reading, he'd change it to *relationship* or *acceptance*...

Of course, no matter what problem you were carrying around with you, this society had an institution whose particular purview that problem was, just waiting for you to commit yourself to its care. For example, there was the welfare office, Alcoholics Anonymous, and tax advisors; there was the church, there were brothels and every conceivable branch and side-branch of psychotherapy, and for real problems there was the automobile association. All of them were happy for you to come or call, and all of them, after a preliminary chat to clarify things, would be grateful to take you in. But who, one wondered, were these institutions actually for? If you felt no desire to go to the brothel, so what, another person would get jerked off there. If you couldn't go to analysis, another person would lie down on that couch. If you didn't feel up to going to confession, absolution would be granted to another.

Under these circumstances it was disloyal—neither proper nor compliant—to give free rein to your grievances. Well, there you go, you shouldn't have missed your appointment at the brothel or the analyst's, or the service on Sunday…

For all that, there was a far more serious thing forbidding him to speak, forcing his complaints back down his throat, or at least making him accuse himself of whining and self-pity. And he suspected that the "anti-Fascist" state he'd grown up in had had a great deal to do with that. – In the twentieth century, you could only complain if you'd gone through Auschwitz…

That last thought was one he'd probably arrived at only upon returning to his apartment in Nuremberg. Hastily he paced the rooms, back and forth, through doors that stood ajar and sometimes closed by themselves, so that he'd have to shove them back open with his shoulder. He tried to fight down his perturbation, but he knew that only alcohol could do that for him now. Now and then he stopped in front of the boxes of books he'd never unpacked, staring at them and trying not to think of Hedda…

Shouldn't he just leave the damn books—altogether he'd spent a horrendous sum of money on them—where they were and go away? After all, he didn't even know an easy way to ship them back East; that was guaranteed to require elaborate organization. Should he abandon them, then, should he just leave the books here and forget about them? Lately he'd been developing an aversion to excessive numbers of books; sometimes he even felt a sort of loathing for them. Once he'd wistfully dreamed of living in a world where every book would be at his disposal…he seemed to have freed himself from that dream.

These thoughts clearly dated back to an earlier time… shortly before the visa had run out, with just a few weeks left, he'd often had the idea to simply head back East. – End this limbo before the deadline, he thought. Pack a bag or two with the things he definitely wanted to take— the so-called manuscripts, for instance, a whole slag heap of bits of paper and notebooks he'd started, which by themselves would nearly fill a bag—and then vanish without a parting word, without a whimper, as the saying went. Then he would have been out of there; probably no one would actually realize he was gone until after the holidays, or the start of the new year. As for clearing out his apartment—which he felt incapable of doing—surely his landlady, who lived in the building, would take care of it. Or it would be taken care of by the trash collectors. He'd cover the costs by way of his publisher. He'd vanish as suddenly as he'd come; the intervening year—his year in West Germany—would gradually become just another of the many half-baked memories he carried around: out-of-focus, dimly lit memories, containing just a few lurid, disjointed scenes that he regarded as what truly belonged to him. Those scenes often concerned what he called his desires. Maybe the whole year in West Germany would appear to him later as one single flareup of desire, one single precipitous scene of desire, stylized and overblown, without beginning or end. And as a time that had threatened to annihilate his desire...at this point he cut his thoughts short.

He could simply leave his key in the apartment; Hedda had the spare key, and his landlady had kept one as well. He'd put a letter on the table to terminate the lease; then he could head out. While the morning was still dark...and a kind of ghost of him would remain. Yes indeed, an inscrutable ghost, rattling his chains, leaving no trace in Hedda's life but devastation. But maybe all those things could be put back in order...as far as he knew, Gerhard had said he'd wait for Hedda. He'd wait for this damn year to end, that was how he'd put it, and then he and she would have another heart-to-heart.

At the station in Frankfurt he'd bought Hedda a bottle of sparkling wine (now standing on top of the fridge in his kitchen); then he'd tried calling to wish her a happy birthday. For half an hour there was a busy signal; then he gave up and ran to catch the train to Nuremberg, which he couldn't miss, since it was the last one that left from Frankfurt. He reached Nuremberg shortly before one, dashed to the nearest public telephone and finally got Hedda on the line. – I wanted to wish you a happy birthday, he gasped breathlessly. I apologize, please, forgive me... – She cut him off: My birthday was over forty minutes ago! – I know, I'm apologizing. I tried to call from Frankfurt, but the line was busy... – Yes, I was talking to Gerhard for quite a while. – C. wondered if he dared ask the reason for her conversation with Gerhard. He bit back the question; the reason for the phone call was obvious:

Gerhard had never once forgotten Hedda's birthday. C. said he'd take a taxi and drop by. He had to talk to her, he was feeling guilty. – Can't you put it off until tomorrow? asked Hedda. Or rather, until this evening? I'm already in bed.

Despite the rebuff he took a taxi to Schillerplatz. The two windows on the second floor were dark. But he knew she might be in the second, smaller room, her bedroom, whose windows looked to the back, onto the sprawling complex of the Tucher brewery that stretched along the back of the row of apartment buildings. He actually thought he saw a faint streak of light on Hedda's ceiling that had to be coming from the crack of the door to that back room. He pressed the buzzer by the front door and held his ear up to the intercom…he buzzed again, getting no reply. Stepping back onto the street, he saw that the glimmer of light on the ceiling had vanished. But he went on ringing the buzzer for nearly a quarter of an hour, increasingly desperate, even though he knew it was pointless…

Whenever a low-pressure system moved in, the entire area from Schillerplatz to Kobergerplatz was blanketed by the pungent smell of malt that rose from the Tucher brewery. It seemed to fill the streets, rising up past head height like a heavier kind of air soaked with the beer's bittersweet ingredients; some days Hedda complained and said she was going to move out. December was mild and rainy in Nuremberg, and it was those nights especially that the smell of malt would absorb all other smells. On the twenty-minute walk to his apartment C. grew soggy and sober; the rain coming from the invisible sky was more like a dissipating smoke; the benumbing brewery vapors seemed to rise even from the dead grasses of the roundabout at Kobergerplatz, and dripped in fluid threads from the bare trees around the square; even the light of the spherical lamps seemed to be stained yellow-brown as they shed endless foamy strings of beads resembling bubbles of spit.

From Kobergerplatz, where Kobergerstrasse began, it was just five minutes to his building. Often, walking past the ten buildings before his, he'd see a certain lighted window in one of them. It was on the third floor in a kind of bay, and the light often burned till morning; sometimes he'd stop to stare up. The woman who lived there, about the same age as he and Hedda, had invited him to visit several times. She came to all his local readings—sometimes with Hedda, though he had no idea what to make of their relationship and never asked Hedda about it—the first time being about five years ago, when he'd met her at an event in Regensburg on one of those short reading trips in the period before his visa. And then that woman—what a strange idea—had sent a yellow leather jacket to him in Leipzig, triggering an argument with Mona, his girlfriend in Leipzig.

He entered his apartment and stepped right onto the telephone, which was sitting on the floor of the dark corridor; there was a splintering noise, he'd crushed the keypad into the plastic housing. Cursing, he set the phone on the kitchen table; fortunately it still worked if he punched the numbers in carefully. He looked around for signs that she'd been in his apartment…then he sat down at the table and started calling her. After he'd pressed redial and waited for the tenth time, Hedda suddenly picked up. Before he could get out a word, she said sharply that he should leave her alone. – Please…he blurted, I just wanted to know when I should come and see you tomorrow. – She said she didn't know if she wanted to see him at all, and hung up.

A wave of panic shot up inside him…however familiar the feeling was—and however unjustified by Hedda's relatively benign dismissal—its onslaught was always unexpected, and he was defenseless against it. It was an indefinable clot of fear that he felt in his body, while his brain seemed to float above him in a void, no longer bearing any relation to him…all that helped was liquor. He took a bottle of vodka from the fridge, filled a water glass more than half full, and drank in quick little swigs.

He knew that the root of this panic lay further back and that it responded to indiscriminate triggers; he couldn't find any pattern in them. Hedda had similar feelings, but she had faced up to them; she was able to protect herself much better than he, and in her case the causes seemed easier to identify. She'd had some experience with psychoanalysis and advised him to try it out too. He'd always resisted the idea; he felt he could get a grip on his own… I am who I am, he said, what is there to improve about me? – How you deal with your fear, she replied.

Was what he'd said really true, was he really who he thought he was? Now that Hedda was trying to talk to him about his fears—almost always in vain—he felt that it only set them in motion…and sometimes he blamed his panic on Hedda…

By the time those thoughts were going through his head, he was on his second or third glass of vodka…once the panic had passed, all that was left was rage and despair. He made coffee, and while it was collecting with a faint plink in the machine's glass pot, he was already pouring his next vodka, and another one right after that…

His bag was still packed! It was out in the hall; all he had to do was pick it up and head back out! Why wait out the three weeks he had left here?

Around six or seven there was a train from Nuremberg to Leipzig he could easily make.

Holding the vodka glass he roamed through his rooms; whenever he turned on the light, light-gray swaths of dust appeared, covering everything, the floor, the shelves, the tabletops, the windowsills. It looked as though no one had visited the apartment for years…which meant that he was visiting it only as a ghost…

Sitting on one of the two boxes stuffed with books and labeled *Holocaust & Gulag*, he took hasty swigs from his glass. As he did, he saw an open notebook lying on his desk; he went over, switched on the desk lamp, put on the reading glasses lying nearby—which only had one arm left—and read the fragment of writing that covered the first page. Evidently it had been meant as a kind of diary—he'd started keeping a diary several times, but quickly dropped it again, or simply forgot about it—or it could be the start of a fictitious diary, something he'd often thought of doing; at the top there was a date from at least five years ago (a time when he was still in the GDR); what had he meant by that fictitious date? The lines were in barely legible, fugitive writing; exactly, writing that was on the run; he seemed to see that he'd jotted it down while drunk.

He read: "I suffered from the sense of having no real place to write. The writer no longer has any refuge in Europe. But that suffering is probably just a cover-up: he's just fleeing from the thought of having lost his gravitas. Lost significance and resonance…

The first two words were crossed out…they must have annoyed him the moment he wrote them down. Now these lines filled him with such abhorrence that he grabbed his bag and fled the apartment.

He came from a world and a time in which women were the suffering sector of humanity, while men lacked that prerogative…men had to be victorious for their Führers or their General Secretaries. And it was similar with desire, women were also the desiring part of humanity…not for nothing was the troubadour Walther von der Vogelweide wearing a skirt as he sat crying on his rock. – Those admonitions were buried deep inside him, tattooed into his soul, and his soul was filled with shame and scorn when facing suffering that pertained to him… Hedda had been indignant at these primitive schemata. She told him: You'd rather stick to your panic attacks, because you don't have to think about them—and you can't. You don't take your real feelings seriously, because you think you ought to be ashamed of them…

He climbed back up the stairs to his apartment…he'd forgotten to turn out the light. With a strange sense of parting (which didn't convince even him) he made one more circuit through the rooms, then sat down on the packing cases and pondered what to do. The catastrophe under the seat of his pants seemed to give him a kind of security. He drank another vodka and called Hedda for the last time. No one picked up the phone…he shouldered his bag and headed to Friedrich-Ebert-Platz, where there were taxis at all hours. He rode to the station and bought a ticket for Leipzig.

He fell asleep on the train even before it pulled out of the station, and didn't come to for hours. Clearly the train was approaching the border, there would be no way to get off now. The line of cars trundled haltingly uphill, through the Franconian Forest or the Fichtel Mountains; left and right of the tracks lay a nocturnal blue-black snowscape, a dense growth of conifers dropped heavy loads of snow from their branches as the train passed. Now and then the locomotive uttered wailing siren sounds as though to warn someone, some watchman up ahead in the darkness. After one of those wails C. came wide awake… suddenly sober and gripped by icy cold; a draft swept through the cars, all empty as though everyone had fled. In all the compartments the windows were open, grimy brown curtains fluttering like Siberian flags; C. went through the car slamming windows and doors shut, but it didn't get any warmer. Suddenly he felt that familiar nameless yearning for Hedda… Why hadn't he stayed in Nuremberg? What was the alcohol doing to him? Had he lost his mind, not staying in Nuremberg with Hedda?… he wondered if these words echoed what Mona had said before his departure from Leipzig. – The border station was Probstzella or Gutenfürst, he could never remember which. It wasn't much farther, and then the cart with beer and liquor would be trundled through the train…

At the border he sat wide awake and distraught in his compartment, the sun already rising; the country outside was turning flat and bare. – It's not for me the sun's shining, he thought, that's all perfectly clear, clear as mud…

He remembered the first time he'd met up with Hedda, in late November 1985, when he'd been in the West for barely three weeks. He was coming from a reading in Bayreuth, and they'd agreed to meet at the station in Nuremberg, where he was stopping over on his way back to Hanau. First they'd gone to a pub, then to Hedda's apartment. And on that first evening he'd met Hedda's boyfriend too. Gerhard, lounging on a sofa in the living room, gave C. his hand from a recumbent position. Next to the sofa stood a bottle of wine that was already one third empty... He's drinking because I went to meet you! Hedda whispered at some point, using the formal you. Gerhard was uncommunicative, regularly taking a swig of wine, raising the neck of the bottle to his lips without sitting up or bothering with a glass. He asked C. if he'd like some wine too. He'd been listening to music, the dramatic strains of Gustav Mahler's Second Symphony; when C. came in, he turned off the stereo. Hedda moved back and forth between the two silent men, amiable, a bit amused, happy even, C. thought; she stroked Gerhard's shoulder when she passed him, and when she set down a glass of wine in front of C. she gave his arm a fleeting, apparently unthinking touch. She said that unfortunately there wasn't anything special to eat, only pickled herring, stupidly enough. Should she whip up a salad with that? – Oh yes, said Gerhard from his prostrate position, herring salad, that wouldn't be half bad!—You'll have lots of chances to taste how good her herring salad is, said Gerhard, switching seamlessly to the informal you.

C. felt uncomfortable left alone in the living room with Gerhard, who also had trouble maintaining his taciturn aplomb, drinking from his bottle in shorter intervals; when he got up to go to the bathroom C. saw that he was a tall man, younger, wearing jeans and white wool socks, no slippers. He had a beard, and behind round spectacles his eyes, alert but sad, seemed to gaze past C. with a touch of hauteur. Left alone for a moment, C. drained his glass in one swallow and poured himself another one, which he also drank at once, leaving just the dregs. By the time the herring salad was on the table, he was already on his fourth glass; he'd missed his train, and the departure time of the next, the last one to Frankfurt, was drawing ominously near. It occurred to him simply to forget about the train; as Hedda talked about literature—her affinity for Peter Weiss, whom she'd met one time just before he died—very different thoughts were passing through C.'s mind. Perhaps owing to the wine he felt rebellion rise within him, a protest against the train that was waiting for him at the station, and simultaneously against the obligation to leave this apartment, where he felt so much cozier than in his makeshift, untidy, filthy, unheated place in Hanau, where he'd trip over empty bottles and toppled stacks of newspapers just inside the front door, where he'd have to clear books and unwashed plates from the chairs to find a place to sit, where his bed was an unruly snarl of blankets and sheets, inextricably knotted and twisted, and so infested with spots of red wine and indefinable other things that they chafed his skin…and he kept thinking: Here they've got everything, and I've got nothing…it seems to me the situation should be reversed.

After a while, chewing herring salad on his sofa, Gerhard said: Why does he have to go back to stupid old Hanau, anyway? Either he sleeps here or book him a hotel room. – Hedda took out the phone book, called a hotel, and reserved a room for one night; it worked out right away, and C. was amazed how simple things were here in the West; again he thought: Here they've got everything, and I've got nothing! – Hedda was talking about the four-volume edition of Peter Weiss's notebooks, and in search of a quote she went into her little study to get the books from the shelf: C. followed to help her look. Hedda stood in front of the tall bookshelves, vainly scanning the dense rows of spines; C. was standing beside her, and she turned toward him and gave him a helpless look… I can't find them, she said. – Never mind, said C., his voice hollow and indistinct, little more than a noise he pressed out through clenched teeth. Everything went black for a moment, then he pulled her over, a bit too forcefully, flung his arms around her, and kissed her on the mouth, holding the back of her head with his right hand to keep her from ducking away. He let go of her, she stared at him; he couldn't tell whether she was surprised, her mouth, slightly open, wasn't smiling, but it looked as though there was laughter in her eyes. He pulled her over a second time, a bit less roughly, and kissed her again, his hands darting over her body almost of their own accord, racing as though he had just fractions of a second to give every part of her body, even the hidden-most, a single fleeting touch. He saw her close her eyes and felt her return his kiss, and an almost mad sense of happiness erupted in his body, instantly flooding him to the tiniest fiber of his being. He knew this moment was unique, unrepeatable, the high point of his life. He held Hedda tight and tried to tug off her clothes, impeded by his own embrace, which he could not relinquish. Hedda helped him; he couldn't tell if she was removing her clothes or his; once she was naked, he sloughed off the rest of his things, roughly and hastily—like peeling off the skin of a boiled potato—and pushed her onto a couch, or was it her bed, which stood against the wall…

He moved over her body and felt he was transforming into a mythical monster or some antediluvian lizard, made of a substance with a strangely soft, almost liquid or even immaterial consistency, yet gifted with a measureless network of nerves whose sole fleeting purpose was surrender, and this substance was instantly fused, as though by a heat storm, with every inch of Hedda's skin. Hedda let out a soft cry, as though fearing he might momentarily incandesce… You'll have a baby, he mumbled, as sunspots burst and burned on his retina. – Hedda opened her eyes, she was smiling, tears clung to her lashes… What did you say? she asked absently.

From the corner of his eye, C. saw Gerhard standing in the open door, evidently about to speak; possibly Hedda's question had been meant for him. Gerhard closed his mouth and retreated, closing the door with silent care behind him.

When they came back into the living room, holding hands and feeling apprehensive, Gerhard had vanished. – He probably went to the hotel, said Hedda. See, he took the piece of paper where I wrote down the address for you. – Hedda called the hotel, and when the front desk answered, she asked to speak to a Herr Rast… Rast, that was Gerhard's last name. – There was no Herr Rast registered, she was told. – Oh, then she'd like to speak to a Herr C., he had to have arrived. – That's correct, said the lady at the front desk. – She said there was a Herr C. registered, and he'd arrived. Only he couldn't be reached right now; he'd gone out.

The next morning Gerhard called and asked how much longer he'd have to stay at the hotel. – C., busy kissing Hedda's neck, could hear his rather indignant voice emerging from the telephone. – Three days…a week, Hedda replied. – Then he'd look for another hotel, this one was a miserable dump… Besides, he said, remember it'll be your birthday soon, December 8. I want to be home with you for that…

Hedda's birthdays seemed to have been the only happy days of her childhood, and they had to be remembered. Or rather, for the first years of her life it had been the so-called name days celebrated in the Russian tradition—the day on which she'd been baptized with her real name—and later they'd switched to the German custom.

Hedda was born in '45 in a camp near Nuremberg, amid a motley mass of Eastern Europeans, all swept along by the wave of the German retreat and temporarily stranded in the outlying areas between Fürth and Nuremberg. They came from all the countries the Germans had overrun, Yugoslavians, Rumanians, Hungarians, and especially Russians and Ukrainians. They all had something to hide, some major theft or minor murder, some betrayal, a wife and child they'd left behind and were trying to forget; in some cases, apparently, it was collaboration with the Nazis. And now they were all stray dogs in the American occupation zone, hoping to make the leap across the big pond to the West.

Hedda had told quite a few stories about her years in that camp; formerly a training camp for elite SS units from the Nuremberg area, it was still fenced in and guarded in the first years after the war. When C., now a sharer in her knowledge, was questioned about it, the first thing people usually asked was: So those were all collaborators, right? The question made C. furious: the West Germans, ruthlessly obsessed with pigeonholing people, simply couldn't picture the scenes that had unfolded on the Russian steppes in winter 1944, amid howling Katyushas whose projectiles made no allowances for a few stray Ukrainians who might be torn to shreds along with the fleeing Germans. In their pathological lack of imagination, the West Germans couldn't conceive that it was utterly irrelevant what group you joined after weeks of blundering through minus-30-degree nights, no roof over your head and shapes lurking behind every bush, ready to butcher someone for a jacket or a pair of shoes. It was irrelevant whom you went along with, Germans or Russians or partisans, for the sheer prospect of a piece of bread when you hadn't seen one in weeks. The Germans thought that by ascertaining the allegiances of the human refuse they'd hounded and flogged all the way across Europe they could rectify the history they'd put out of joint. The master race of Germany's economic miracle couldn't do without its racial inferiors.

Hedda had once told C. that she'd probably been conceived right in his neck of the woods, in Leipzig. Much later, in the early '80s, when her first book appeared, the publisher advised her to take a pseudonym, her Russian name being practically unpronounceable for German readers. She chose a name that sounded as Germanic as possible: Hedda Rast. She took her boyfriend Gerhard's last name, even though they weren't married. And her first name harked back to childhood difficulties with the aspirated German "H." In the first years of her life she'd spoken nothing but Russian, not becoming fluent in German until she went to school; it was hard for her to avoid the guttural Russian "kh," or turning the "H" into a "G," and for that she'd been rebuked and mocked. C. was irritated by the pseudonym at first, telling her she'd given up her identity. – If you mean my Russian identity, Hedda responded, we always had to keep it hidden, ever since our time in the camp.

In those camps, the great rumor was *America*. Everyone wanted to go there, and perhaps a few actually made it. An American visa, that was the dream everyone dreamed. A steamer ticket, an entry visa, a residency permit! Anyone who'd landed in the camp was prepared to do literally anything for a visa, prepared to sell everything: convictions, faith and honor, wife and child. If their underage daughter was consorting with the GIs outside the camp gates, all the better.

The American authorities—if you even got an interview—scrutinized each word like a counterfeit coin, or, still more often, covered their ears to keep out the imploring effusions in Russian or Albanian. – At first they asked: Are you a Nazi? – Later they asked: Are you a Communist? – Who knew what those American majors wanted you to be? – Or they'd ask: What do you know about the Russian atom bomb? Nix? No? – They'd wave you away: Go back! Go down! Back to the camp…

Back in the camp, they'd lapse back into their half-sleep, their lethargy. It was typical of people with no visa: by day and by night, even while awake, they were always sleeping and dreaming without noticing it. At night they lay awake, dreaming of a ship that would take them away, by day they slept, and the ship drifted through their dreams, the long-drawn wails of its horn filled their ears, and the Statue of Liberty loomed colossal, reaching up its torch. They were always at the point of waking up, but they didn't, they couldn't wake from their half-sleep, they never wished to wake from their deep sleep, they couldn't wake up, or they would have had to realize that the ship did not exist. And so they remained stranded in their interim state, sitting asleep outside their houses or barracks in camp; on the tables whose legs dug into the sand stood the vodka bottles they clung to, and they swayed in their sleep on their chairs as though on a rocking ship. In limbo they drifted off to the next limbo, an orphanage somewhere, an old age home, or the graveyard…

Their daughters meanwhile forgot how to speak Russian by the time they were thirteen or fourteen. They picked up a hodgepodge of American expressions and stuffed chewing gum into their mouths because it seemed to enhance the timbre of that universal language. They slathered lipstick on their lips, tucked tiny purses under their arms, and wobbled on high heels, chewing, smoking cigarettes, through the alleys where the American soldiers hung out. They didn't speak Russian or Serbian now; with artificially husky voices they spat out English sounds, Tennessee slang as broad as mashed chewing gum, or certain words from Harlem so wicked they would have blushed if they'd known what they meant. They all wanted to marry a nice American boy, but here they also lagged hopelessly behind the German fräuleins, whose skirts were tight too, but not unequivocally too small for them, not cobbled together so shabbily and ineptly that the seams threatened to split with every movement. Their Slavic farmgirls' feet barely even fit in the pumps, so they stalked across the cobblestones with swollen blue ankles constantly twisting; it was a kind of botched processional dance that provoked laughter when immersed in the mellowing shadows in the evening, when the heat turned blue over the rubble heaps that were gradually yielding to new houses. They had no ground beneath their feet... and when they returned to camp at night, they caught the eye of the men who sat outside drinking, unable to stand the stench in the barracks. When the tired girls staggered past, the men cursed them as whores. And now that they were known as whores, it seemed natural that the men should reach out their hands for them. And so they were constantly fleeing from their fathers, brothers, uncles, and the friends of the family, whom one thing only could wrest from their sleepy stupor: the craving to clutch at their daughters, the whores. – In the towns the camps got a bad name: they confirmed the notion that the people from the east were inferior, and had won the war due solely to their overwhelming numbers.

Perhaps the only good day of the year, for the girl who would later call herself Hedda, was her birthday. – On that day I really was the princess, she'd told C. one time. There were scant resources to brighten the day for her, but all those resources were deployed, with a traditional Russian disregard of whether there'd be anything left to eat the next day. The inhabitants of the barracks came together, and the girl was the center of attention. Everyone brought her a little offering, and there was singing, full of fervor, and in those songs that Russian pride erupted once more; lost people reclaimed their territory, and their territory was in the songs that ascended to the skies, telling of the infinite steppes through which the Volga carved endless gleaming curves; they had never owned any territory but the infinite one of their songs. Lo and behold, they had all come to celebrate the day of her birth, that particular day on which the little girl had appeared on earth was a special reason for all to rejoice, and to drink for once not from bitterness, but for joy. And they would sing and drink on into the night, when the child was already in bed, feeling a sense of happiness and belonging that she never knew otherwise.

Forgettable German birthday celebrations were no equivalent; they served rather to train children as dutiful consumers. C. was in the habit of observing birthdays quite casually or even negligently, regularly forgetting even his mother's and his daughter's. He sensed that this was hard on Hedda and that she was trying in vain to hide it. The year before, when he'd known Hedda for just a few weeks, he'd failed to turn down a reading on her birthday even though she'd invited him to Nuremberg. And then he'd actually forgotten to call her that day. Later he claimed he'd felt awkward about celebrating her birthday with her boyfriend Gerhard there. Hedda replied that Gerhard had actually been disappointed when he hadn't come; he'd been looking forward to seeing C., because he'd started to take an interest in him as a writer. C. realized that he had a deep-seated problem precisely with that sort of nonchalant attitude, which he regarded as a Western phenomenon. He regarded that behavior as the freedom of happy, competent people with an insouciant and prodigal command of all the things for which he harbored a smoldering crater of greed...with ease they commanded love, physical closeness, sexual desire, so he believed; they took those needs as something matter-of-fact, and insisted upon their fulfillment as though that were a perfectly normal right. For them it hardly differed from the desire for a cold soda on a hot summer evening, C. believed. – When he encountered anything resembling that matter-of-fact attitude, envy surged and choked him, resentment and rancor filled his gorge; he'd never have thought himself capable of such low-down emotions. Later the feeling verged on madness, he could literally call it up inside him with the simplest combination of thoughts, soon with practically all the thoughts that plagued him in his paralysis...there were times when he was afraid to think of Hedda at all. He crawled back into his shell and thought he was the ugliest creature in the world...he sensed his self-hatred was liable to kill him if he didn't focus completely on self-preservation.

Over the course of the past year Hedda had ended up leaving her boyfriend Gerhard. Early in the year Gerhard had gone to Papua New Guinea for two months; he was an ethnologist or anthropologist (C. wasn't quite sure which) out there in the tropics on an assignment from UNESCO. C. stayed at Hedda's place in Nuremberg the whole time; he'd moved in right away, just two or three days after Gerhard's departure, prompted by no more than a tentative remark from Hedda: She was by herself now; he could go ahead and visit more often. – He'd taken the very next train and hadn't budged until the two months was up. C. always sensed that Gerhard knew everything, that it was clear to him what went on in his absence at the Nuremberg apartment, which was actually his. As time passed he called less and less often, and when C. sat nearby eavesdropping, he sensed that the conversations were getting shorter and more monosyllabic. When C. returned to Hanau two months later, it seemed to him he'd suffered from an almost perpetual guilty conscience in Nuremberg; he'd felt like a wrecker, even a murderer, he'd suddenly feared for Gerhard's life. And on top of that he felt like a parasite who'd nested in someone else's dearly bought, hard-earned life and was shamelessly using that person's property. And all that thanks only to an unearned privilege, a completely questionable "talent" that people insisted on seeing in him, but that bore a strong resemblance to a hubristic false front behind which he found fewer ways to prove the truth of what he pretended to be. Less and less was he able to be the character he played in the literature business…or maybe he wasn't playing himself up, maybe the literature business was playing itself up using him as a character? The difference, for him, was merely one of degree, of abstract nuance. At night he sat in Hedda's kitchen, loathing himself. He didn't dare go over and get into Hedda's bed, though he knew she couldn't sleep either: she was troubled and tormented by the impenetrable, inexplicable darkness that persisted over there in the kitchen despite the fact that he'd lit all the lights. He felt more repulsive than his worst lies and betrayals had ever made him feel; all he wanted was to sit still and wait until he dropped dead. It would be a death that suited his cowardice: simply wait until his breath ceased and his thoughts crashed; simply call a halt to his heart. It was a suicide befitting a charlatan like him: waiting for death to take its place inside him and reveal itself as his true *I*…

By day he made love to Hedda, almost without respite, to the point of extinguishment, to keep his true feelings from finding any room inside him. In the first few weeks he advanced on her with a desire and abandon that alarmed her; within a very short time he lost several pounds, and the constant couplings began to cause him physical pain, he felt shattered and drained,

nearly every inch of his skin was chafed and hypersen-
sitive; reality upended in his head, and he found himself
perceiving things from an elevated plane where everything was skewed and shifted, diaphanous and unstable,
where things connected in implausible ways, arbitrary or
random. He completely lost his sense of time, he never
knew when one day had ended and the next had begun;
he hardly slept except during the day, and the rest of the
time he lay on the sofa, drinking from a bottle of wine
he kept beside him, just as he'd seen Gerhard do. Hedda
began to struggle against the frenzy of his desire, but soon
realized that he was following an imperative; dimly she
sensed that he was waging a sexual war against his past,
and that it was a battle for his survival. She reckoned on
his natural exhaustion, but she couldn't have known that
his exhaustion would be total—it would take his lust back
to a nadir from which it would never recover. She didn't
know that ultimately he was sleeping with her in order
to unman himself. Once, when he was lying underneath
and she was sitting astride him, in his lechery he'd said an
obscene thing to her: Fuck me to death! – She didn't suspect (and he didn't know himself), that these words had a
deeper, almost diabolical meaning for him, one that in his
frenzy he hadn't even intended.

The evening before Gerhard's return, C. left for
Hanau. He was convinced she was relieved at his departure, but her farewell embrace contradicted that impression. In her gaze was something he pondered for a long
time. There was love in that gaze, but perhaps a love that
was more sisterly...he couldn't explain it. Certainly, there
was compassion in it, too, but at the base of that gaze
was the search for someone with a kindred fate. For a few

seconds they stood together, their gazes touching: they had the eyes of companions in fate brought together by some unlikely chance.

A short while later Hedda broke off her relationship with Gerhard (without informing C. beforehand); Gerhard actually found her a little apartment on Schillerplatz, and then she moved out of his place. C. could only guess how their break-up had played out; she didn't say a word about it. C. didn't see her until three or four weeks after she'd moved out, and when he did, he thought there was still desperation, even madness in her gaze. One time, when she was still at Gerhard's, C. had tried to call her and got Gerhard on the phone: C. flinched at the wave of icy hatred surging from the receiver. But what had he expected?

Now C. was on the spot: Hedda hadn't said a word about it, but he felt called upon to end his relationship with Mona in Leipzig. He sensed that Hedda had been avoiding the subject for a long time already. Of course he avoided it too, but in his mind he constantly felt tormented by it. Now and then they did end up talking about it, and Hedda let him know that she found his behavior unacceptable. His way of keeping silent and simply doing nothing, simply stealing away while Mona—there'd once been love between them, after all—was left in the dark. Just vanishing into thin air like a coward! – C. responded that he still had some manuscripts at her place in Leipzig, or at least he thought he did, and he'd have to go back one more time. Then he'd say his farewells… – That's an elegant way of putting it, said Hedda. – Of course I'll tell her first, he said. Some opportunity will turn up, a phone call, or I'll write her a letter. First, though, I have to find out when she starts her psychotherapy in Halle, it's for a month or two, and it keeps getting postponed. – Inpatient therapy? asked Hedda. – Yes. And during that time she won't be reachable. But I do want to reach her before-hand…hopefully the therapy hasn't started yet. – So you don't even know that? – No, said C., feeling Hedda's critical gaze almost physically. – That's another cop-out, she said. Dumping her and then passing her on to a psy-chotherapist. Don't you think that's just a way for you to evade all responsibility?

Meanwhile he'd found out when Mona was supposed to be staying at that clinic in Halle. It could be that she was back in Leipzig already…he'd last spoken to her in October. She didn't have a phone, and she'd either have herself connected with him from the post office—which was a lot of trouble, you had to put up with a long wait— or she'd call from the apartment of some friend or other. She'd said she'd be back from Halle in early December, though that might be delayed by a week or more. C. couldn't quite remember what other things they'd talked about…

Now he'd come up with the idea of taking a trip out to see Mona and clarify things with her. The thought instantly made him break out in a sweat.

What was he supposed to tell her? This is probably my last time here, I'm going to stay on in the West, I've got another woman there…

You know her name, it's that Hedda Rast you've always been jealous of…

Should he say: I'm in love with that Hedda Rast…yes, exactly, her, that Russian writer who'd sometimes answer the phone when you called. That's just the way it is, we're meant for each other, I can't leave her now...

He sat in the station restaurant in Leipzig, clutching his beer glass to get a grip on his fear, wiping away his sweat. He'd gotten to Leipzig in the afternoon and had been sitting in the restaurant ever since, undecided on what to do. Should he head out to see his mother (hadn't that been his plan?) or to West Leipzig to see Mona? Or he could go visit Martha, the wife of his friend H., he was sure she'd be glad to see him. He pictured Martha, eyes flashing at him through her thick lenses, taking those glasses off and wiping them so she could see him properly. The thought of Martha had a soothing effect.

Martha and her husband were on friendly terms with Mona; maybe it would help if he consulted them about his problems first? At least he knew he could talk to Martha about it; Martha had always been on his side.

So should he tell Mona nothing for now? Should he tell her that he was going to extend his visa soon, and she'd hear from him then...she should please try not to lose patience with him! – What he really wanted to do was turn around and go straight back to Nuremberg... after all, Hedda didn't even know he was gone yet!

It was awful to think of standing in front of Mona now and telling her that he'd left her. That he'd left her months ago, actually a whole year now, she just hadn't known it. Did she really not know it yet, had he never given her a hint? – What would happen if he told her out of the blue? Screams? Tears? Would she throw things at him? That would be the best-case scenario! She'd collapse, that was the likeliest thing: she'd collapse, and his appearance on her doorstep would be tantamount to murder!—He was already sitting on the tram, on his way to commit that murder...

He bolted to the door and got off at the next stop. A lukewarm drizzle was descending on Leipzig, or rather a filthy musty soup of moisture that fog and fumes had melded to twilit ambiguity. He was standing at one of the stops in front of the central stadium; on the other side of the street was the DHfK, the GDR's best-known sports college, its massive buildings barely visible in the downward-bleeding dusk. On the road beside the tram tracks, car chased car, headlights already on, nothing but rushing clouds of filth and drizzle. Leaning on the iron railing that separated the tram stop from the road, C. drank the last third of the bottle of liquor he'd bought at the main station and had nearly finished while waiting for the tram. – He was too drunk to show up at Martha's, he thought. So he'd have to go see Mona...and there he'd have to force a decision...

Taking the next tram, he went one stop too far and had to walk back down Georg-Schwarz-Strasse. He passed the building where H. and his wife, Martha, lived; there was no light in their windows, though with the city now in twilight, they would have had the lights on. He walked up Uhlandstrasse, parallel to Spittastrasse, where he'd lived with Mona. About halfway up Uhlandstrasse you came to a little square where a narrow street on the left led to Spittastrasse, heading straight toward the building—number 19—that had been theirs. From Mona's window on the fourth floor you could look straight down the narrow street to the square, which was lined by a few trees that actually turned green in spring.

At Mona's no lights were on either...she was out. Or she wasn't back from her clinic yet. He stepped through the dark-green wooden door into the courtyard, so narrow and crooked that the inhabitants' trash cans practically filled it. He opened the wooden door to the wing where she lived, also dark green, and hard to shut; as usual, it made an ugly tortured sound against the half-crumbled stone slabs of the hallway. He stopped at the mailbox: his name was still stuck next to Mona's on the brown, rusty metal receptacle at the right end of the row. White paper gleamed through the pattern of holes on the door... Could there be letters for him in the mailbox? – He climbed up to the third floor, the wooden steps creaking; as usual, he was out of breath by the time he reached the apartment door. His name still hung there too, a makeshift piece of paper with his handwriting, attached by one thumbtack; Mona had always called him a slob. He put his ear to the door and listened: inside there was not a sound to be heard. Suddenly he wondered if he even had a key for the door...he couldn't quite remember if he'd taken one, if Mona had given him a key when he'd left last November. Or if she'd given him a key on one of his rare visits over the past year. If that was the case, it ought to be some-where deep in the pockets of the traveling bag at his feet.

One more time he put his ear to the door and listened for sounds inside the apartment...it was silent as a coffin in there. He was tempted to press the white doorbell, but let it be. Then he shouldered his bag and went back down the creaking stairs.

As he did, he tried to imagine how the apartment looked now. No doubt he'd constantly encounter his belongings: on the little writing surface built into a book-case—for lack of space in the tiny apartment, which wouldn't have fit a desk—on that sloping, brown-stained wooden panel there were surely still papers of his...maybe even some forgotten manuscript pages. There would definitely be a whole stack of mail he hadn't thrown away because he hadn't answered it...and now he never would. And then there was a little lamp clamped to a bookshelf, and behind that dusty lamp were books he'd always guarded like gold: books of poetry from West German publishers, Apollinaire, Cavafy, T. S. Eliot, *Nadja* by Breton, *How It Is* and *From an Abandoned Work* by Beckett. – He'd bought new copies of all those books in the West, but they lay there in a pile untouched. Here they'd been his treasures, rarities he'd obtained through humiliating contortions, some of them stolen at the Leipzig Book Fair. Now they were gathering dust too...

Inside, he was probably holding still because he'd heard a noise at the door. He was sitting in the tiny smoke-filled living room, bent over the writing surface, scribbling away at something. He sat in his familiar defensive posture, his back to the door, behind him an invisible shield radiating from his cramped muscles that protected him from interruptions and prying eyes. That person was writing without cease, what he wrote was long since irrelevant, for he wrote now for no one but an anonymous god. For that god his sentences flowed as they always had... Characters, characters? he thought. That god had never interfered and demanded characters from him...

Why hadn't he unlocked the door and stepped into that living room? Maybe then he could have seen which of them was alive and which one was the ghost...

So how is Mona doing, anyway? – Down on the street, almost at the end of Uhlandstrasse, the question came. C. wasn't asked how he was, but how Mona was doing. He was always fine; for years now, with patient tenacity, he'd been staying on top of things and doing fine, according to the reputation he'd acquired. A young man (who seemed vaguely familiar) had stepped into his path and asked about Mona. – We haven't seen each other for a bit, the young man went on, it feels like quite a while to me. But how about you, it looks like you're not doing badly? – No, said C., no, I'm doing fine. – I promised to visit you two, I promised Mona, the young man said, while C. waited for the penny to drop, to recollect who this person was. She was planning to return just before Christmas, so when is she getting back? – Who… Mona? asked C. It seems there's a bit of a delay. – The last time I saw her was about two months ago, she mentioned something about Halle, but she wanted to be back just before Christmas. – I have to get to the station, said C., I'm going to see my mother. – I don't want to keep you, but if you could tell her I'll come by a bit before the holidays, the way we agreed. It won't bother you if I come…I know you're always writing. – Yes, said C., pointing his thumb in the direction of Spittastrasse. Up there's where I sit, you know, where I'm always sitting and writing. – Of course I know, said the young man, who seemed to be one of Mona's students. And I won't bother you, really…

At the tram stop he sat on the sill of a bookshop's window to wait; here, with his back to the glass, in the niche of the display window, he found some shelter from the moisture descending from above. Trams kept coming from the direction of the train station; in the opposite direction, heading downtown, traffic was stopped. The trams on the other side of the street poured forth boundless multitudes that were slow to disperse in the chaos of traffic; cars were backed up next to the tram stop, throngs of cyclists rang their bells piercingly, and pedestrians scuttled about in between... At any moment, C. thought, Mona would be getting off one of the trams; he suddenly expected to see her wedged in among the people, harried and shoved, carrying her luggage, the many too many bags she was bringing back from Halle. What would he have done, would he have gone over to greet her?... I doubt it, he thought.

At last a tram heading to the station arrived, and he got on. A short while later he was sitting on an express train to Berlin.

What would have happened if he'd run into Mona at the tram stop? At least he would have been sure of having a place to sleep that night. Now he had to go to Berlin and hope for a lucky break on West Berlin's Savignyplatz. A lucky break couldn't be ruled out; at Savignyplatz he generally ran into lots of people he knew.

At Mona's he couldn't have slept alone, or at least that would have raised tricky issues. He'd much rather have gone to Martha's to sleep...it was too late for that, he was incapable of making decisions. – Once, several years ago, Martha had said a thing to him that he'd never forgotten. – My cunt can do without your prick, but not without you, she'd said; it had been a kind of deliverance for him.

With Mona he would have ended up arguing (the kind of argument he was already having with Hedda now); he would have had to make all kinds of pretexts, surround himself with smoke and mirrors, for instance claim—or admit?—that he was impotent yet again. Which Mona wouldn't have believed, or would have taken personally. She would have been right not to believe him, and wrong

to take it personally. Mona would have insisted that he
didn't love her anymore…but that wasn't true, he did love
her, yet he didn't want to sleep with her. He loved Hedda
too, yet no longer wanted to sleep with her. Or wasn't able
to. He didn't love Martha, but he wanted and was able to
sleep with her. He was practically terrified of the moment
when he'd start loving Martha…

What Mona really wanted was to marry him, he felt
he knew that, though she scrupulously avoided the subject…she knew it was out of the question for him, he'd
told her that early on…but: Did he really know that it was
so far out of the question?

He'd never had the potency (so he believed) to work
his way through decades bunkered down in a marriage. If
he heard the word *duty* he broke out in a cold sweat; his
stomach turned when he saw a double bed somewhere.
He was a guy for doorways, park benches, and pissoir
nooks; once his desire had been slaked, he lost interest. He
had a problem with closeness and distance, that was how
Hedda had put it one time. She was probably right: He
liked closeness only at a very great distance. There were
other noteworthy things that Hedda had said that he kept
chewing over. – For you, she'd reproached him one day,
love is just an interim arrangement!

Remembering these words, he felt a twinge of
pain…a sense of loss (quickly turning to envy); there was
something he lacked, and he couldn't find the reasons why.
– For him love never achieved the level of normalcy, he
told himself. When it stopped being a state of exception,
he stopped believing in it. For instance, he never slept in
the same bed with Hedda, and against Hedda's desire for
him to do so he had a never-failing weapon: he snored.

But he didn't snore when he slept by himself, at least that was what Hedda claimed.

He blamed his aversion to sharing a bed (or so he'd explained it to Hedda) to the fact that until the age of ten or even twelve he'd had to sleep in a double bed with his mother to save space in his grandparents' crowded apartment. That apartment consisted of practically nothing but an oversized kitchen with a few tiny vestigial chambers attached to it, one of which was filled almost entirely by his parents' conjugial bed. Throughout most of his childhood he slept next to his mother in the place of his father, who had vanished in the cauldron of Stalingrad; only his grandmother's death resolved the situation. Every night of all those years that he could still recall, he had been intensely preoccupied with suppressing an erection, or—if a lapse in concentration allowed one to occur after all— with hiding it from his mother. Ever since that time, he could only fall asleep lying on his right side—that was how he'd always arranged himself, with his back to his mother—in a position known as the stable side position, as he later learned during army medical training. It was the position for transporting wounded men who'd gotten a bayonet to the belly: the right leg extended the body in a straight line so that it occupied as little space as possible; the left leg, bent at the knee to form a right angle, was folded over the groin, with the anchors of the knee and foot ensuring a stable side position in which even an unconscious man could be left unattended.

That was how he lay in bed, anxious to leave as much space as possible between himself and his mother; the vulnerable bit of soft tissue that sprouted between his legs was in the dead zone beneath his angled thigh, where the summer heat cooked it through. His mother was probably lying on her left side; he heard her breathing even when he tried to ignore it. His eyes and thoughts were trained on the darkness, on the wall of the room right in front of his face, drilling through the masonry and out to the street beyond. It was dark and hot there…but behind his back it was also dark and hot.

In the heat he dozed off, but woke in alarm a few seconds later: Was he uncovered? Had he thrown the covers off, was he poking his rear end out toward his mother? Only the width of a door separated her from a tall mirror on the left side of the bed, and maybe she could see him in that mirror. Didn't that sole glimmer of light in the black bedroom, reflected by the mirror, fall right on those two scrawny curves that he was thrusting out into the open? Just in time he flung the much too warm cover over his lower body; his mother stirred, a labored breath audibly left her body… Had that sigh had an exasperated sound?

No, in her sleep she seemed to be thinking of his father, plying his bloody trade in Stalingrad. – Nonsense, the war had ended several years ago, his father couldn't possibly still be alive. And now he was condemned to fill his father's bed…

In the daytime, too, the existence of that organ between his legs preoccupied him more and more. He'd have to go on living with it till the end of his days; suddenly that realization could no longer be suppressed. There were quite autonomous symptoms of growth to be observed in that body part that up till then, if mentioned at all, was acknowledged with formulaic diminutives, and it was as though a kind of rebellion against that mocking tone had stirred inside it. Of course rebellion was fine with him, but he'd have liked to have control over it. But the prick—that was a term he'd picked up from his schoolmates—stood up against its owner as well…so maybe he wasn't really its owner? The thing belonged to a power whose true burgeoning lurked in the future. It began by distending at the most inappropriate moments: for instance when he happened to think of it on the street, at the municipal baths, at school, and especially in bed.

On afternoons when his mother wasn't there he'd stand in front of the mirror in their shared bedroom and investigate the thing, and when he did, it grew visibly at the touch of his fingers. In fact, it had started growing at his mere gaze…the thing wanted to be looked at, it was struggling for a respect that had been denied it. – He'd read a thing or two about hypnosis in some obscure books; it had to do with willpower, a capability that according to his mother he utterly lacked. This might be a chance to test that willpower: in front of the mirror he made his prick grow—this brought an inexplicable sense of bliss— and then tried to hypnotize it to make its power ebb again. This last effort gave him a bad feeling; the thing refused to cooperate, it exerted a force that crippled his will…but he'd read that it sometimes took years of willpower train- ing before hypnosis really worked. He resolved to prove his mother wrong in her poor opinion of his will…at least he'd prove it to himself.

But his victories always proved fleeting, apparently even dependent on the seasons. In the winter he had far more success keeping that organ down; it couldn't be seen under the thick down comforter anyway…but in the spring it would grow visible again. It was embarrassing; however many books you read, there was never any talk of

its visibility. So the main thing was to keep it invisible...
which was best achieved by making it disappear. It was
absurd, but this preposterous appendage had to disappear
like his father...into a kind of Stalingrad, in a cauldron
where everything was ground to a pulp, where nothing
could get out again. There'd have to be a bloody carnage
leaving—as in his father's case—nothing behind but an
official notification with the dry remark: *Missing*.

In the summer, when it was alarmingly hot, he was
given no covers but a thin sheet beneath which everything
showed quite clearly. And it wouldn't even be fully dark yet
when his mother went to bed. When she came in—sometimes unexpectedly as though she'd been lurking behind
the door, eavesdropping—his hands would dart up under
the sheet to his chest; however lightning-quick that reflex
was in his half-sleep, she had to have noticed something.
Her face showed what she was thinking: The boy's head
is filled with smut, I always knew it!—All too often she
complained that he'd fallen in with a bad crowd...by that
she meant the older boys who'd already left school or were
having to repeat a grade. For instance, they'd measured
the length of their pricks with a ruler he'd had to procure
for them...but then they'd chased him away and he never
saw his ruler again.

In the morning he woke in a light-flooded room and
realized to his horror that he'd flung the sheet from his
sweaty body. He jerked his head around: his mother was
no longer lying next to him. She'd already gotten up, the
room was pitilessly bright and still, the whole apartment
filled with silence. How long had he been lying this way?
Probably for hours...he was alone with his nakedness,
and everyone knew it, they knew everything about him.

His nightshirt had ridden all the way up to his neck, he was lying on his back, legs slightly splayed, and from the midpoint between them rose the only organ he still felt. And it was to blame for the silence that surrounded him. Provocative, impossible to ignore, it raised its head and sunned itself.

Around Savignyplatz in Berlin-Charlottenburg, C. knew he could always find someone with a place for him to spend a night or so. The bars along the square were peopled day and night by the East German poets who had emigrated, been expatriated, or been granted a multi-year visa; they called Savignyplatz the "Bermuda Triangle," saying that if you ended up here, all you could do was go under. – C. sometimes felt he should have gone straight to West Berlin as soon as he'd left the GDR. It hadn't occurred to him, no one had suggested it, because no one felt he was one of them...

And whenever he went to West Berlin, his mind was always set on a different area (not far from Savignyplatz) that he also referred to as a triangle...

Arriving in Berlin, he continued straight on to Friedrichstrasse Station. On Friedrichstrasse, first he went to a café called "Kleine Konditorei," next to the railroad bridge and across from the border checkpoint, to drink several cups of coffee in quick succession. In the men's room at "Kleine Konditorei" the sight of his face in the mirror appalled him: he looked haggard, gray, alcohol-scarred, ten years older, his bloodshot eyes gleaming like a frustrated madman's. He splashed his face with water from the faucet and dried it with toilet paper; the towel was unusable, a slippery rag that seemed to have been dunked in perfumed soap.

Then he walked across to the border checkpoint, try-ing to put on a resolute face dominated by "his mission." In fact, it was the face that performed the mission when crossing the border: the face smuggled the appended per-son through the checks, and in every case it was a false face. In the best-case scenario, it ought to be above all suspicion, but that was ultimately impossible, since suspi-cion was the very premise of the checks. In actuality a face above all suspicion was infinitely suspicious...every time he crossed the border he felt like an agent of the Stasi—or he would have loved to feel like one—but that feel-ing struck him as an imposture, a transparent, suspicious imposture. – Despite his focused face, he was in some utterly different dimension as he crossed Friedrichstrasse, forcing several cars to brake with a screech; unalarmed, he gave the angry drivers friendly nods. A moment later he was standing in the relatively short line at passport control.

You know what you should really do? said the border official behind the window of the little booth. – What? C. was still playing the preoccupied, very busy man, and the comment made him jump. – You should really get a shave, the official said. You hardly look anything like your passport photo anymore. – Oh, said C., I'll get a shave by the time I come back home tomorrow, you'll see. I just forgot my razor over at the Hilton... – Well, hopefully it won't get stolen over there, the official said with an unex-pectedly friendly grin. – C. got his stamp and hurried on down the narrow corridors along the iron railings—he practically felt like a suitcase on a conveyor belt—to the last steel door, where another inspector stood. The man waved him through after glancing at his visa stamp.

After that, in the yellow-brown tiled hall—a revolting color—he never had the nerve to turn around again and look at that last border official...probably for fear of being called back: Actually, come back a moment, mister! In unmistakable Saxon dialect, a voice he could practically hear resounding through the air. No, maybe it was the border guard's gaze that he felt on the back of his neck. – Could they really call him back again? In the yellow-brown hall he was already on West Berlin territory...he assumed! If he heard a voice, he probably didn't need to respond anymore, he could just ignore it and walk doggedly on. Would they come after him and take him by the arm, still bland and low-key? But the grip, already insistent, might instantly change into a policeman's: Give me your passport, it'll take just a minute!—Should he tear free and run? Maybe shove his bag in the guard's face and flee. Up on the platform, he'd be a goner if the train didn't come right away. Probably every other person there was a Stasi agent. Ridiculous...what would he do if they nabbed him at Zoo Station and bundled him into a car with a chloroform-soaked cotton wad under his nose? No one would care, no one would even notice.

He didn't turn around until he was on the stairs going up to the city train. The border guard wasn't even looking his way; he was looking at his watch, waiting to be relieved. No one had called him...yet the hall seemed to have a strange smell of chloroform. Its repulsive yellow paint seemed to transpire the smell, it was a dull oily paint with a pungent salty tang, the smell of old stations that could never be heated properly. When the word *Lubyanka* appeared in the books he read (from the *Holocaust & Gulag* section), he always pictured the prison's corridors in that color. It was the *Lubyanka* that he imagined transpiring the cold, sticky, blinding smell of paint and chloroform, a smell that had spread all the way to the western border of the so-called GDR and would never disappear from that country...

He wouldn't shed the chloroform smell until he was standing on the city train (you could never get a seat at Friedrichstrasse Station), or actually not until the next stop. When the bums got on, for instance: they practically invaded the train, taking over, laughing brashly, yelling their packs of dogs into submission, and plunking themselves down on the floor without a qualm. They were drunk, ragged, bleary-eyed, and insecure...but insecure in a different way than C., in a way he almost envied; they were at home here on the train. They were at home even when they were caught without a ticket, still cracking filthy jokes as the cops dragged them off. He managed just once to mingle with the bums undetected and take a clandestine swig from the bottle of whisky he'd bought in Probstzella; the bums didn't bat an eye. That dispelled the chloroform smell from his nose.

Lehrter Stadtbahnhof, Bellevue, Tiergarten, Zoo Station; he went down the stairs, tossed the empty whisky bottle into a garbage can, and wandered aimlessly through the station passageways, where he soon lost his bearings. At some point he came across a back entrance to the Heinrich Heine Bookstore and tried the door handle; it was still open. That bookstore always seemed to be open, day and night, a book paradise; leading with your right shoulder, cautiously trailing the left, you sidled down narrow chasms between precipices of books, and still you kept toppling the teetering book towers. The bookstore was an atomic pile of literature; if it had imploded, this would have been the place where the force of the human spirit finally bored its way to the earth's core. C. wriggled his way single-mindedly through to the checkout, to the left of which stood a small bookcase stuffed with Surrealist and Dadaist publications, mostly from small publishers. He bought a book called *Maintenant or the Soul in the Twentieth Century* with pieces by Arthur Cravan, a peculiar, enigmatic figure from French surrealist circles. Cravan was like a character invented by a novelist: a boxer who'd written poems and other things. And he had published the journal *Maintenant*, though only five issues had appeared. For a while he'd been championed by André Breton; once, in 1916, he'd boxed the American world champ Jack Johnson, getting knocked out in the first round. Then he'd disappeared overseas—evidently meeting Leo Trotsky on the ship—and died in Mexico while boating at just over thirty. – When C. first read this grim biography, his first thought was: That won't happen to me, I'm going to survive this century!

The slender paperback cost just twelve marks; when he paid, he saw to his horror that he'd have to break his second-to-last 100-mark bill.

It was after eleven by the time he was sitting in the Presse-Café on the other side of the street. This café (open around the clock) was always his first stop when he arrived in West Berlin: he had to put his thoughts in order. And he'd put his thoughts in order over and over again in the Presse-Café after spending hours, half the night, with a hollow belly, corroded soul, and no way to stop walking the streets he'd connected in his mind to make that "triangle." After that, breathing heavily, bright red in the face, he'd go back to sitting at the café…

With a window seat, you looked straight out at one of the city's hot spots; a mere pane of glass separated you from the unleashed human mania for movement. At the intersection, the traffic coming from under the train tracks on the left jammed, the glut of cars trying to get off Hardenbergplatz jammed, the traffic from Budapester Strasse jammed, and at the end of Joachimsthaler Strasse a Tatar horde of gleaming machines stood aquiver, waiting for the light to give the signal for the onslaught. Above all this swirled the psychedelic smoke of the luridly tinged exhaust fumes. A jam of pedestrians formed in the thick of things, heedless of the frantically blinking traffic lights, standing in the middle of the street and chattering about a soccer game. A crazy old man towered in the middle of the intersection, shrieking and flinging whole stacks of printed flyers high into the air. Sirens wailing, police cars sped toward the kiosk on Hardenbergplatz, a pack of policemen charged from their vehicles, jumped a bunch of dealers, stretched them on the sidewalk, and handcuffed them. For a few seconds all the lanes of the street were swept clear; flickering colors played on the moisture of the December night as it sank wearily onto the asphalt. The sad sky was Jackson Pollock, painting the street with multicolored tears and magical daubs. C. felt his brain slowly start ingesting the madness of the colors; a sentimental frenzy began to whimper in his skull. The Polish waitress knew exactly what was unfolding inside him; she kept coming by, bringing him coffee and liquor and soothing him with her sarcasm and rolling *R*s. It didn't matter what happened to him, for the moment drunkenness and fatigue were exactly the state his body agreed to. He stood up—thoughts decaying in his head, oblivion in all his limbs—paid, and went on his way.

Instead of heading straight to Kantstrasse, which would have taken him to Savignyplatz, he crossed Joachimsthaler Strasse and kept walking down the right-hand sidewalk toward the Kaiser Wilhelm Memorial Church. Here you passed a whole string of X-rated movie theaters, striptease joints, and sex shops that lined the entire block on that side. At the end of the block he turned a sharp corner onto the end of Kantstrasse. If you kept walking along Kantstrasse, passing under a massive, ugly concrete building propped on pillars and heading back in the opposite direction toward Joachimsthaler, there was another conglomeration of porn theaters and the like. And up on Joachimsthaler there was another whole row of them. This route was what he called his "triangle"...

He remembered spending entire nights here, moving from pub to pub but never daring to enter one of those establishments. His greatest desire was for someone—the way he pictured it, it would have to be a woman—to invite him into one of those dim caverns. For him this triangle of streets was a magical triangle down whose legs he paced hour after hour, increasingly short of breath, bent over, fixing his gaze on the ground like a dog, worrying all the while that he was starting to attract attention... A person constantly running down this street can't help attracting attention, he thought. – So he'd hasten his steps when he passed the glittering entryways where the display cases hung, with photos behind the glass and announcements of the programs in the offing. He slowed to a stroll only once he'd regained a more innocuous stretch of the street. Each time he got back down to Joachimsthaler Strasse, the apex of his triangle, he'd think: That's enough now...

From the corner he just barely made it to the Presse-Café, where he drank a coffee and a brandy and had a rest. More and more often, ordering gave him a coughing fit; his nervousness, the excitation he couldn't let show, vented itself in convulsions of his throat; the waitress said to him in her Polish accent: Don't smoke if you can't take it...

He knew he'd never manage to fetch his bag and walk over to Savignyplatz (not by a long shot); instead he'd head back toward the Memorial Church...or, for a change, he'd walk down Joachimsthaler first, then down Kantstrasse to its end, then around the corner back to the Presse-Café... he hadn't yet peeked at any of the displays, and now, coming around the corner, he walked slower, then stopped to light a cigarette, standing as though by accident outside one of the entrances; his gaze probed one of the cases, but it was much too far away. He raised his head from the still-burning lighter, took what seemed an accidental step and managed to get jostled by a passerby... Beg pardon! he murmured, stumbling two or three more steps toward the entrance. Behind the glass of the case were splayed thighs, slender and of an almost unreal hue; unless one of the hands was resting between the thighs, the triangle in the middle had a glossy red star sticker over it. Maybe the star would have been left off in one of the cases he could glimpse farther down the passageway...

When he'd orbited the magic circle ten or more times, when exhaustion set in and his café breaks grew longer—his feet were aching and the ache spread farther and farther upward, his whole skeleton hurt, his thighs cramped all the way to the hip, his shoulders and arms seemed many times heavier—he told himself he'd be able to escape this part of town only once he'd gone into one of those establishments or movie theaters. He sensed that that wasn't at all what he wanted, he wanted to go on walking until he got blisters—though he had blisters already, his heels were burning like fire—trapped for nights, for days in the cloak of his desire, carried away by his dead-end addiction, blind in his obsession...and getting blinder and blinder the longer he panted onward, knowing that he could never see what he wanted.

He knew the routine in those establishments: you went into a tiny booth, where you put a coin in a slot with a red arrow pointing to it. A blind went up, and you looked through a glass pane into a lit-up room where a kind of conveyor belt moved in a circle. Several unclothed women would be prancing on the conveyor belt, performing limber balletic movements to rhythmic dance music. When the belt carried one of them in front of the open blind, she would sit or drop to her knees, spreading her legs toward the glass pane or aiming her buttocks at it... but one of her hands would still be resting between her legs, and the instant she began to remove it the blind would go back down. You'd put another coin in the slot...

There must have been a little light in the room, visible only to the woman on the conveyor belt, that lit up a fraction of a second before the blind went down...

He berated himself because he still hadn't tried to find a place to spend the night. He knew how nights like that ended, this wasn't his first. Early in the morning, in the unformed time between night and day, in some café or other (not the Presse-Café, he didn't dare go there in this phase), stranded, tattered, with a face scoured by the night's disappointments and wan as the morning—that gray premature birth that hovered in limbo as he kept himself afloat with coffee and brandy.

How was he supposed to make it over to the East in this state…in this confusion, with the smell he'd soaked up from the entries to the peep shows? Outside the always-open doors of those institutes—invented for the sole purpose of his torment—invisible clouds collected on the sidewalk, imbued with the ruined men's effluvia…you inhaled the lost sense of self of the dark groveling figures who went in and out of those doors; you retained, days later, their gasses in your clothes and your hair—their blood, sweat, and tears, their cagey panting, their flatulence, the smell of their burned-up semen. And all that mingled with the scent of the immaculate women who danced before them, taking breaks for mild disinfectant baths…

Drinking in a café in the gray light of dawn, he was utterly godless. He was cast out from the world and felt shattered to the very last bone. That eye he'd hoped to find somewhere amid his triangular route, that eye hadn't looked at him…and he hadn't seen it. His trinitarian path had proved to be an endless desert march along a dry dead periphery. He wondered if he ought to walk to the checkpoint at Friedrichstrasse Station for early morning exercise, or if he had money left for a taxi…

No, of course he couldn't cross the border. At one point, shortly before finally extricating himself from his triangle, he'd gone a short way inside the entry to a peep show to take a hasty look, as though in passing, as always with the semblance of disinterest, at the disemboweled lower bodies in the display cases. From farther within, where the corridor turned a corner and the rhythmic flicker of dark red light and the goading drone of obnoxious percussion wafted out, an elderly man had suddenly walked toward him, in a coat with a summery look to it. – Here, want this, you can have it, the man said, holding out a thin, rolled-up magazine. C., looking away in alarm toward one of the display cases—that was the moment when he was forced to take a real look at the gaping bodies with the silver or pink stars between their legs—took the magazine and said a polite thank you. The man nodded, gave C. another glance with his dark sad eyes, and left.

It was a porn magazine in gaudy color...he got his bag out of the locker at the train station and stuck the magazine under the rubber bands holding together the four thick volumes of Walter Benjamin's complete works that he'd been lugging around from West to East and back again for what seemed like half an eternity now. He'd never had his bag searched at the border before, but there's always a first time, he told himself. It didn't take much imagination to picture his predicament when they discovered the magazine amid his pawed-through clothes. The highest-ranking border official, in a voice audible to everyone lurking in line behind C., would quote the title that stood out on the cover in provocative letters: *Anal!*— The two drawn-out vowels would instantly silence the bored murmurs in the yellow-brown, chloroform-smelling hall. The officer would thumb through the pages, shrug his shoulders, shake his head, and then, still much too loudly, he'd say: You know you can't take this thing into the country? – I don't want to take it into the country; I'm leaving it with you! C. pictured the most harmless variant of the situation. – You'll have to, you'll have to! And now go get your entry stamp...

Those thoughts kept going through his head as he sat in the airplane to Frankfurt. Huddled in his window seat, he took hasty pulls at a cigarette; there was sweat on his brow that he wiped off with his sleeve. He'd just barely made the plane; en route to Tegel Airport his taxi had kept getting stuck in the afternoon traffic jams, the airport shuttle bus full of passengers had already left, and they'd had to drive him out in a Pan Am car to the plane waiting on the tarmac. When the plane lifted off, the first thing he felt was a fit of nausea—evidently the alcohol and the sleepless nights kicking in. He ordered a whisky from the stewardess, who gave a friendly smile and said he'd have to pay extra for the expensive stuff.

He remembered the very first time he'd flown from Berlin to Frankfurt, an utterly cloudless day with a good view over the countryside from the plane. – Are we flying over GDR territory yet? he'd asked the stewardess as she passed. – Yes, we have been for some time, she replied. – A sense of liberation had welled up inside him: so there it lay, that GDR; the majestically droning plane took barely half an hour to cross it. And that patch of ground wanted to make history, liked to describe itself as a steadfast bulwark of the progressive portion of humanity, or some such... What a wretched backwater!

And yet he was perpetually justifying himself to that country! If he ever got to the point of being able to write again (though now that point seemed to be receding farther and farther into the distance), then, given that he hardly had any other topics left, he might be forced to write about the magic triangle he'd just left. But how could he justify that to his Ministry of Culture? He'd already done it; he'd searched for a way to explain it to himself. He'd justified his relentless roaming around that glittering circle of streets next to the Zoo Station with the notion that he was on the lookout for a mystery. But for what kind of a mystery?

For a mystery that seemed to reveal itself bit by bit the more coins you stuck in a slot?

The mystery was not the opened leaves of that sex hole up there on stage (which, with luck, you could catch a glimpse of)... If you could pay, the entire free world had no more mysteries at all. What was up there was freedom, and freedom was damn good business in this world. There was no better business than freedom, it was as simple as that. If people demanded to wallow in an ocean of idiocy, then that was what they were offered: idiocy galore with topless waitresses.

Did the mystery he couldn't fathom lie within himself? – He'd come out of a hole, and he'd have to return to a hole in the end...and yet he didn't know his origins. What he knew about them, what he was able to know about them had always been too little for him. – He didn't know how he'd begun...didn't know how (nor when, nor why) he'd begun to write, dark chaos hid all those things from him. And because he didn't know, he didn't know why to keep going. Maybe his country over there (down there, beneath the airplane) had been right to shake its collective head at C.'s mad notion of wanting to be a writer. Everyone had been mobilized to shake their heads (to deny what C. took to be his existence); they'd induced all his acquaintances and relatives, his so-called family circle, his friends, and his lovers to shake their heads and deny him…they'd done their best to murder him! And they'd succeeded, just a puny remnant survived…

And they'd induced him to shake his own head, deny himself, and forget how he'd begun…

Yet even now he sprawled on his face in front of them, begging for one single, barely noticeable nod…

He recalled the shock that he'd gotten the first time he saw himself on TV…and that repeated every time thereafter: Could that be him, he asked himself, appalled, that bloated creature on the screen struggling in vain to make itself smaller? Did he correspond to that jittery monstrosity gasping for air and words in the flickering glass, visibly straining toward the edge of the box and squirming in distress at the questions the interviewer asked in his vain attempt to shed light on things? Did that jellyfish have anything to do with him? – Only in some way far beyond the scope of the TV screen. The only way to show him was a figure on the run, with the camera firing away at his back. – It was a similar experience when he heard his voice on the radio: a squashed Saxon dialect, the mushy whine of the southern suburbs of the Eastern Zone, that squishy whimper (used by most of the party bosses) in which every word sounded revoltingly false and supercilious. It was a language hostile to the electronic age… and the audiovisual innovations of the multimedia world found no way to bend that language to their ends except as the butt of scorn and ridicule…

Did that mean he was stuck peering out from inside that moribund system he'd come from?

He went on gnawing on that thought even after finding a seat in a big fast-food restaurant in the Frankfurt train station…in the back, up a few steps on a separate level behind a wooden railing. Up here sat people who'd detached themselves from the constant stream of travelers, mostly foreigners who clustered around the tables and seemed immersed in endless passionate discussions. On all sides you heard Turkish, Arabic, and Eastern European languages; up here no one noticed if you drank too much. There were another two hours before his train left for Nuremberg; he could have plenty more to drink, or he could take a stroll through the neighborhood around the station…

Wasn't this the very state he needed to justify: his instability…his inability to love…his inability to sit down and write? What should he do…why was he here? – Only Hedda's presence kept these questions from grinding him down. Her affection, her loyalty, her tenderness kept that from happening…so why was he constantly on the run from her? Because his questions couldn't be suppressed…

He had three weeks left until his visa expired (he was repeating himself!), and he could go or he could stay, ultimately it all depended on Hedda…but what burden did that saddle her with? – He no longer had a country to justify himself to: an eon separated him from the probing gaze of the minister who had issued him the visa. Now that minister no longer existed for him; he was free to prowl the red-light districts of the West and bemoan the prostration of his prick, but he didn't have to answer for any of it and could write whatever he wanted without anyone giving a hoot. – In a certain sense I'm stateless, he told himself as he got drunker and drunker. Stateless

like Hedda's aged father, lying in an old-age home near
Nuremberg, waiting things out, barely speaking a word
and refusing to get up. All day long he read *Pravda* or
Izvestia, or gazed absently into the gray German sky or listened to the jackhammering German construction noise
beneath his window...the old-age home had been remod-
eling for the entire year now, the old-age business was
booming. And through that man's waiting brain rolled the
endless expanse of the Volga's big bend, the shimmering
river that no longer existed for him. And now and then
his thoughts might drift to his wife, whom he'd loved and
then stopped loving, from an excess of love and because
that love was full of guilt, for Hedda's mother had killed
herself in hostile, gray Germany when their child was ten
years old...

No, he had to justify himself to no one but God now!
To that so-called God up there, much higher than an airplane, that old authority whose erstwhile greatness was
gone... Now we're finally equals! he thought, raising the
neck of his beer bottle into the air before pouring the rest
into his glass.

He had practically no memory of how he'd started
to write, but he could think back to the time when he'd
written only for himself. He'd written for himself alone,
and no one had known a thing about it, and evidently he
hadn't even complained. He'd actually been embarrassed
anytime someone found him out and wanted to know
what he was writing, and what for. And back then maybe
he really had been writing for God...it was a long time
ago, as though in a different era. He'd been at the point of
forgetting that time, but suddenly it was starting to interest him again. His writer's block had called it to mind, his

inability to put to paper a single line he could accept. Now he'd sometimes find himself wondering how to return to that distant childish state: writing for God or for himself, which was the same thing on some very banal level…

But it was impossible, he was an employee of the literature business, and there was no returning from that point. The literature business was an itch you could never get rid of…

The only option was to have a breakdown and never write anything again. Play the imbecile…and then maybe write on the sly without letting social services get wind of it…

He was making a tremendous effort to break down, but something in his body refused to play along. Before getting on the train to Nuremberg he'd bought a fresh bottle of liquor, and he already knew he could stomach this one too…

Maybe it was due to the alcohol that the word *God* kept floating through his head these days… A softening of the brain, that was another way to put it. All of a sudden he was returning to his childish faith and starting to bargain with the man upstairs. And certainly Hedda was partly responsible; she often spoke of God, embroiled in constant conflict with him. Her quarrel with creation was a specialty of the Slavs, her ancestors' outrage lived on indelibly inside her. She raged against God, sometimes resembling an Eastern holy warrior, accusing him of protecting the wealthy while sending disease to decimate the poor, breathing life into them then mercilessly condemning them to death, so often in agony. Often she went so far as to call her God a beast… C. sat by mutely, having no arguments to offer, which she probably took as disapproval. It wasn't disapproval, he was simply shocked in the face of what seemed to him the deepest possible faith in God. It was the faith of Dostoevsky or Rachmaninov, and no argument could hold against it.

That was why C. was suddenly thinking about God again; when he was a child, he recalled, such thoughts had occupied him almost constantly, but he'd never mentioned them, he was ashamed; in that period just after the GDR was founded, religious thoughts—though not punishable—were held up to broad ridicule. For Hedda, the dialogue with God was a given; she hadn't been cut off from her roots, however little she realized it.

The West had never had that sort of religious tradition that went on growing in an almost vegetative way. God had a different name here, he was called a "denomination" and made his appearance in questionnaires, in sections asking for information on "affiliation" and "membership." The churches that supervised that terminology made it clear from the outset where non-members belonged: on the margins. Doing business on this basis, the churches had made great progress, and at last ended up where they'd always wanted to be: ghettoized. That ghetto consisted of clearly demarcated realms, of buildings that called themselves "houses of God," whose occupants dealt mainly with finances. They'd found a foothold in every one-horse town, each with their display case outside the door. For C., that facilitated the comparison with another sector of the economy: the one dealing with the realm of sexuality that lay beyond the bounds of church- and state-sanctioned matrimony. Those forms of sexuality were ghettoized as well, relegated to certain demarcated urban areas that you couldn't set foot in without overcoming a certain inhibition…a house of God was another place you couldn't enter without first breaching something like a barrier. Those two institutions were connected by something unspoken and untouched: the secret bond that tied lust to renunciation.

Sorry, mister, but this isn't valid, the conductor said, handing back the ticket he'd just inspected. – C. stared at him, uncomprehending. – Your ticket is invalid, it's expired, the conductor insisted. Maybe you have another one in your wallet there? – C. came to his senses, searched his wallet, and actually found the ticket he'd bought in Frankfurt half an hour before… How many tickets was he carrying around with him, anyway? There was a whole stack of them in his wallet, and that was minus the ones he'd sent to the reading tour organizers to claim his travel expenses. – It seemed to him he'd been traveling around and around in circles for the past several months.

He could easily imagine that he was already on his umpteenth back-to-back go-around: he'd arrived in Nuremberg in the middle of the night, tried to phone Hedda, she refused to see him, and in a huff he took the next morning train to Leipzig…from Leipzig to Berlin, from Berlin to Frankfurt, from Frankfurt back to Nuremberg…only to flee straight to Leipzig in the morning, and so forth, and on and on like that to the end… to what end? Until his visa expired, exhausted, until his limbo was over (it would never pass), until he could stop loving Hedda, until he couldn't go on any longer…

Until he was pulverized by this orbit of idiocy, he kept traveling, circling a God who refused him his love. Who refused it because he'd chosen C. to write. But C. wouldn't play that game, no, he'd refuse to write until he'd seen

some love! And one side in this war—either God or he—
would have to capitulate...

He was already thinking that maybe he should go
straight on to Leipzig the next morning (with the three
weeks left on his visa he'd be able to do that a few more
times); he'd look up a good connection as soon as he got
to the station in Nuremberg...

But before leaving Nuremberg he'd go to the bank
and take out money, to avoid being short of cash again as
he orbited. In Berlin he'd had to spend two days crashing
with an acquaintance (someone he'd run into at one of the
bars on Savignyplatz), waiting for his publisher to wire
him money so he could pay for his plane ticket. – GDR
citizens residing in West Germany only temporarily had
a serious disadvantage (serious for C., since he was constantly traveling): despite their equal status as enshrined
in the West German constitution, they could get neither
checks nor check guarantee cards, and they could take
out only a limited sum each month. C. had an account
with a small private bank whose only branches were in
Franconia, the part of Bavaria around Nuremberg. For
that reason, most of C.'s money was deposited with his
publisher, and he had to have them remit it to him. At
the moment, though, he hadn't yet exhausted the sum of
money allotted him for the month of December; he could
take out another thousand marks.

As soon as he walked into his apartment, he saw that
Hedda had been there: she'd had the demolished telephone replaced, and fetched his mail from the mailbox
and stacked it neatly on his kitchen table. He called her,
and to his surprise she answered immediately. – I've been
waiting for you, she said. You ran off to your mother's

again, like you usually do, right? Or did you go see Mona?
– Yes…no, C. replied, should I come over?

I didn't see Mona, I was at my mother's, he said,
drinking coffee in Hedda's tiny living room.

Isn't she back from treatment yet? asked Hedda.

I have no idea. Why do you want to know?

I do have an idea. She is back. She called three days
ago. Or maybe four.

She called? What did she want? – C. tried to remember where he'd been three or four days ago…perhaps he'd
been in Leipzig just then. Standing outside her apartment
door, listening, while she'd gone to her friends who had a
phone, and was trying to call him in Nuremberg…

How should I know what she wanted? Naturally she
wanted to talk to you, not me, said Hedda.

C. bit back his reply; he went to the kitchen to get a
fresh cup of coffee. Leaning against the stove, he listened
to Hedda's voice through the open door:

I was over at your place; no need for you to be surprised about that. First you act like a telephone terrorist
all night long, and suddenly not a peep. That got me worried after all. That evening I went over to your place, and
the moment I came in, the telephone rang. It was stupid
of me to pick up…

It wasn't stupid. What did she say?

She jumped down my throat, of course. Who was this
on the phone, what was I doing in your apartment, you
can imagine the sort of thing. She didn't even let me get a
word in, I should have just hung up…

I'm really sorry about that! said C.

I tried to reason with her, but it was impossible. She
started yelling and crying…and then it dawned on me.

You didn't break up with her at all…though you kept saying you did!

Yes, said C., yes, I did say that…

And that's what you need to explain to me! And I'm asking you not to hide in the kitchen when you do.

I think I just forgot, said C., coming back into the room with his coffee cup.

You forgot to break up with Mona? I'm used to surprises from you, but this is taking on a whole new dimension…

C. wondered how great a danger was lurking in this conversation; after a while he said:

Probably I was just too much of a coward…and I was too much of a coward to tell you, either. After you broke up with Gerhard, I felt obligated…I felt pushed to do the same thing…

I didn't push you, I didn't even ask you to do it.

Yes, I know…

But you told me you'd done it…you were practically even bawling because it hurt you so much to leave her!

Impossible! Was I really bawling?

You told me quite convincingly about a phone call you'd made to break up with her. I fell for it because you seemed so shattered, you were very authentic. You practically shed tears… I think you even did shed a few tears…

C. was silent.

There's another explanation for the whole thing, said Hedda. You just wanted to keep a haven available for when you go back to Leipzig. After all, you never did really decide what you want to do when your visa expires. Maybe you'd leave me and go right back to Mona without missing a beat. You kept that option open. Very practical…

But now you've decided it for me, said C. Now I'm staying for sure.

Do you think that still matters to me?

I don't know...

You strung me along for half a year, you were practically always lying to me...

I didn't mean to lie to you!

It's all the same to me if you go back to Leipzig three weeks from now. It doesn't matter to me what you decide, if you stay here or not. I'll do fine without you... – Now it was Hedda who had tears in her eyes.

Appalled, C. reached for her hand, but she slapped his fingers.

It's final, he said, the decision has been made, and I'm staying here. Whether you're happy about it or not, I'd stay here even without you. I can't live in the East anymore...

And what you're doing here, do you call that living?

I don't care what you call it.

And I'm starting not to care either. I *don't* care! said Hedda. I'd rather we stopped talking about it...

When he left, he tried to hug Hedda goodbye, but she wouldn't let him. From his apartment he called her again and told her that he'd accepted three invitations to readings in February and March already, and that they were in West German cities. Wasn't that more evidence that he'd never had any intention of going back East?

Maybe you just forgot where you'd planned to be at the time, Hedda retorted.

He'd been telling the truth: he really had committed to events that coming February and March, and the dates were written down in his calendar; he'd arranged them in the fall without giving the slightest thought to the cutoff point imposed by the visa. – The mail on the kitchen table included a letter from an American university inviting him to give a talk and do a reading tour in the USA in mid-April; immediately he sat down at the typewriter and accepted the invitation. He didn't even know if he really wanted to go to America; he knew he was apt to be daunted by undertakings of that sort, but it was as though he were searching for an anchor, for obligations that would tie him down in the West. Tie him down near Hedda...

Now he stood there like a liar; was that what he really was? – He sat in his study at the table that served as a desk; the hounds belonging to the butcher next door yelped in the yard under his window. Those squirming vermin howled as piercingly as a whole horde of Cerberuses, nipping each other and whimpering, no longer capable of guarding the entrance to Hell. C. couldn't stand it anymore and went out on the street... Was this liar who he really was? – He sat on one of the benches that stood in a circle on Kobergerplatz; the fine rain that was falling hadn't let up since early December; the fluid atmosphere seemed to fizzle like frothing beer in the gravel at his feet. Now and then a fit of laughter rose up inside and convulsed him. With his cupped hand he shielded his cigarette from the moisture that flowed grimily down his face; above him the invisible, stagnating sky was stirred up, the contaminated clouds indulging in constant shameless incontinence...

Wanting to love...yet being unable to—didn't that have to make you a perpetual liar? Delivering a desperate performance of love, yet always knowing that you didn't have the stuff for it? Being unable to love, yet hanging onto a woman with every fiber of your being—as a man, that made you a walking lie. He was a conglomeration of lies, but all the same he knew that without the woman he loved so wretchedly, he'd die…

Another laughing fit shook him; he tried to pull himself together as he saw a couple on the other side of Kobergerplatz standing in a tight embrace under an umbrella. They were a very young couple, kissing and shielding themselves from him behind their umbrella. – All the same he averted his gaze, perhaps because the scene had a touch of kitsch, and looked in a different direction. – He wondered when he'd first experienced that. – That first time he'd been nearly thirty, for sure; his former classmates had long since been pushing their baby carriages around town. But he'd spent years holed up in various dens and dark corners trying to write, always haunted by the fear that someone might be watching. And several times a week he'd gone to various sports clubs, where he'd trained his body until it was almost perfect…that unloved, narcissistically mistrusted body that refused ever to get sick. But still he'd never kissed… when he thought about that, a dull sense of shame welled up from him. He knew he'd robbed himself of any kind of existential meaning. And he'd even taken pride in the thought that his body refused to age; well, it couldn't age, that was what a living corpse couldn't do! That was a fact, he dragged around the shame of a weird somnambulant corpse; an embarrassing anachronism who must reveal to no one that he'd actually died long ago. For years he'd had a lurking awareness that it was ultimately senseless to go on existing like that. With that infinite desert of omission inside him that he'd never be able to cross, that he could never find his way out of…

Sometimes he'd make an advance on a woman, ambushing her from amidst his desert, dragging her back into his Berber existence. For a while, a scant year if it lasted a long time, his insatiability would keep her breathless, until the desert gradually got the upper hand again. It was as though in each woman he'd seek the taste of life that he'd never come close to in his childhood, in his adolescence, and the endless years they call the years of youth. All those years had seemed like an endless torment to him, like being shut up in a coffin...outside it was bright, and through cracks and gaps the bitter blooming scent of the seasons drifted in, but around him was motionless darkness.

Every woman sent him into a state that felt like a mad race to catch up (and he knew perfectly well this only frightened most women off), to make up all at once for everything he'd missed; he saw each woman as, literally, one last chance to win the struggle against his meaninglessness...the last chance before he finally succumbed, before fate finally choked him off...yet in that very moment of struggle he'd already given up. Even as he loved, he'd already resigned himself to love's impossibility, which ruled him like a merciless dictate. He knew that none of the loves he'd missed could be made up for, he knew that it was over and done with...he couldn't start his life over from the beginning!

And with that sense of despair he'd press his face into the woman's lap and try to taste her essence...the essence of the female, the essence of nature, the taste of life, the taste of the earth. He tried to discover the nature of female lust, to fathom it, to drink and devour the rivers of her lust, the real taste of a woman, as foreign to him as the atmosphere of a distant galaxy. He burrowed his mouth as deep as he could into her openings, constantly tearing the fine membrane that held down his much-too-short tongue behind the row of teeth in his jaw...it was futile, it was over, done with. In a panic of forlorn desire he sought to tap the unknown to the fullest, the musty ceaseless smells of smoke, the sweet and bitter solids and fluids, the enigmatic colors shifting in shudders of feeling, that organism that for him would always remain impenetrable. And when at last he drew back, emerging from the swamp between the spread legs with damp hair and the chafed red face of a newborn, eyes filled with the acrid waters of origin, flowing with tears, he stared into the blurry, wide-open maw, and it seemed to laugh at him, the laughter of an unattainable freedom...

He hunkered sodden on his bench, and by the time he tore himself away, he felt he was dissolving; the rain seemed to have transformed him into a heap of cold flesh with a layer of textiles stuck to it, heavy with damp and smelling of beer. When he reached Schillerplatz, he saw that Hedda's windows were dark...a familiar experience: walking for hours through the night, on the lookout for a lighted window. Those luminous rectangles against night's black background had always been the object of his yearning...what went on behind them? He knew what had gone on behind the illuminated windows of his childhood home in the small town of M.: bickering, outbursts of hatred, brawls, all against all, armed or unarmed, accompanied by yelling and screaming; in the end he was always the one kicked into the corner with everyone ganging up against him. Behind the windows he gazed at from the street, the lamps weren't swaying, neither chairs nor pokers were being swung overhead; peace prevailed...

Of course he knew that it was often a deceptive peace. But he also knew that in weak moments he would have been happy to exchange his state of mind for a deception. – In this century, could you even get by without lying?

He remembered once calling the twentieth century the century of lies. – The entire century was one big train of lies, he'd said to Hedda. In the form of a lie and loaded with lies that train had moved forward, moved through, moved past, with a locomotive as its symbol of leadership...and it would go on moving just like that for the remaining years of the century. The lie of progress formed the tracks for that train. And it had hauled the cattle cars across the country, he'd said, cattle cars filled with people barely recognizable as such, to Auschwitz, Vorkuta, Maidanek, Magadan, beneath a sky that was a web of lies.

It's the most mendacious century, there are no errors as in previous centuries, there's nothing but the scientific lie. It's as though human history has stalled amidst a gigantic trash heap of lies. All the governments of this century have ruled with lies, the gangs, cliques, sects of politicians, party bosses, and ideologues have exercised their power everywhere on the basis of lies; the word *power*, no matter whose mouth it issues from, whichever theoretical nuance tinges it, signifies nothing but the power of the lie. The air of this century is infested with lies, the cities are sick with lies, the earth is rotting in lies. If truth was required for a century to exist, the twentieth century never would have been...

But is all that any reason for you to lie too? asked Hedda. – He didn't know what to say to that.

The stars and candles of the Christmas lie were

already glowing in many windows on Kobergerstrasse...
He'd walked up and down it twice already; he felt like a
character in a novel who'd been deserted by his creator.
Whoever had invented the character had left it standing
in the middle of the street, somewhere between beginning
and end, no longer sure what to do with it; amid the ver-
biage of his conclusions it gradually began to decompose.
God had ultimately decided that his hero was a tedious
creature, and had abandoned him...

He'd reached Schillerplatz yet again; the rain was
pouring down. Up above, the windows of her apartment
were dark...should he ring again? – No, it was pointless;
the only thing he could do was take the first morning
train East...

In this century the hero of the novel had met a miserable end, he went on thinking as he turned and headed
back toward Kobergerstrasse. That had become clear
around the middle of the century, when the deportations
came to light, the pictures of the cattle cars crammed with
people, when the first films showing heaps of corpses
unreeled on the screens, hectic and grisly, when the reality
behind the lies was revealed. The life of a novel character—its confusions and sufferings, its obsessions, its misfortune or fortune—was inconsequential, it was foolish
and banal compared to the fates that had unfolded in
the camps; the stories of novel characters were no longer
worth a thing, not even the stroke of a typewriter key,
reduced to waste fit for idiots. The modern epics for people who wanted everyday stories from everyday life were
soap operas on television; novels, however, were a waste of
even the cheapest paper. God had turned away in revulsion
from the tripe of novelistic lives; now and then his finger

pointed to the lives of those who had survived Auschwitz. Thinking people tossed their books into the trash bins; used book dealers were no longer buying the tacky stuff. The innocence of storytelling was utterly lost now that accounts of the Gulag existed (which, incidentally, meant big business for the publishers). The so-called innocence of storytelling had become a sickness far surpassing any type of dementia. – For a long time after arriving in the West, C. had wondered at people's literal revulsion toward everything that went under the heading of "serious liter-ature," but it could hardly be otherwise in a country that had been educated about the concentration camps. It was no surprise that a whole host of literati (and a growing host, at that) was suddenly crusading against the omni-presence, the dominance of the subject of Auschwitz: ulti-mately what they were advocating was for everyone to go back to reading the idiocies they produced…

When it came to transporting his books to the GDR—a problem he needed to tackle, since it would surely require elaborate organizing—C. thought all he'd want to bring were the two boxes labeled *Holocaust &* *Gulag*…

He was standing in front of the house on Kobergerstrasse, where a light was still burning in a slightly projecting window bay. He asked himself if he could ring the doorbell of the woman up there in the state he was in, the way he was dressed…it was all too clear that he was going to the dogs; he was alcohol-scarred, haggard, sleep-deprived and unwashed, and hadn't shaved for days; his clothes were so heavy with the beer-stinking moisture that they practically sagged off his body, and wherever he stopped, he left puddles. Besides, he didn't know what to talk about with the woman…he had all too clear a memory of his desperate attempts to adapt to the niceties of conversation the first time he had visited her. – Could he possibly feel at home in boring old Nuremberg, she'd asked him. Sometime she'd like to show him some pictures from Hong Kong, where she'd recently been. She'd been visiting her daughter who, barely twenty, had gone to join her father, the woman's ex-husband, who was living in Hong Kong. And now she was wondering if she should go to Hong Kong too; anyway, she was planning to visit again soon, though of course it cost an arm and a leg.

C. was sitting in her brightly lit living room with comfortable and, as people put it, modern furnishings, with a cup of coffee on a knee-high table in front of him, looking at the color photographs—they seemed to show a kind of science fiction world with gigantic advertisements in mostly Chinese writing—that were being dealt out before him from a whole big stack. – Am I going too fast for you? the woman asked. – Not fast enough, he thought, as she laid the pictures in front of him more slowly. – Really nice photos, said C., and felt that his voice sounded oddly lifeless. – You have such an authentic Saxon accent, she said, we love hearing that here. – Something inside him blanched when he heard phrases like that, it was probably his liver or his spleen, but fortunately the pallor didn't show in his face. He decided to talk as little as possible so as not to occasion another such compliment; meanwhile, she talked on undeterred: Did you know my parents came from there way back when? But that was before the war, I wasn't even born yet…

It cost C. an effort to stay for an hour; a shorter stay would have struck him as rude, but back in his apartment he saw that he'd failed to make it an hour anyway, he'd spent at most fifty minutes with her. He thought of giving her a call: Could he come back and take a closer look at the photos? – A few of the photos had actually sparked his interest: two or three shots showing the entertainment districts of Hong Kong at night, exploding in a mad glitter of colored lights. – I'd like to take another look at those three photos...would he have been able to say that to her? – She'd commented on the photos by saying all the pretty, colorful images came from bad neighborhoods, surrounded by drug dealing, child prostitution, and so on... – Yes, said C., you always have to keep that in mind. – He knew all that, but he'd been interested in the pictures anyway, without daring to let it on. They'd shown larger-than-life figures of women painted or pasted on the walls of the entry halls to some of the establishments, in obscene poses, naked lower bodies and legs spread wide. Seductive kitsch in lurid pop-art style; openings had been cut out at the crux of the thighs, apertures through which you could peer into an unknown interior, and you saw men standing in front of those pictures, holding their heads up to the openings and looking inside. Slender, delicate Chinese men in dark suits, grinning at each other, libertine and derisive.

Filled with senseless haste, he'd merely glanced at the photos. He sat at the coffee table drinking his coffee, sensing that he wasn't built for the products of the textile industry: whenever he leaned forward to pick up the coffee cup, the gaps between his shirt buttons gaped to show the undershirt stretching taut over his belly, which the stranglingly tight jeans forced up and over his belt. The longer he sat, the more tightly and uncomfortably he felt squeezed into the armor of the clothes against which his body bridled in vain; the shoes he'd recently bought on Breite Gasse—after hours of pacing back and forth indecisively amid the free market's shoe surplus, his feet hurting, a pain that had never abated since making that purchase—clamped his burning feet like medieval torture devices; legs fidgeting, he looked as though he'd take to his heels at any moment. Meanwhile, she'd gotten up several times to pour him more coffee; he watched (trying to be discreet) as she tugged the tight skirt down her clearly sturdy thighs and straightened it at the hips; she moved around the coffee table with a mixture of restraint and coquetry, an extremely charming mixture... You just don't know how to hide your hot ass, do you? he thought. – When he took his leave—it must have seemed abrupt— she blanched slightly, sunk in her armchair; then with a pained smile she saw him to the door.

In his apartment he stripped off his clothes and poured himself a large shot of liquor. His clothes lay on the carpet in front of him in what seemed a putrid heap of indefinable material hostile to humanity, oozing moisture and smelling of beer and gasoline. He carried a chair into the bathroom, climbed onto it and scrutinized himself in the mirror over the sink...the scene reminded him of looking at himself in the mirror in his mother's bedroom at the age of twelve or thirteen, standing on a chair, naked. His body steamed, and for a few moments the glass of the mirror clouded...as the mirror gradually cleared, he saw himself: he didn't need to hypnotize his prick anymore; it had hidden itself away, abjectly and all on its own, into the tangle of his pubic hair. The mirror showed the torso of a shivering whitish male body, awfully close to old age, a damp, sticky, useless body, bloated, neglected, done to death, a perpetual object of hatred and scorn from God and all the world. Up on the chair he started to teeter, whether from the alcohol or in a fit of disgust, and had to sit down; he sat gingerly on the top rail of the chair back and propped his hands on his thighs. Now his face appeared in the mirror: no, that wasn't his face: it was a strange face, indignant, driven into a corner where there was no escape, the witless fear-twisted face of a boxer down for the count who can't find a hole to hide in.

In his room he lay on the mattress that served as his bed, with all the doors of the apartment ajar, hearing the rain through the cracked-open window of his study. The howls from the Cerberuses in the butcher's yard came infrequently now, their whimpering drowned by the pestilential rain, just now and then a few long-drawn-out whines rose from below, drilling into his nerves and giving voice to his fear. Should he go back East one last time? He still had a few days left before the visa expired!—No, he had to hold out here; if there was any subject left for him to write about—if he ever wrote again!—it wouldn't be found in the GDR. What was over there was dead, it was past. The atmosphere that could still move him to express himself—if anything could—was the one on Schicklgruber's autobahns, where the West German was in his element. Or the atmosphere in the pedestrian malls like Breite Gasse, where there were enough characters to satisfy all the literary critics' desires.

Half asleep, he saw himself standing in the middle of Breite Gasse between his two book boxes, which were so battered and torn at the corners that the books were almost falling out; all around him life surged in the afternoon sunlight, the ceaseless celebration of *shopping & fun*, pleasing in the sight of God. He'd been standing there for quite some time, looking rather battle-weary, unshaven, unwashed, and greasy...what was he waiting for? He was waiting to be carted off. – But no one paid any attention to him, and to the left and right the consumer revolution paraded, the absolute zeitgeist sashayed through the soup of sun. – That zeitgeist, C. said to himself, won't make it over to the GDR, not in a thousand years... Breite Gasse in Nuremberg, that's the center of the world (or Königstrasse in Stuttgart, the Zeil in Frankfurt, Tauentzienstrasse in West Berlin, or the underground shops in the train stations). For the world is where sellers and buyers meet, faces aglow, at the entrance to Elysium...

Shopping Makes You Free, say the attractively lettered words over all those entrances...

There are so many entrances because not only can you go in, you can come out again. And they stream in and out, and onward through the pedestrian mall in their constant doings and dealings, all sensing they're being filmed by the TV cameras at the beginning and end of Breite Gasse. And that's why they're all beaming, beaming amid the fusillades of jubilation that soar into the air over Breite Gasse and rain back down again. And they're all wearing their company's logo on their chest or their back, the emblem of their global brand or the snappy slogan of their manufacturer: *Coke Is It...* – Yes indeed, they're nothing but walking advertisements now, and so they've achieved their goal. At last they have their names. And so capitalism has achieved its goal, thought C. – And to maintain their identities, thought C., they all carry their number around with them. – He can hear them communicating. – Hello, hello, calls VW No. 116611, hello, hello, I just got a real bargain!—What, just one bargain! exclaims Mitsubishi Motors No. 501134. I've already gotten two bargains, and my wife's already got three, three honest to God genuine bargains!—Three bargains? responds VW No. 116611, that just can't be...where on earth do you get bargains like that? – But it's true, really it is, interrupts Nike No. 174517 (that happens to be the number tattooed on Primo Levi's forearm, thinks C.). It's not far, a hundred yards back that way, that's where those bargains are. We already got four real genuine bargains there!—Hearing this, Becks No. 54123 stops in his tracks, turning pale: Where? For God's sake, where? Microsoft No. 79669 has to prop him up, pressing one of her pointy breasts into his armpit. – Meanwhile, Bayer AG No. 100200 walks by beaming with joy and gives a wave. Four bargains, five bargains, six absolutely genuine bargains! Just marvelous, really...

The next day he woke up and saw that the sky had brightened somewhat; a tiny sunbeam might even have entered the room. – How did I used to write...what did I used to write? That was usually the first question he asked himself when he woke up and realized that he couldn't get back to sleep again. That for better or worse he'd have to proceed into the day... Hedda had once told him that he slept like someone who had to wrestle with invisible oppressive forces. Maybe, she said, it would help him to find out what it was that he was fighting even in his sleep. – He thought about it and came to the conclusion that he was actually fighting against waking up. He furiously resisted waking to this existence that was utterly unknowable to him, that he felt to be a menace, makeshift, contingent on every chance influence, empty of truth. As long as that thin sleep covered him, he had some slight protection, for that time his loneliness went undetected, he didn't feel the silence that surrounded him.

Ever since he'd stopped writing, he'd been inexorably delivered up to this existence. And what was worse, he couldn't even manage anymore to lay claim, in his own ego, to the things he'd written in the time before his visa…the things the critics had praised him for, the things for which he'd received literary prizes and the fellowship that had brought him to the West. No, where that was concerned his ego shrank away to nothing, his books suddenly struck him as part of a craven compromise with the unknown monster that was his existence, as a bargain with that beast that hounded him even in his sleep. Certainly, he'd wrested his texts from the beast, but it played along in a devious way: it let him get away with certain things under the condition that he wouldn't try to kill it. And indeed he had desisted…he hadn't touched the beast, he didn't even dare to look it straight in the eye. And thus he gave it the opportunity to seize him again at any moment.

So it wasn't surprising that he was suddenly thinking back to those early years when he'd written stories and poems just for himself. Notebooks scribbled full of what was still a schoolboy's handwriting; he'd burned most of them at some point (only now and then would he find one or another of those notebooks in his mother's chaotic apartment in M.); he'd burned them because they embarrassed him, they'd been filled with blind, unfulfilled yearnings, whereas the world demanded that you keep your sufferings secret…now his published books embarrassed him, and he would have liked nothing better than to burn them. It was impossible, they were published…they'd been sacrificed to the beast, and the beast reveled in them…

What was that beast? – It was his existence: his existence with no origin, his life with no history…

People laughed at that and said: There's no such thing as an existence with no origin!

He wouldn't reply to that; he'd think: You're absolutely right, I have no origin, and I have no existence.

The void exhaled me, tossed me out into the open, and it's crouching invisibly before me and yawning, the beast! At any moment it can suck me in again. And I followed it (I performed my dance in front of it)…it granted me a few pages, a few images of its aesthetic bestial majesty…a few thunderbolts of remote bliss flickering in the void. All that I put onto paper, then I burned it, burned it in the stove of the smoke-browned kitchen or, later, burned it in public. And so I truly was a man who dealt with fire, and that made a drought, a gigantic thirst become a part of me…

Once he'd told Hedda that he'd taken a sudden interest in the time when he'd started to write. When he'd written solely for himself, and perhaps for some distant unknown being. – She, who'd started writing much later than he had, and still remembered everything about it, advised him to pursue the question at all costs. She'd always suspected that that time was utterly obscure to him. Besides, he'd often complained about the muddled conjectures that were made about him. He hadn't felt offended by critics' cavils, she said, he'd fumed instead about their paradigms, calling them *appallingly simplistic*. – Unfortunately I don't know where to start, he replied, because I feel as if I was writing long before I ever started thinking about my life…

Was he already hankering to write about the time of his visa? she asked. By chance—when she was over at his place having the broken telephone replaced—she'd seen a notebook on his desk with the title "The Visa" written on the first line. Maybe you want to start with this time and think back to that time you can't remember. Maybe you've reached a boundary where you've started needing to remember, she said.

He hadn't replied to that…he knew perfectly well why he'd written down the title without ever beginning a piece underneath. The notebook with that heading had been lying on his desk for a long time, near the edge, covered with papers and writing implements. He'd forgotten about it, but just recently he'd dragged it out again and opened it…he'd put down the title in April, right after his first trip to Vienna, back when his relationship with Hedda was suffering its first frictions.

That was when Hedda began to ask what he planned to do after his visa expired, while he evaded the question. – It was nine months before it ran out, which was too early for him to start thinking about it, he'd replied. – At that time he was living in Hanau, and she suggested that he move to Nuremberg; she said she didn't want to live with Gerhard anymore, she'd find herself a place of her own. Soon after that she suggested finding a place together, in Nuremberg or some other city. – C. was at a loss to make a decision, procrastinating endlessly; it wasn't like him to make a commitment…nor did he have any idea how he planned to end his interim arrangement once his visa had expired.

How had he managed never to ask himself what Hedda would do once he went back East at the end of that year?

No indeed, he'd never asked himself that question; he'd been thinking of nothing but the end of *his* interim state…hardly sparing a thought for the fact that he had long since sucked Hedda into this state with him. – When she read the title he'd written down—"The Visa"—it must have given her the idea that for him that time was essentially finished already. She knew—he'd explained it to her himself—that he wrote all his work retrospectively, for him stories had to be over with before he could write them down…

He tried to recall how Hedda's face had looked when she'd asked about the empty notebook with that title… it had been contorted by fear, he suddenly realized. The mental image of her fear yanked him to his feet and sent him roaming his rooms. And in that mental image, the distress in Hedda's eyes seemed to grow as the end of the year approached…it was virtually impossible to forget the fearful gaze with which she scrutinized him; he couldn't look her in the face anymore, he always felt her gaze on the back of his neck. Only in a bar was he able to banish these thoughts from his mind; he accused himself of destroying Hedda's life, at least in part—she'd been safe with her boyfriend Gerhard and he'd come between them, he was horrified…he could only drown his self-hatred in floods of alcohol.

He was a typical product of the GDR—he told himself—both physically and psychologically, down to his brain cells and nerves, down to his unconscious reactions he was a result of the interim state that called itself the

GDR…and it was impossible to live with that! – And because he couldn't live with it, everyone who crossed his path was compulsively dragged into his non-life. He was one of the human stopgaps from whom the GDR was assembled, the very precondition for its existence, people who were constantly insisting on their idiosyncrasies and their *self*, the same way the government of that country had the word "sovereignty" hanging from its snout in a permanent speech bubble. In that country, sovereignty was the very last thing you had. – And even if I managed to decide to stay in the West now, thought C., it would probably be too late…

On the phone he told Hedda that he had the notion that the visa didn't have to be restricted to the one stipulated year. It's hard to explain, but this could be a chance to look back at my past…if I returned to the GDR, I'd settle back down into my past. But now I can visit my past by drifting back from time to time, I suddenly have temporary emigrations to my past. I feel as if I'd only just now gotten the authorization for them.

Will you be able to live with what you find in your past? asked Hedda; it struck him as an odd question.

I don't know yet. It's as if I were looking down a mountain…or more like a slope. In my childhood there were slopes like that, slag heaps. And it's getting dark, I can't make out anything below, but it has something to do with me, there's no doubt about that. I know quite well that it's unpleasant or even horrifying, dangerous, the thing that's waiting for me if I go down. I'm afraid of what I'll have to see, I'm worried I'll never return from down there…

Is down there where the idea of the interim comes from? Hedda asked.

There's nothing solid there, at any rate, nothing you could cling to or build on, there's nothing but brutality, lies, and evasion, the only sure thing is loss. It's the swarming of an awful squalor...

That's a strange dream, she said.

What kind of a time was it, then, when he'd written only for himself? He had trouble remembering, there was a mechanism of suppression blocking it. – I'd written even before that, from my childhood onward, but always in secret, he told her. And writing in secret makes for a weird picture in itself. As a child I was a puny, underdeveloped champion of fear...the fear of silence. The hell of that childhood was wordless, mute, its nature was silence. And I began to fill that silent hell with words...with a tiny teaspoon, the little spoon from a child's tea set, I began shoveling words into a vast empty hall of silence... what a disappointment! And it seems to me that I ended up by hiding my writing even from myself. Then when I became an industrial worker, I kept trying to go on writing in secret...and those years seem to me like one big era of lies...

Back then he'd sometimes wondered whether writing might actually be his calling...that was the sort of thing you'd read about, it was how writers justified the existence of even the dullest books. But who could have issued the call? After all, he'd always written (perhaps absently missing the call), writing in surfeited childish disgust, disgust with himself, burdened by his endless afternoons in the empty summertime apartment. Wearied by the pen scratching the dry paper, he'd felt his eyelids drooping, but he went on writing, and so he'd floated onward through the slowly drifting air that seemed tinged in the evenings by suns already past...

Suddenly one day he had woken from that absent state. After finishing a three-year apprenticeship, he unexpectedly found himself in a world from which there seemed no escape. He didn't know quite what had startled him awake: he was in an enormous machine hall filled by a din like a tank convoy on the move. He realized that he was right out on the production front. It was the crucial front in the state's battle against its demise, you couldn't escape it, at least not unscathed; here the most you could do was move between the different front sectors. Looking up, he saw that he was planted in front of a gigantic gray-green horizontal boring mill: for a time, one or two months, he was supposed to observe and be part of the workflow at this machine until he understood enough about the piecework system and until he was able to insert himself into the complex structure of the mutually dependent operations, so that he could then be deployed at a similar machine, beginning with a much smaller one. He saw the man who was operating the giant boring mill: a wiry figure somewhere between fifty and sixty, with a wrinkled, shuttered face whose piercing little eyes followed the workflow at the machine with the quickness of a weasel, never missing a thing. Five times a day the man would poke him in the arm with the handle of a hammer, jabs that would keep getting harder and more frequent because C. kept falling asleep on his feet, leaning against the table of the boring mill. They took their breakfast and lunch breaks without interrupting the running of the machine; never taking their eyes off it, they'd sit on a bench between the tool shelves; C. only drank soda, while the man drank beer (which was against the rules) and ate salami sandwiches whose soft pale bread slices showed his black fingerprints, a mixture of lubricant and gray iron dust; C. watched the man eat his sandwiches with relish, regardless of the fingerprints, and thought: Couldn't he at least eat darker bread? – A short time passed, and C. was eating sandwiches with black lube spots too. For eight hours the man would hardly speak a word, and C. was silent the whole time as well, wordlessly performing the few maneuvers that the man dictated with a turn of his head or a look from his angry eyes. Once, after another poke from the hammer, C. opened his eyes and turned his face toward the man; though unconscious of the look he was expressing, he saw the man turn deathly pale and stagger back in an attack of fear. The man spent the rest of the shift hiding behind the machine; the next day C. was transferred to the smallest boring mill at the edge of the hall, where he had to produce an endless, monotonous series of tiny simple workpieces, slave labor with the shortest conceivable per-piece times, leaving him not a minute to glance up for eight hours in a row. Later he was suddenly horrified at himself: it was his first realization that he'd come within a hair's breadth of committing murder.

He'd spent three years as an apprentice learning the same profession as that taciturn man with the wrinkled dyspeptic face: he was a *boring mill operator* and thus one of the elite technicians in the factory's machine shop. How had he even managed to learn the profession? He could hardly remember a thing about his three-year apprenticeship…what remained was the recollection of clashes with the instructors, when he'd been publicly pilloried. Ultimately, the only thing he'd learned during his

apprenticeship was how to keep on growing lonelier...
he'd started on that path in his childhood. During the
apprenticeship he continued down his path into loneliness without ever turning back...

Of course he could never call that state by its name;
the very word *loneliness* filled him with horror. He knew
it was a state he had to start fighting against immediately;
it was hostile to life and humanity. When that loneliness
filtered through to his consciousness, he'd have to start
a war against it—a war against himself—perhaps a life-
long war, in which he'd be fighting a lost cause from the
outset...

In the years of his apprenticeship, he recalled, he'd
always feared insanity. He kept reading books in which
insanity played a role...and he kept seeming to observe
the symptoms of insanity in himself. On the one hand he
felt a certain masochistic satisfaction when he found those
signs, on the other hand they frightened him. And he also
worried when the symptoms weren't there...then he felt
entitled to nothing more than the preordained existence
of a perfectly average worker. – But he kept detecting
those symptoms, they'd recur; he had to keep them under
control, for no one could be allowed to notice them...that
made him unapproachable, impenetrable, impregnable.

The apprenticeship was the last stage before embark-
ing on his fate as an industrial worker, his odyssey through
a multitude of factories and construction sites, moving
back and forth from one to another, largely against his
will. It was the odyssey of an isolated man amid the yelling, conniving, compulsively slaving masses with which
he tried vainly to connect. – After getting away from the
boring mill, which didn't leave him a minute to think, the

first thing he did was apply to transfer to the machinists in the fitting shop, where he'd earn two hundred marks less; after a long struggle he got his way.

He'd suppressed a great deal from that period, leaving his memory groping in the dark. When he tried to penetrate the darkness, he instantly came up against feelings of guilt that made him recoil in alarm. – To talk about this, he said to Hedda, I'll have to talk about a time of lies. The roots lie in the atmosphere of those years.

It was the time when the country he lived in had developed into the *GDR*, ten years after it had been given that name; the abbreviation suppressed the word Germany, even as the entity went on functioning as a sector of Germany. That function waned and waned, however, until it lapsed entirely: the symbol of that being the walling-in of the GDR. – During that period the things he wrote about had taken form: a process, it seemed to him, that had not only been attended by mendacity, but virtually pervaded by it, subverted in a manner no longer to be resolved. When he occasionally stopped to think, he had the impression that his entire existence consisted of pretenses, a perpetual enactment of deceptive maneuvers behind which the truth content of his mental state was vanishingly small. And because the truth was lost, he ultimately found himself in a position to mistake his own deceptive maneuvers for the truth. He found himself induced to believe his own untruths, forced to act according to prompts from his own imagination, no longer sure whether his thoughts had arisen from a sequence of falsehoods or whether they weren't ultimately based on some remote truth lost along circuitous paths. – He recalled the verbal fusillades that Stalinist cultural functionaries directed against writers and intellectuals who had fallen out of favor: if that invective applied to anyone, it would have been him; in his case they would have hit home, because at that time perhaps he really was a *parasite*. – In the end the only way he could see himself was as someone in retreat, he said. Fleeing from a world that regarded his desire to write with incomprehension, if not outright hostility…

As if that didn't happen to every writer, said Hedda. As if every writer hasn't once had to live with the feeling that the world wants everything and everyone with the sole exception of you…

To this day I suspect that I was acting like that on purpose, without actually having the right to, he explained. Maybe it didn't even have to be that way, maybe I didn't even have to be retreating. – He said it was hard to describe, how he kept looking for a way out via the warren of lies and tricks into which he'd maneuvered himself…the only path back out seemed, once again, to lead through lies.

Only through lies, yet again?

Apparently there was no other option for him, eighteen or nineteen years old at the time. Or he would have needed some awareness of his function as a writer, even at that age. Wouldn't that have been asking a bit much? He would have had to have some inner mission, but that was impossible, given his origins. How could he suddenly explain that he felt out of place in the factory, that his real aim was to become a poet? He would have had to grasp that he had that sort of propensity in the first place. In what way might he have learned that, by what yardstick might he have gauged it?

He had woken up in the racket of that industrial

hall and realized that he couldn't continue his journey. His journey in his head, his journey through dreams, that lonely child's journey that he'd embarked on years before…

He recalled leafing for hours through a little literature lexicon containing brief biographies of a whole range of poets and writers. There were several pages of portraits of the best-known writers, the size of passport photos, lined up side by side. In not one of the pictures could he detect the slightest similarity to his face. Nothing of what he took to be the characteristics of a poet could be compared, even with careful modification, to any trait of his. The poets possessed lofty brows, narrow aquiline noses, prominent cheekbones, and big wide-open eyes whose gaze perfectly fit the mode of their poetry, either veiled or glass-clear…he presented quite a different picture: his eyes were narrowed to a slit, peering out from behind a protective wall of pretense. And he showed no symptoms of the illnesses of the poets that you could read so much about: they suffered from consumption or syphilis, had too many white blood cells or too few, were menaced by strokes or mental derangement. For him it was just the opposite: his body was filled with raw, indestructible, practically implacable health; he wasn't cold in the winter, nor did he sweat in the summer; his eyes could make out the tiniest letters on the chart on the optician's wall; time after time he'd been called up to the front of the classroom to demonstrate exemplary breathing techniques with the smooth workings of his abdominal muscles. He wasn't admired for what he wrote (no one knew anything about that), but for his athletic achievements, for which he was known throughout town. There wasn't a single swimming competition from which he didn't emerge as the victor; his adversaries were beaten the moment he entered the water; one time, on the cinder track in the town stadium, he'd finished second in the hundred-yard dash, by a hair, because he'd been daydreaming and missed the starting shot, and years later he was still fretting over the defeat; in his gymnastics club he was the first one to do complete circles on the pommel horse; in boxing matches he knocked opponent after opponent out of the ring even while he was still working as an apprentice, and later on he joined the town boxing team.

All that was merely the apparent truth, it was the façade, he'd told himself, the insignia of a false life. – He had reached a point where he'd had to recognize the show of that earlier life as a lie. And it was a recognition that nearly killed him…

All that he'd been in that earlier life was gradually crushed, picked to pieces, pulverized—that was the impression that lingered from that time. If ever he met a person who showed any kind of interest in him—he wasn't even talking about signs of affection—he failed to notice; all the senses within him that could have registered such a thing had been torn out. All possible ways of reacting to love had shrunk back to nothingness; everything inside him was geared toward defenses, barricades, armor, and each avenue approaching him was blocked by a labyrinth of lies and deceit. And the reason for all that was to gain a little, tiny piece of free time…a piece of time left over that no one had noticed, that belonged to him, in which he was undisturbed, the use of which no one would ask him about, a piece of time in which by chance he'd find a path to himself, a piece of time snatched from the eight-hour

workday, or snatched from the eight hours of his leisure time in which he was paralyzed, dead, or engaged
in a desperate, futile search for himself, that he snatched
from his eight hours of sleep…a piece of time that had
been forgotten and lay unused, unnoticed alongside the
twenty-four-hour day…a piece of time that he robbed
from the production front, that he pilfered from the Cold
War, from his government, the self-sacrificing elders in his
so-called family, that he carved from the flesh of inanity,
that he stole from the People's Police and the army, that
he snatched from the Free German Youth, the Society
for German-Soviet Friendship, the steadfast solidarity of
the sister nations at his side, the millions embracing and
longing ardently for peace, a piece of time that didn't exist,
that he had still managed to find somewhere and to flee
with from Stalin's prosecutor Andrei Vyshinsky…time in
which he could quickly cover an empty page with a text
that he somehow extracted from himself.

I am a poet! He occasionally had the presumption to
make that inward claim. – The next moment the thought
would alarm him, because it called for proof that didn't
exist. In fact it would have called for two proofs: one to
show to the world and one to show to himself…taken
together, they would have been tantamount to a proof of
God's existence. But as everyone knows, there is no such
thing.

And God was silent on these matters, as he'd always
been. At least he made no objections, and that was as
much as could be hoped for. And God even seemed to
overlook his lies; evidently he weighed truth and lies on
different scales.

It was impossible to find a common denominator for

what made a poet. Except perhaps for the inner unrest that distinguished all of them, that all bar none seemed to know, at least in a certain segment of their lives. It was known to be found even in one who never moved from the spot, who left his four walls only when it couldn't be helped. In a character like that, the inner unrest was even more powerfully at work, now accompanied by the consciousness that you could never get rid of that unrest by giving in to it—by moving place to place as many others did, as though that could answer the perpetually recurring question of whether or not you were *free... Freedom*, you thought you knew what that meant, but if you tried to express it, the magic word resisted every explanation. And yet the word was typical of writers: they had to be free (whatever that meant), independent, so that they could freely chase their inspiration. They were constantly on the trail of that inspiration—perpetual travelers or wanderers, or at least they were walkers, lonely walkers. Aimless, yet always alert and attentive, they wandered the cities, or left the cities behind them to ramble through the countryside until they were lost in the twilight.

One mental image that fascinated him, that he thought he would never forget, was a young man striding in the last light of evening along a barren ridge. He was visible only in silhouette, the wind beat in his face, his coattails fluttered, he held his hat clapped to his head. Bent over, he climbed higher and higher until he appeared at the very top of the hill; now he gazed around, and into the abyss below his feet; bare bushes lashed him with their switches, and behind him tattered clouds swept on toward the fading light. – C. wanted to describe an image like that...he'd begun many of his writing attempts with that image.

There was another image he tried his hand at just as often: A line of little boats heading into a bay, evidently from a sailing ship anchored out at sea. They headed into the semicircular bay, making for the beach; now and then their silhouettes seemed to dissolve as they crossed the broad track of shimmering light the low sun cast across the water, seeming to set it on fire.

Presumably there were dozens of scribbled pages that began with similar images. They were buried in forgotten, yellowed notebooks that he'd hidden somewhere and could no longer find. These irretrievable images occupied his imagination, but there was nothing he could do with them, nor with the images of sunsets that had passed, but whose light still underlay the darkness.

Thanks to his iron constitution, he could be assigned all kinds of work, the doctors increasingly refused to give him sick leave, and he acquired the reputation of a malingerer...which in most cases he was... Since he tried to shirk work as often as possible, they always kept an eye on him at the factory, rarely leaving him unattended; his superiors charged him with tasks where he couldn't escape their scrutiny...he felt hounded, got drawn into irresolvable disputes with his foremen and unit managers, squirming in front of them in a web of excuses and lies... when asked the reason for his slacking, he had no reply but lies...

If he'd stuck to the truth, if he'd said that he was occupied nonstop with thinking about his attempts to write, they would have given him the reply he anticipated (and occasionally received): In your free time you can do whatever you want, but not during work hours! – There was no escaping that reply, and it was exactly what he would have told himself, if he'd been taking the needs of the factory into consideration...

And when he asked himself why his free time wasn't enough to write in, why it wasn't long enough for him, he felt like a liar in his own eyes. After all, in his afternoons and evenings he easily produced pages at a time, writing in a surge of emotion in which he himself hardly seemed involved...and afterward he couldn't believe the things that had appeared so fluently, so unresistingly on the paper. And with that he provided the very proof that his free time did suffice to write in.

He was chasing some chimera, some proof that he was a *real* writer...he was chasing after some unreal notion, a phantom, an idealized figure from the past. No one would have believed he was a real writer, no one believed it of him, no one could believe it, not with all the will in the world, and he didn't believe it himself. And yet he wrote several pages almost every day...maybe writing those pages wasn't really what this was about for him, he was a liar...

The texts he wrote that way deepened his unbelief still further; they were rooted in the void he felt himself to be. They sought to give expression to his nonexistence, or even to exaggerate it by utterly renouncing the solid ground of reality; their rudimentary plots played out in invented surroundings where neither light nor darkness prevailed, where a shadowy figure, isolated and aimless, hurried past other shadows through the fantastic landscapes of a shadowy existence, and that figure was concerned solely with its own dissolution. – No wonder editors sent these writings back indignantly if he ever submitted them anywhere. – And those rejections were further proof that the idea of being a poet was hubristic, that it was based on a tangle of lies…

The rejection letters he received from East Germany's literary editors were dictated by appalling mental laziness…it took him an extremely long time to be able to say that. They advised him to look for a decent job already… and later, when he'd started publishing in the West, he encountered the same thoughtlessness from the other side. They were impressed that he'd gone into the bondage of the East German workplace, that he'd submitted: for him the recommendation to look for a decent job had been tantamount to proposing suicide. He still didn't know quite how he'd weathered that assault against his self, or whether he even had weathered it, and now people wanted to give him a bonus for "certainly not looking like a writer" (that was the basic tone of the reviews he read in the West), that he didn't have anything "delicate, cerebral, or coddled" about him… What crudity, what anti-intellectualism! he thought. The reviewer who'd written that, she couldn't have known that he was still fleeing from the life that had forced that visage upon him. The little intellect he had was still on the run from the death chambers of industry, he was still in the process of breaking from the life in which money was earned with honest labor…

One question remained unanswerable: Why hadn't he tried more systematically, more seriously to liberate himself from that life, instead of hiding in a labyrinth of subterfuges? Why had he kept on participating, why had he never actually *gone on strike*? – He was left on his own with that question, the sole idiot in his story…

Some mornings he'd sink down on one of the wooden benches that stood between the rows of lockers in the overheated changing room. The room would be empty; in these first few minutes after the shift had begun, it would still smell of the half a hundred workers who had just sloughed off the remnants of their nocturnal warmth and gotten into their clammy oily clothes to go down to the halls, growling like snappish dogs, and disperse behind their workbenches or their machines. He'd be left behind on the upper level of the changing rooms, perhaps hiding in the adjoining baths; the last of the other workers would turn out the light as he left. Down in the hall the rhythmic punching of the time clock could still be heard, where the punctual herd stood in a long, winding line; meanwhile the first howling noises were already rising, the machines were being switched on, their distinct voices merging to a triumphant roar that shook the factory to its foundations.

The factory howled as though an arsenal of airplane motors had revved up. – In the upper level of the changing rooms there were several windows into the halls—former skylights, as the changing rooms and baths had been added to the building later on—one of which could be forced open; C. climbed onto a bench and looked down into the three halls separated only by the pillars of the craneways. Down there, under the pall of noise, under clouds of oil fumes and iron dust, the productive forces swarmed like the seeming chaos of an ant colony…and he was looking down on it from above.

He climbed down from the bench, and as he turned around he happened to glance at one of the mirrors that hung in the changing room. – It isn't true, he said, recognizing his haggard face, it's the other way around! This world of work, the factory, the economy, this world of progress is the lie and the deception. But what I write won't be a lie, and you'll vouch for that, nameless God!

Then he left the factory, going out into the still-dark town…at that hour there was hardly a soul on the street. Work had begun in the factories, and before the shops opened the town was still, dark, and empty; the winter cold, with dawn looming, was aggressive and keen; he shivered under his thin work clothes, sensing that he was growing weak and would soon have no choice but to flee back inside the factory…they'd catch him as he slunk back to his work station (to warm himself up, to shake off his loneliness); again he'd have to talk his way out of it some-how, again he'd have to come up with lies…his life as a poet was built on lies, his stories and poems were based on lies…perhaps it was even a lie that he was alive! And he looked up toward God, he begged the creative force of the heavens to lend support to his lies. He called on God to turn away from the universally visible truth and back up his lies…

When the cold refused to let up, he was transferred to the stokers in the boiler room. Only for four weeks, they promised him, but when the month was over they didn't summon him back. The stokers were understaffed, and the winter was shaping up to be a long one, the ther-mometer seemed to have frozen solid at a point far below zero; during long periods of sub-zero weather, the boilers had to be stoked for three shifts a day without interrup-tion even on the weekends. After a while he realized he'd been detailed to the boiler room because they didn't know what to do with him up in the fitting shop. – C. soon found that it was best if the boiler produced the highest steam pressure between three and four in the morning, meaning that it was enough for him to put in the bulk of his boiler room work starting half an hour after midnight; it took good physical fitness, you had to be able to shovel coal at a truly frightening tempo. The other stokers shied away from those demands; they were happy to switch shifts with him, so for months he only worked the night shift, which suited him fine, and he settled into the arrangement…

At night the boiler room was the only living cell left beneath the fitting shop. Sometimes he passed like a sleepwalker through the deathly-still factory halls where the cold stars glittered through the tall glass façades. The snow behind the glass looked blue and seemed spread for all eternity across the lifeless hilly expanses that stretched up to the bare trees of the park behind the factory yard. In the darkness of the halls his footsteps crunched on metal filings, the tread of a ghost, preternaturally audible, echoing twice or three times over in that gigantic cathedral whose religion was labor. A few months ago he'd still worked here himself; now he knew of a cell filled with glowing energy that lurked in the beyond beneath the concrete floor, a cell under his command, and suddenly he'd become the cathedral's secret god.

When he came to work at nine thirty in the evening, he'd sit right down at the long, narrow table in the boiler room and start writing. Slowly his thoughts would think their way through the beginning of a story, then reach out faster and faster. He was always writing the same stories, with just a few variations, and they had no value to anyone but him. These stories were mostly set in the woods… in the woods of his childhood, which had seemed endless to him, and he tried to replicate that endlessness in these stories. You saw a solitary figure walking through the woods, up the hills, hills stretching out as though in an uneasy dream.

As in the poems of Nikolaus Lenau—a poet he'd often read in his not-so-distant youth, confounded, riveted, repelled, then smitten once again, unable to set him aside and forget him—the seasons played a key role in his texts, which refused all classification. An isolated figure strayed through the woods' arrested seasons; you didn't know what it had escaped from, for the world it fled was not depictable; the real world had grown so alien to that figure that all its senses were thwarted, it had sunk behind a shadowy terrain, and the fugitive no longer knew quite which world he'd come from. And now he was anxious to escape the desolation of the woods. They were weird tales with no rational basis, in which the inert woods breathed, hostile and forbidding.

Now that C. was working in manufacturing, the woods of his youth had receded into the distance; he sought desperately to surround himself with the vocabulary of those woods, but they were nothing but words now: trees and leaves, water and clouds, grass and swamps and autumn. Little by little the proof that his stories had any meaning slipped away from him. – He wrote faster and faster, but his characters never got anywhere, either because that would have lain beyond the realm of these stories' possibilities or because he ran out of time and had to stop writing in the middle. The next day there would seem to be no reason to go on writing the story.

While he wrote, the factory and all its meanings surrounded him. There was a shift in the frozen reality towering over him: all at once it was irrelevant whether the world showed him a face that was real or unreal. He saw himself immured in the crypt beneath a massive church with which his relations had broken off...in the cellar where he dwelled, you no longer corresponded with the administrators, you only corresponded with God...

Or it was as though he were sitting in the hull of an old steamship, in the energy center of a gigantic listing freighter where no one else lived but vigilant rats. He'd been given power over the heart of the steamship, his judgment determined whether that battered ship in need of an overhaul would stay the course to its distant destination. But it wasn't real power: the ocean's untamable water raced past the ship's sides, in his quivering cavern he heard its rush and din.

Then, in the morning, the first ray of light would reach him, he'd detect it with childish gratitude: from above, through a little window at ground level just beneath the sooty, scorched cellar ceiling, sun spilled in; the dust-dim, cobweb-hemmed square of glass flared with the light that was finally encroaching across the wet pavement of the factory yard. Now the night was over; he'd stagger home in the foggy morning light to sleep away the day—one of those stubborn spring days that refused to warm up. And in those autumn days that rapidly grew colder, it was still dark in the morning when he started on his way home. In the evening he headed back to work; the night had already begun, there was little life on the streets, the harsh night wind swept the last frail tissue of sleep from his brain. Beneath it the first fragments of sentences already lay exposed, needing only to be shaped. He had several hours to sit at the table, the long table that stood as though on swaying ground. He seemed to have deliberately chosen the narrow end of the table; from there he surveyed the whole room, keeping both the boiler and the entrance in view, and he wrote at last, with the long table tapering away in front of him, covered with a sea-green, darkly patterned oilcloth. It was astonishing how easy it was… strange, what endless preparations he'd needed for this almost effortless writing. When he'd written for a time, the present seemed thrust away, and he sat swaying, his feet hooked around the legs of the chair, as though in the hull of a ship at the bottom of a wave trough, where the rapid current carried him, where the organism of the sea throbbed beneath the floor.

Sometimes he had no idea what he'd written the night before. In the first few hours a story more than ten pages long had flowed onto the paper. Ten pages of an old grade-school exercise book with a light-gray cover already yellowed at the edges. He'd filled the ten pages almost without glancing up, in a kind of unbridled inspiration that refused to let the pen rest. He hadn't kept to the thin bluish ruling of the pages, the paper was covered densely up to the edges with hasty, forward-flowing waves of writing that grew smaller and smaller, toward the end barely legible.

Once the story was finished, with no more than the pause that the turning page granted him, he'd immediately begun a second story, since he still had half an hour left before he'd have to stoke the boiler. The second story had come into his head while he was still writing the first one…he pressed ahead with his writing until his task at the boilers could no longer be delayed. Then he hid the notebook in his yellow leather portfolio and began without delay to scrape the cinders from the fire grates. Atop the embers that remained he shoveled new coal…coal, coal, more and more coal, he was burning the Scythian woods of his childhood. Then he cleared the ash from the lower chambers of the furnace and adjusted the flue vents to ensure the optimal combustion rate. That was followed by quenching the ash and the cinders, which lay in great heaps in front of the boilers; the jet of water pierced the heaps, and at once the boiler room was filled with explosive plumes of steam, with fountains of still glowing ash; he stuck the metal nozzle of the hose into the mixture of ash and cinders, which instantly boiled up and—seething, spitting out smut and sparks—absorbed seemingly endless quantities of water, until at last the heap stopped smoldering. He turned off the water and shoveled the still-steaming material into an iron drum to move out of the boiler room using a crane; each night he had to move six to eight of those brim-full drums. Finally he cleaned the work area, sweeping the remains together, washing the concrete floor and the boiler fronts with the hose, letting the jet of water flood the oilcloth of the table as well, then washed off the windows, the tiles, the sink at the back wall. Then he went upstairs and took a shower himself.

When he came back, a milky cloud bank would be suspended beneath the cellar ceiling whose lights blazed out surreally. Drops of water trailed from the black lampshades, the whole boiler room was dripping and trickling with condensing steam, the puddles in front of the boilers mirrored a lurid glow, sparks hissed in them, red and white reflections sprayed the room with baffling fire. In the flues the fire had swelled to a roar, steady as a train or a ship's motor; from above, from the still-dark factory halls, lashing, echoing impacts could be heard as the steam shot through the pipes. Damp warmth filled the boiler room, an oppressive, subtropical warmth that smelled like a brooding moor. Billows of steam kept forming and resolving into moisture on the cellar ceiling; the roaring of the flue seemed to metamorphose into silence in the boilers, so the omnipresent murmur and trickle of the water could be heard... Rainforest! he thought. Somewhere behind the boilers a few crickets woke in the dark corners where they'd been hibernating and began their mechanical chirping. He sat back down at the table, took out the notebook he'd hidden in the yellow portfolio, and started writing again...

In late April 1986 he'd gone to Vienna for the first time to give a reading, and he'd been looking forward to it. – I love Vienna, he thought, for me it's a city of literature...but he was afraid of being disappointed the way he'd been in Paris several months before. And he was smarting from the fact that he'd had to leave Nuremberg again because Hedda's boyfriend Gerhard was back from his trip to Papua New Guinea. C. was back living in Hanau, where his drinking had become a full-time occupation. He told Hedda he'd use the time in Hanau to write, but she knew he wasn't doing any writing there. He didn't call her for weeks, telling himself he was worried that Gerhard would answer the phone; she'd asked him more than once if he wouldn't rather move to Nuremberg; he couldn't decide, he put off answering. As long as he stayed in Hanau, Hedda wouldn't find out what kind of figure he cut in reality...

Most of the books in the *Holocaust & Gulag* section were ones he'd bought in Hanau, and they were scattered all through the apartment. On the floor, on the armchairs, on the repulsively brown, scuffed sofa whose sagging seats had gone greasy black from years of use. Scattered among these books stood the bottles, always within reach: liquor bottles, wine bottles, beer bottles, most of them open, impregnating the rooms with a persistent haze of evaporating alcohol that seemed to cloud the daylight and nauseated him first thing in the morning. In the middle of the main room, amid the bottles and the toppled bookstacks, lay the mattress he'd removed from the unbearable bed and a heap of prickly wool blankets in whose tangle he slept...at completely odd times, whenever the alcohol happened to exhaust him. Sometimes he'd vomit from the mattress right after waking up...all he needed to do was slide his hammering skull to the mattress's edge and the undigested alcohol gushed silently from his gullet, stinking, the color of black blood, mixed with a few chunks of bread and unchewed slices of pickle...when he got his breath again, he'd use a book to wipe up the hellish swill that had gushed from his body and scrape it into a plastic bag; the book, from the *Holocaust & Gulag* section, would go straight along into the bag; usually he'd buy a new copy that very same day.

A further category of books that had joined the others littering the floor and among which he lived like a scuttling reptile were ones on various forms of psychotherapy and psychoanalysis (a book trend in the West as well, and he'd submitted to it); he felt judged by these books...he consulted them—perhaps a stupid idea—whenever he was brought to extremis by reading about the crimes of his century's dictatorships; these psychological books were no help, though. In them he merely reencountered his torments, and found confirmation of his suspicion that only precarious strokes of luck had kept him from becoming a tool of those dictatorships. His wretchedly provisional attitude toward life was all that had kept him from seizing the first rung of the ladder that led to atrocity...

These books meticulously pointed out the things that had shaped him; after reading them he'd feel as though a curse weighed him down...admittedly he rarely managed to read them all the way through, but with some unerring masochistic instinct he'd hit on the chapters swarming with paradigms that denied him any capacity for love.

It was as though he were combing those books to find a psychological logic according to which his love for Hedda was inevitably doomed to fail...

He knew that Hedda loved him and was waiting in Nuremberg for him; he knew that she desired him and was tormented by the fact that he couldn't be with her; he knew it, yet he was unable to surrender emotionally to that love. He sensed that he, too, harbored a desire for her, but he believed himself incapable of communicating that desire. No matter how he tried, a dissenting voice would instantly pipe up inside and accuse him of lying...and that dissenting voice was always lying in wait, with the force of an old, inherited curse. Every feeling of love that budded within him was instantly denounced by that voice and revealed as an attempted fraud...the Argus eyes of entire state religions seemed to be keeping watch over the sincerity of his feelings. He'd long since ceased to know when—whether in the beginning or the end or some-where in between—his feelings had ever been sincere. Inside himself he found no vessel that could, in good con-science, hold Hedda's love...evidently he stemmed from an inferior tribe, in which every attempt at communion rotted away into squalor...

He recalled his attempts to override that dissenting voice: it would let him have his way for a while, then seize a moment when he turned weak and label his revolt mere playacting...

When he couldn't write, only alcohol enabled him to tolerate himself. Now the alcohol and the psychotherapeutic literature (which he read with an obsessiveness resembling his alcoholism) had formed an alliance: he felt altogether subhuman, and had black and white proof of it.

He went to Vienna hoping to tear himself out of that state of mind for a few days, breathe different air, maybe even get an idea to write about; he arrived on the night of April 29. – He spent the whole next day wandering through the streets around his hotel, not far from St. Stephen's Cathedral; Vienna was muggy, already hot as summer. Quickly C. sensed the peculiarly oppressive mood that seemed to have seized the whole city; the restaurants were nearly all empty, the tables outside the cafés stood vacant in the sun, with only the occasional gust of wind ruffling the tablecloths. And the waiters standing in the doors in their traditional white aprons seemed to register those stirrings of air with particular suspicion: were they getting stronger or not, what direction was that wind coming from? – They gazed into the sky, whose blue was flawless, with just a few little white-gray puffs of cloud floating far off at the edge, not moving. Those little clouds seemed to be the focus of everyone's attention...

C. soon found out the reason for the tense mood: several days before, on April 26, in Chernobyl in the Ukraine, a nuclear reactor had gone up in flames, and the news coming out about the disaster was growing more and more horrifying. In his lair in Hanau he hadn't noticed a thing, but now the news finally reached him; it sounded like a catastrophe that no one could quite get their minds around yet.

What was the meaning of that incident in Chernobyl? – When C. thought about it later, he felt that on that April day in 1986 the world had experienced a *turning point*. The industrial age had experienced a turning point. The blind faith in humanity's technological progress had been shaken as never before, and it had happened within a political system that celebrated the notion of progress like no other. Belief in the world's controllability had suffered its heaviest blow to date…

Until just a few years ago he himself had been a figure from that industrial age, albeit one of its countless marginal figures. He was a character from a backward, obsolete epoch, he was a thing of the past…

As he walked through the streets, he had the impression that all of Vienna was waiting for evacuation measures to take effect. People hurried down the streets around St. Stephan's as though under some incalculable threat; they ventured outdoors only on essential errands and then shut themselves up in their houses again. Meteorologists voiced the conjecture that the next rain to fall on Vienna would come from clouds that had passed over southeastern Europe, and hence would be radioactive.

On the evening of April 30 he had to give his reading in a small auditorium resembling a theater foyer; and he'd been announced as a writer from the GDR—in other words, from a country with the same political system as the one that had caused the catastrophe of Chernobyl. He sat at a podium slightly elevated above an audience of at most twenty people who fixed him with their perplexed gazes. He read three shortish passages, with interludes by a pianist playing a grand piano. In the middle of the second passage he had the creeping feeling that he was dishing out utterly alien gibberish. The people stared at him as though they expected him to explain or at least apologize for the disaster that the East had inflicted on humanity. In the last section, reading poems, he felt a sudden surge of defiance. He read more quickly, more loudly, barely pausing between pieces, ultimately hurling the poems into the audience with furious pathos as though he were shouting down dissenting voices before they were even raised. The audience, making a visible effort not to seem disrespectful, displayed stoical patience. The faces in the front rows were filled with astonishment and doubt, gradually hardening into resistance. The scattered, skeptical applause trickled off into the concluding piano music.

Late in the evening he walked through Vienna one more time; he lost his bearings and suddenly had no feel for the direction of his hotel. – He wanted to drink, that he sensed, but not in so-called pleasant company, not making conversation, receiving compliments and at pains to answer with the same; he wanted to drink the way he was accustomed to, speechless, dark, and hasty, until something came to life within him, until the beast from the forest that threatened to waste away inside him stirred and emerged from his eyes...

He came to a narrow street lit with loud colors, where insistent music blared from the doorways, where the usual swanky affectation of an entertainment district prevailed. Here people were still around; here, mostly in groups, roamed the restless and the addicted whom no global catastrophe could dismay. He had drunk enough by then, and managed to walk without hesitation into the first peep show he came to. In front of him the ring- and chain-laden hands of a bearded man with a gleaming bald pate turned the pages of an album where photos of scantily dressed girls were filed away. He tapped one of the pictures at random, not really looking, paid the specified sum, and was shown to a booth whose door he locked behind him. He was barely able to take a real look at the young woman performing her show in a set-piece interior behind a pane of glass barely a yard away. She'd invited him to sit down, but he remained standing, he even came a little closer to the glass, with a strange sense of duty vivid in his mind. He tried to look into her face, but the face revealed nothing but inaccessibility; it existed at a distance that could not be measured spatially…he was still seeking an explanation for this when, with natural grace, she removed the skimpy pieces of clothing she'd been wearing when she came in. – He wasn't here to look at her face, he thought, focusing on her body, on the breasts, on the thighs that smoothly stretched and spread…but suddenly he believed he no longer saw a thing. It was true, he saw nothing, it was as if one of his brain functions had been erased: he stared between her open thighs and couldn't see anything, no, that woman was invisible to him, death clutched him by the throat…

He went to the ticket booth, paid the sum again, and tapped the same picture in the proffered album. This time a barely perceptible smile seemed to play about the woman's mouth when she appeared behind the glass. The scene repeated itself, she began her mincing movements, she undressed; in front of him, a few inches behind a pane of bullet-proof glass, writhed a beautiful woman's body with its gleaming skin, and suddenly shadows crossed it, miasmas, everything blurred. He felt tears rise to his eyes, he clenched his teeth to get a hold of himself (he had no idea whether she could see him behind her glass), he bit the inside of his cheek until he tasted blood in his mouth, and then he left the show.

Outside, he leaned against the wall; a cold wind brushed his sweaty forehead, there was the smell of rain. He walked away from that district and into darker areas, hardly knowing what he had just experienced. – His senses had failed him; in the crucial moment he'd been struck with a kind of blindness. The body of a woman had offered itself to him: she turned, bent, crouched, but it had been impossible for him to make out her image; she had reached into her lap and opened her labia, that he knew, but he hadn't seen it…

He found himself near his hotel, more by chance, after a bafflingly short distance; a fine drizzle started, smelling more of dust than of water. Here, mid-block, the sidewalk passed beneath arcades, along rows of columns; he walked on under the arcades…and suddenly he recoiled. He was looking at a wall with closed window shutters, closed long ago, it seemed, from their peeling paint—at first glance the building looked like an old bankrupt theater—and on those shutters hung posters: with his face! – There were three or four windows at street level, and posters with his face were hung on all the double wings of the wooden shutters. With something approaching horror he turned away, and saw the same posters hung on the pillars behind him…they were the posters for his reading, which was already over.

Was it really his face? – It was his face, clearly recognizable, but the fact that it hung here, lined up in a row, was devoid of all verisimilitude. He couldn't say why it was, but he both could and could not recognize himself… maybe it wasn't his face after all? – No, that face on the posters had nothing to do with him…only through some inexplicable ill-fate had he, C., ended up behind that face, which had been photographed in an absurd mix-up and used on the posters for lack of a genuine likeness of him. The picture on the posters was the picture of a dead man…it wasn't possible that the life of that corpse had been his, his story, the one that lay behind him…

And I must end the story, there's no more point to it, he thought. I must put an end to this story at once.

I'm beaten, he thought, well then, my number's up. I'm beaten, it was bound to happen! – Finally he got kicked hard in the side, somewhere below the short ribs—at that point he'd already gone down—and passed out for some indefinite period of time. But he must have gotten kicked more; they were wearing the crude brutal footgear that fashion dictated, *boots*, they used the English word, yellowish suede things with treads. Once he managed, with effort, to pump air back into his lungs, he sat up on the pavement and felt the sore places on his body. He'd noticed one more thing before the stars in front of his eyes went dark: the hand of an unseen person slipping unerringly into the pocket of his leather jacket and pulling out his wallet.

Still sitting gloomily on the cobblestones, he gradually recalled how it had happened. He'd been walking home from a bar down narrow dark streets that some instinct had always warned him against, especially since they weren't much of a shortcut; he'd had quite a bit to drink, quite a bit too much—he was staggering down the middle of the street. Through the fog in his brain he'd heard rapid steps, two or three men were suddenly running after him, and before he'd quite registered it, there was a loud impact on the back of his head. He turned and swung his fists in the air, much too slowly, nothing but shadows before and behind him; a volley of blows rained down on his skull, wrenching him off his feet. Later he told himself he'd lain down on purpose to end things as painlessly as possible.

That had been about an hour after midnight; for an hour his birthday had been over. It was two by the time he got back to his apartment, where he took an ice-cold shower. Then he sat naked and shivering on a kitchen chair, smoking. Strangely, his hand kept reaching for the telephone, but there was no use dialing Hedda's number, he knew that; he'd already spent all evening trying, and that had just driven him madder and madder…

The day before had been his birthday, he'd turned forty-eight—not a day to celebrate, not particularly. Still, Hedda was disappointed because yet again he'd agreed to a reading that day… What are you getting excited about? I didn't forget your birthday this time, I forgot my own, he said. Besides, I'll be back by evening. – That was true; the reading was in a nearby village, a kind of artists' colony in a former farmstead, where a group of women were doing so-called painting therapy, thirty- to fifty-year-olds, several of whom knew Hedda, who had given them the idea of inviting him in the first place; they were offering a reading fee of six hundred marks, money he didn't want to pass up. – Why hadn't he suggested that Hedda come along, when she could even have driven him there and back in her car? If he honestly admitted to himself what had kept him from suggesting that, it was the fact that in the village he'd be reading to twenty-five women, no one but women. – The reading was scheduled for the afternoon; if he'd expedited things just a bit, he could easily have been back in Nuremberg by seven. But he hadn't gotten back to his apartment until twenty after ten.

Immediately he rushed to the phone to call Hedda; as the dial tone echoed from the receiver in relentless monotony before the switchboard terminated the clearly futile connection, he realized that something in the kitchen was altered. The whole time he'd been staring at that alteration with the shrilling receiver clamped to his head, hurting his ear: next to him, over the back of the second kitchen chair, hung his yellow leather jacket...

He hadn't worn the leather jacket in years; one day it had ended up over on Schillerplatz, where he'd left it hanging in Hedda's closet...

Now it was here, hanging over the chair and lending the kitchen its shabby yellow cast...why did he suddenly think this jacket was giving off a barely perceptible whiff of chloroform...?

He took an open bottle of liquor from the refrigerator and drained the remnants in one swallow. In that instant he realized that he hadn't checked his mail yet...

He dialed Hedda's number again, but hung up before it rang. Like an automaton, with precise but remote-controlled movements, he took all his things from the light summer jacket he'd been wearing, then put on the leather jacket and filled its pockets with that paraphernalia he always carried around with him: cigarettes, lighter, passport, reading glasses, and wallet. Carelessly, he put his wallet in the leather jacket's tight, narrow side pocket, where it practically stuck out a bit...

At the pub he'd rapidly tossed back beer and liquor. He stood at the bar, keeping the bartender almost uninterruptedly busy; there weren't quite two hours left until he'd stop serving, and C.'s inner unrest was so powerful that each glass of alcohol seemed to sizzle in it like a drop of water in a forge. Behind him was the smoke and racket of the overfilled pub; the babble of voices, vying with the disco music tootling from the loudspeakers, made him increasingly nervous. From time to time, after every other glass, he'd go to the telephone—there was a pay phone on the wall by the restroom—and give Hedda a call. Each time the phone spat his ten-pfennig piece back out again...

Whatever else had gone on at the bar was plunged in darkness, the images were tangled, distorted and unstable, he had considerable gaps in his memory...all he remembered was that when he tossed a fifty-mark bill onto the counter to pay his tab, the barman had stared at him with raised eyebrows. He had to put down another twenty to get any change back...

Later he thought he recalled that each time he'd returned from the phone to the bar, a table of young men near the exit had fallen silent; they seemed to stare at him inquisitively as he staggered past. But he hadn't paid any attention...

He found that change—a crumpled ten-mark bill, still damp from the barman's dripping hands, and a few coins—in the pocket of his pants. Limping around, he searched his apartment for money, finding a few coins here and there, on the windowsill and desk...when he thought he had enough for a bottle of the cheapest booze and a pack of cigarettes, he got dressed and headed for Friedrich-Ebert-Platz, where there were several French-fry stands and beverage kiosks run by Turks, one of which was open all night; the police tolerated it, because that way they knew where the bums would congregate…

Returning with the bottle in his hand, he ignored his mailbox a second time. He was afraid of finding his duplicate key there, the one he'd given to Hedda…

Most of the so-called bums were found at the train station, despite the greater risks they seemed to be exposed to there; the nights were warmer in the spacious underground passages than near the kiosks on Friedrich-Ebert-Platz. – C. sat on a staircase, watching them furtively; he had a staircase all to himself, he didn't belong to them, they paid him no mind. His fate was nothing compared to what they'd gone through: he'd been ditched by his woman, that was all. Maybe the same thing had happened to some of them once, but afterward they'd gone downhill so quickly that the original reason was already forgotten. They'd stopped thinking about how alone they were, they didn't even notice anymore. The majority of them were men (not counting the packs of dogs that scuffled at their feet), but as a rule there'd be a few women too. C. felt a pang in the region of his heart as he watched them get ready to sleep, past midnight: two or three of the men bedded their unwashed, matted heads on a woman's lap, their bodies stretched on rolled-out strips of corrugated cardboard. The woman enfolded the men's heads as best she could between her breasts that dangled in a filthy blouse, and a smile appeared on her puffy face; she nursed a cigarette and drank from a can of beer; the men gave satisfied grunts and dozed off. The others formed a circle around the little group, settling as densely and comfortably as possible on the hard stone steps, and the dogs crawled into the gaps, producing a warm heap of animals of indefinite species ingeniously fitting themselves together. Breathing, wheezing, whimpering, they rested, and the noises of their bodies were like a curious song in which all the notes were in tune with one another. C. hadn't been able to sleep in days, and for a brief moment he felt something approaching envy... Envy was a feeling that was constantly lurking within him, seizing him momentarily wherever he saw the least semblance of human warmth or closeness. A moment later he felt ashamed and made off down the narrow street. He walked across the castle rock and passed through the dark side streets near his apartment, where he peered warily to the left and right: clearly there was no need to worry about being mugged a second time now that they had what they'd wanted...

Much more than the streets, he dreaded his apartment, that cell split in three where he breathed dust and felt besieged by the tireless barks and yelps of the horde of squirming hounds below his back windows. Why hadn't he listened to Hedda and moved out long ago? Why hadn't he moved in with her? She'd kept suggesting that they look for an apartment together...

To fight back against the racket of the hounds, he played records for nights on end. The neighbors complained about that, though not about the yowling of those damned mutts; they were on good terms with the butcher next door. – Three or four times in a row he listened to the first album by the *Paul Butterfield Blues Band*, which he'd unearthed in a bargain bin on Breite Gasse several days before. The first song, written by Nick Gravenites, started with the lines "I was born in Chicago / in nineteen forty-one"; it must have seemed made for Paul Butterfield, who really was born in '41 in Chicago. He was dead now, and his guitarist, Mike Bloomfield, always clad in elegant suits, was dead too; orgies of alcohol and drugs were the cause. – C., born the same year as Butterfield, was still alive...

If he wasn't mistaken, he was still alive. After soaking himself brim-full with the blues on that record, he felt sick and went down to the street. He'd been having that feeling for weeks; every couple of hours he'd feel sick and filled with frantic unrest. A senseless frenzy came over him, and he couldn't tell whether it came from outside or emerged from inside him. When he got up to Schillerplatz, he saw that Hedda's windows were dark. There was no point in telling himself that there couldn't possibly be a light on at this hour...she was gone, there was no doubt left about that. She had vanished; she was having others deny any knowledge of her whereabouts...she'd given up, she'd probably stay vanished forever! Fortunately, no bars stayed open this late around here, so he was back in his apartment a short while later. By then the whimpering of the Cerberuses in the butcher's yard had quieted down. He didn't dare touch the liquor in the refrigerator...if he got the bottle out now, he wouldn't be able to make himself pour it down the sink; it had been going on like this for days. He had two blue Valiums left in his traveling bag; if he halved them, and things went well, he could get some sleep for the next four days...

The signs were unmistakable: the yellow jacket over the back of the chair, the key in the mailbox, no word of explanation, no farewell letter; it was the cleanest break you could imagine. – For days he'd phoned all over the place like a madman, coughing, out of breath, acting like a total nuisance; meanwhile, his ribs were growing back together again and the swelling on his face was subsiding. Once he could get his breath a bit, he would hurl himself down on his mattress every night and bellow with pain; he couldn't cry, so he squealed like a stuck pig; it was a miracle that no one called the police on him. – It really did seem that Hedda hadn't told anyone where she'd fled to; all her friends claimed to be equally mystified. He thought of Munich, it was quite possible that she was staying in Munich, lately she'd been writing something set there. But her friends in Munich had nothing to report either; C. asked them to call Gerhard, Hedda's ex-boyfriend, for him; they promised to do it, then didn't call back. The next day they said Gerhard didn't know anything either. – He just doesn't want to know, C. yelled into the phone, he's just pretending… – No, they said, that's not how he sounded, he was worried and distraught…

Then the woman on Kobergerstrasse whose light was always on at night mentioned the word *Haar*. – C. hung up, sat down at the kitchen table, and tried to think (meanwhile the agile beasts in the yard were yowling more shrilly): Could Hedda have checked herself into the clinic in Haar…where he himself had once undergone withdrawal treatment? He knew it was on Hedda's recommendation that his acquaintances in Munich had persuaded him to take that step. – He suddenly remembered occasional hints on Hedda's part that the thought was not alien to her. – When all else fails, there's always the psych ward, she'd said once before; she was talking about the anxiety attacks she felt dogged by. Her anxieties, he suddenly realized, had been so bad that he'd once nearly cancelled a reading so that he could stay with her in Nuremberg; at the last moment, tormented by guilt, he'd gone anyway. Toward the end she'd been quite good at hiding those anxieties from him; she'd lulled him into a sense of security...I'm doing better than you think! Words like that were still echoing in his ears. – On the evening before his afternoon reading to the women's painting-therapy group, an argument broke out: She didn't even factor into his thoughts anymore, she charged. – He could easily have cancelled the reading, his birthday provided an excuse. But the six-hundred-mark fee had been more important to him. Returning to his apartment after the argument, he'd been worried—it seemed to him he'd left Hedda in some strange kind of distress. Were her anxieties returning...had she felt unable to be alone that night and the day after?

It was too late to answer that question. And the six hundred marks were gone as well; he clearly remembered the moment when the hand slipped into the pocket of his yellow leather jacket and pulled out his wallet. He didn't care about the money; he'd been too busy coping with the kicks that were slamming into his lower body... He'd feared for his life.

At that moment he hadn't realized that he feared a life without Hedda...

One night about a month before that, on one of his benders, he'd strayed into the so-called red-light district near the train station, ending up at a sort of pub where he sat at the bar and stared at a TV screen that was reeling off scene after scene of copulation; he felt embarrassed by his situation, as clearly no one besides him was paying any attention to the screen. He was distracted by a young woman who asked if he'd buy her a drink; she was evidently one of the several scantily dressed ladies hired by the bar to encourage solitary male guests to drink. He found himself with her and the sparkling wine she'd ordered in a so-called séparée, a red plush hole in the wall crammed full with a corner sofa and round table. In that dimly lit cave, curtained off from the outside, he'd been so taciturn that she finally asked what he wanted here, anyway. – I want to see your breasts, he said. – She said that would cost him another round of sparkling wine. – He couldn't remember whether she fulfilled his request; the third time she sent him out for sparkling wine, he'd gone to the toilet, seen that the stairwell was empty, and seized the opportunity to sneak out of the bar…

He had no further memories of that night; he couldn't even find the street with the bar. Ever since being attacked, he kept an eye out on the streets for characters he might have encountered in that bar, hustler types, he called them. They'd come and taken the money he'd cheated them out of, taken it twice, almost three times, over. But that was just speculation, in reality he knew nothing. And there were plenty of those types in the city; somehow they all looked the same, despite their colorful getups: flowered shirts, golden chains on their chests and wrists, moustaches and colorful tattoos; they always had fresh haircuts, and always seemed to be coming straight from the tanning salon or the massage parlor. It was pointless to give them a wide berth, the whole city was full of them…

A peculiar apathy began spreading inside him, seemingly due to the fact that he was spending more and more time sober. He forbade himself from drinking, telling himself that he simply had to fight his way to lucidity. In his sleepless nights on the mattress, sweating and plagued by bouts of nausea, he realized he was more preoccupied

with alcohol withdrawal than with losing Hedda. He'd
barely thought of her all day, nor the day before, perhaps not even the day before that. Only now and then
would that mania seize him, and he'd start abusing the
telephone. He'd call her apartment on Schillerplatz for
half an hour on end, at the point of cracking up, a state
he'd emerge from more exhausted than he'd ever been
before... Even after shoveling tons of coal he'd never
been that spent, he told himself. He lay on the mattress
unable to move, while panicky thoughts chased each other
in his head, long series of self-reproaches with which he
smashed his consciousness to pieces: Why hadn't he ever
gotten his act together and looked for an apartment with
her? Why couldn't he make a place for himself in this
world? Why hadn't he managed to break up with Mona in
time? Why hadn't he gone to Greece with Hedda?

Why hadn't he slept with her more often? And why
had he obsessed about other women instead? Why hadn't
he been able to talk to her about it? Why hadn't he loved
her...?

Current events were almost completely passing him
by; he registered some things now and then the way you
pick up marginal matters. He didn't read the newspaper,
didn't switch on the radio (he'd always gone to Hedda's to
watch television), and he didn't talk to his publisher on
the phone. He barely felt any surprise at the things he did
hear: embassies being occupied, masses of people leaving
the GDR, the opening of the Hungarian border, the West
German foreign minister visiting Prague. Demonstrations
in Leipzig, Berlin, and Dresden, the founding of new par-
ties in the GDR: New Forum, Democratic Awakening,
Social Democrats...the GDR's fortieth jubilee...the

Honecker government stepping down. – The events remained remote…or they filtered into him for a few moments, then slipped off again. Why was he so apathetic? Was it true that he hadn't loved her? Could it be that he just hadn't felt it? Hadn't realized it, because he was ignorant? Surely he had loved her to the best of his means, which were slender, perhaps too slender, but there had been love inside him, he knew that now. He wouldn't be talked out of it, he'd loved her despite his inadequacy…

Why hadn't he realized it? Why was he so alone, why were there no answers inside him? Why did he forget her birthday, why did he forget to call her…it was too late for that, it was over. – Oh, this capricious September!

The months passed, and they had nothing to do with him. Maybe he'd asked himself the wrong questions, maybe he should have asked whether he'd even ever lived. Whether he'd ever woken up to life. Always, as far back as he could think, it was as though he'd been half-sleeping, just about to wake up. And he couldn't wake up. But you had to be awake, you had to have lived to have any part in love. But he had yet to find out whether he had lived.

They were here now too, the beggars, the homeless, the so-called bums; they loitered outside the train station, they hunkered cross-legged on the stone floor of the tunnel leading to the trams, heads hanging, with white plastic cups set out holding a bit of small change. The ones outside the station doors weren't as humble as in Nuremberg or Frankfurt; scruffy Eastern Europeans grabbed you by the sleeve and gurgled repeatedly: *Pleaseplease money, Deutschmark please…*

You had to tear yourself away by force; when you looked them in the face, you saw they hadn't been members of the secret police; those guys were doing better, those guys were probably doing great. These here had been at most pitiful little informers.

Leipzig's main station had barely changed, not yet, but its façade was plastered with that mind-boggling flood of lettering that neutralized freedom of opinion— still new and unfamiliar—by leading straight to illiteracy: election posters as yet untouched by age; ads for all kinds of trinkets and trash; posters for stomach-turningly well-intentioned exhibition openings; flyers for saunas, partner massages, and courses in Asian healing or erotic arts. A great deal of paper washed off by the rain had been tracked far into the station, leaving trails slippery as soap. Inside, all the walls were thronged with flimsy wooden kiosks that seemed to be shoving each other aside; the masses of them made the station hall feel cramped. The fast-food sharks' kiosk culture had transformed the downtown area into a dump of makeshift shacks; everywhere it looked as though the trash collectors had been striking for weeks.

C. had no problem with anarchy, and not much of a problem with messes, but this wasn't anarchy, it was the dictatorship of haggling and idiocy. The small predacious fish had come first—the washed-up businessmen and the tricksters, the junk car salesmen and the bargain-mongers—and that had put such a damper on the East Germans' sense of freedom that now they wanted their Wall back. The big sharks were still waiting, they had time, they preferred to keep investing in Thailand for now; the word *Germany* dangled from their snouts, but clutched to their hearts were suitcases filled with stock certificates; back in 1933 they'd waited first to see what sort of plans that little dachshund with the funny black moustache had, and that had paid off. Now the East German police were joining forces with the young Nazis, or at least handling them with kid gloves, and the Reds were being pilloried everywhere, which was starting to improve the investment climate.

He had just been to see his mother; it was early March and still quite cold. He'd arrived in Leipzig that morning intending to catch the train for Berlin after visiting the Leipzig Book Fair. Then, though, he recalled his last visit to the Book Fair—the last one still held in the GDR, in the year that brought Germany's reunification—when he'd suddenly been racked by feelings of disgust and fled the exhibition hall; the scribblings of journalists, dissidents, and professional victims were creating a furor and being feted; meanwhile books by real writers weren't being pilfered from the stands anymore, lonely and foolish they gazed out from the shelves at their former audience.

Over the station was a tiny sun utterly devoid of warmth, glittering glaringly and piercingly white. Though it was a weekday, there was little activity outside the station, and inside, in the two great pillared halls, there was an echoing void; just a few drunk bums skulked around the beer and sausage stands, their noses peeking frozen blue from the tangles of their beards. – C. hauled his body full of black sloshing bile up to the upper level (along with his traveling bag, heavy with books, those old East German editions); people gave him a wide berth, you could see right away that he had the evil eye. He plunked his bag down in the middle of the broad rectangular space at the end of the train platforms. The clocks to the left and the right, on the east and west sides of the station (a terminus station, a thing that had always seemed blatantly symbolic, but that was a thing of the past), showed different times (though it had to be around nine); their innards had turned sclerotic from the dry fumes and filth, and they hiccupped, at the point of a heart attack; from some far distant unseen corner of this continent of a station the blows of a jackhammer lashed out with a hiss, shot up along the roof without an echo, much too quiet to count as noise, but the pigeons reacted as though pursued by rifle fire. Other than that, the icy hall was empty and still.

He'd pictured himself lying up on the roof sometimes, in the fantasies of rage and anger that helped him fall asleep, lying up at the very front, at the upper edge of the façade, hidden behind the stone embellishments and frills, behind a machine gun aimed at the city; he gazed through the sights at the admonishingly raised finger of the Karl Marx University (where he, a member of the *proletariat*, had been shown the door one time when he came to see his girlfriend Mona...), or he aimed the barrel of the gun at the monstrous modern building where the Stasi had its headquarters (according to legend, they had built the block nine stories down into the ground so the torture computers could work undisturbed); and sometimes even now he saw the smoke of the city from that vantage, how it streamed dark and aimless in all directions, with tangled skeins of little dark birds lingering in it as though to warm themselves, those unidentifiable urban birds gone mad.

The station was as empty as his dreams. The early trains no longer ran these days; the last, late trains no longer ran either. And at this hour all the trains taking workers to their shifts had already left; they weren't packed, as they'd once been. They were just barely occupied, for there was no longer that plethora of factories to distribute them among (and why should there be, now, at the end of the industrial age?). But they still pulled out of the station, with a rumbling of iron, out through the arched portal past the end of the platforms, into the open, into the light, where the delta of the tracks fanned out. C. had been left behind by himself...he was no longer a worker, and that blackened his name; grief clouded his heart. Grief that wafted into his heart from the gloom beneath the station vault, mingled with the incomparable smell that old stations have emanated for a century. It was the smell of shabby old dark-green trains that have already pulled out of the station. The smell of their rust-red iron chassis, their smell of old grease and bitter dust. Train cars stranded a long time between stations, on out-of-the-way, forgotten lines, in steppes, in forests, on old, strange-smelling tracks; cars that have taken on the smell of the old gravel spread between the ties, black and gray, oil-smeared and sand-crusted, and the smell of old waterproofed wooden ties, with the desert swathes of gravel between them, old black granite with its salt taste, with its smell of welding flames. Granite that the old cars, brought back at last from oblivion, carried back to the stations, so that the stations smell of desert, of gravel...of coal, of earth, of the filth of the ramps and platforms across which life's animal and human flesh has been shunted and loaded. Of endless routes of gravel, crossing the lands and finally petering out in the sea. And so the trains passing over the gravel carry the smell of the sea into the stations. The iodine taste of the sea, the salt smell of the sea, the smell of pure limestone, of chalk, of iodine, the wild smell of storms, the bitter smell of the doldrums, the stale smell of a lead sky. The blue granite smell of the sea and the smell of old steam locomotives that have pulled the long trains full of gravel to the ports. And the smell of the great freight ships full of gravel that have sunk at sea...

And the stations smell of so many things to grieve for. But there is no grieving for the sea at the stations, nor for the sky that pours down the iodine smell of the sea at the stations, nor for the sun that quenches the bitter wet salt of the sea at the stations...

In the arched portal far down at the other end of the station a light was rising, the archway filled with light like a rising sun. And under the roof of the station, light lanced in rays, the filth on the glass of the vaulted roof blazed and filled the hall with light. There were nine rays to be seen up there; it was a magic number. And in the rising sun at the end of the station, three letters loomed dark against the blazing panes of glass, *AEG*, three letters standing for an electrical corporation, and that victorious symbol gave the sun its name.